# THE DEVIL IS A PART-TIMER!

**SATOSHI WAGAHARA**
**ILLUSTRATION BY 029**
**(ONIKU)**

1

# RÉSUMÉ

**NAME**
SADAO MAOU

**DATE OF BIRTH**
NEVER THOUGHT ABOUT IT

**AGE**
200 (OR SO)

**ADDRESS**
DEVI
VILLA
SASA                    YO

**TEL**
00

**PAST EXPERIENCE**

| 1741–AROUND 1799 | WAGED WAR ACROSS |
| 1870 | ACHIEVED POST OF DEVIL |
| 200X | LEFT POSITION OF DEVIL KING |
| 201X | PART-TIME CLERK, M |
| 201X | CURRENTLY HERE |
| | |
| | |
| | |

**QUALIFICATIONS/CERTIFICATIONS**
LEVEL 1 ARCHITECT (DEMON REALM), D
DANGEROUS MAGICAL POTIONS, WYVERN
ACCOUNTANT LICENSE, CONSULTANT (SMA

**SKILLS/HOBBIES**
WORLD DOMINATION, CUSTO

**REASON F**
I AM
FOR

**PER**
I W

**COMMU**
WITH MY
AN BENT TO
IT TAKES BUT TO

DEPENDENTS
ECTED FORCES OF
MONIC ARMY

"Listen, Emilia the Hero, and cower in fear! Someday I, too, will land a full-time position in this place!"

### Satan, the Devil King [Sadao Maou]

Defeated by the Hero, he made his way to Japan from the faraway land of Ente Isla. He is currently holding down a part-time job at the MgRonald fast-food joint in front of Hatagaya station, angling for a full-time position while he conspires to conquer all of Japan.

DO

# RÉSUMÉ

**NAME**

Emi Yusa

**DATE OF BIRTH**

Autumn    ↑

THINK OF SOMETHING, MAN.

**AGE**

17, BUT ...

**GENDER**

F

**ADDRESS**

Urban Heights Eifukusho #501
Eifukucho Đ-Đ-Đ, Suginami-ku, Toky...

**TELEPHONE NUMBER**

090-xxxx-0211

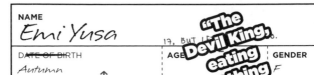

"The Devil King, eating nothing but plain eggs for breakfast? Are you kidding me?"
—Emi

| PAST EXPERIENCE | |
| --- | --- |
| 19XX | born on Western Contin... |
| 20XX | assisted with famil... |
| 20XX | assumed role of ... |
| 20XX | assumed role of ... |
| 201X – Present | contract employe... ...vice Center |

**QUALIFICATIONS/CERTIFICATIONS**

event planning assistant; crop ... ...st of English for
International Communicat...

**SK...**

...studies, ...

...

## Emilia the Hero [Emi Yusa]

As the Hero of the land of Ente Isla, she fought tirelessly against the Devil King, ultimately pursuing him into Japan. She now works at a call center in order to earn some cash, but what happens when the two of them reunite in Tokyo...?

K...

**COMMUTE TIME**

Nearest station: Eifukucho,
Keio Inokashira Line;
approx. twenty-five-m...
commute

# RÉSUMÉ

**NAME**
Shiro Ashiya

DATE OF BIRTH

AGE
1500 (ish)

*Don't remember when I arrived in Japan.*

**ADDRESS**
Inside Devil's Cast...
Villa Rosa
Sasazuk...

TELE...
Um...

"**Your Demonic Highness, would it hurt you that much to plan out your living expenses a bit more?**"

| PAST EXPERIENCE | |
|---|---|
| | fought in nu... foot soldier bef... ...tan |
| Circa 1750s | ...of Devil King Satan |
| Circa 1850s | |
| 1870–1910 | ...ral and chief commander of ...nt, Ente Isla |
| 20... | ...der of invading forces, |
| 20... | |

QU...
ma... smith; handler of dangerous
m... ...tructor license; level 1; Demon Realm
Lit... ...amination; demonic interior decorator

SKI...
As... ...ooking, telekinesis,

REASO...
I don't remem...

PERSONAL GOA...
I wish to re... ...of wor...
worthy of... ...eated...
well as a fis...

COMMUTE T...
A househo...
work fro...
be awak...

**Great Demon General Alciel [Shiro Ashiya]**

The Devil King's right-hand man and closest confidant, he joined Satan on the journey to Japan. Scrimps and saves all he can as he attempts to discover a way back to Ente Isla, even as he assumes a pseudo-househusband role in Maou's apartment.

**NAME**
Chiho Sasaki

**DATE OF BIRTH**
September 10, 19XX

**AGE**
16

**GENDER**

"Wow! That was amazing, Maou!"

**ADDRESS**
Hatagaya ■-■-■
Shibuya-ku, Tokyo

**TELE**
0

**PAST EXPERIENCE**

| March 20XX | grad... | ...uya ward |
| April 20XX | en... | |
| 20XX | ... | |

**QUALIFICATIONS/CERTIFICATION**
Level 3, English Proficie...
Level 2A, Kanji Characte... ...tion

**SKILLS/HOBBIES**
arch... ...ing ...ooking...

### Chiho Sasaki

A sixteen-year-old high schooler working alongside Maou at the MgRonald in front of Hatagaya station, she is currently smitten with Maou and his indefatigable drive to realize his dreams—no matter how evil they truly are.

...iety thro... ...r to contribute
..., I've a... ...working at

**CO**
ten mi...

**FA**
No...

...ho Sas...

HERO OF ANOTHER WORLD VS. TEENAGER OF JAPAN!
"I swear, he and I aren't like that..."

MgRonald

# CONTENTS

SATOSHI
WAGAHARA
ILLUSTRATION BY 029
(ONIKU)

THE DEVIL IS A PART-TIMER!

1

YEN
ON

NEW YORK

THE DEVIL IS A PART-TIMER!, Volume 1
SATOSHI WAGAHARA, ILLUSTRATION BY 029 (ONIKU)

Translation by Kevin Gifford

HATARAKU MAOUSAMA!, Volume 1
©SATOSHI WAGAHARA/KADOKAWA
CORPORATION 2011
All rights reserved.
Edited by ASCII MEDIA WORKS
First published in 2011 by KADOKAWA
CORPORATION, Tokyo.

English translation rights arranged with
KADOKAWA CORPORATION, Tokyo,
through Tuttle-Mori Agency, Inc., Tokyo.
English translation © 2015 Hachette Book
Group, Inc.

Yen On
Hachette Book Group
1290 Avenue of the Americas
New York, NY 10104

www.hachettebookgroup.com
www.yenpress.com

Yen On is an imprint
of Hachette Book Group, Inc.
The Yen On name and logo are
trademarks of Hachette Book
Group, Inc.

The publisher is not
responsible for websites (or
their content) that are not
owned by the publisher.

First Yen On edition:
April 2015

ISBN: 978-0-316-38312-7

10 9 8 7 6 5 4 3 2 1

RRD-C

Printed in the United
States of America

THE DEVIL FOCUSES ON HIS CAREER FOR MONETARY PURPOSES

The bank account had been wrung completely dry.

The reason couldn't be simpler: He had used up all the money.

On what? Well, first, there was that long-sought-after refrigerator. That was a mandatory purchase, he felt, given his qualms about the food-preservation situation, what with summer looming in the distance.

Next, there was the bicycle. It was a record-breakingly cheap fixed-gear, but for the commute to and from his part-time job, it worked.

That, and the washer he bought. He figured at first that the Laundromat would suffice, but the time and annoyance involved came to be too much. Definitely another appliance he wanted squared away before summer arrived.

He had made all of these purchases with cash. And now, his remaining balance would barely cover a stick of gum.

"You should be more careful with how you spend your money, you understand."

The condemning voice beat against his eardrums.

"...What, did you want me getting sick off rotten food all summer, then? You want me to wear the same outfit every day?!"

"I said nothing like that." The calm, serene voice still had a chiding air to it. "But think about this. Your account might be exhausted, but you do have a job, yes? And a steady one at that. It would be simple to figure out your income for the next few months. You could have easily paid for all of this on credit."

"Don't like taking loans."

"...I honestly don't think you're in the—"

"Plus, there's all kinds of fees and things for that! I don't like paying for things that I can't see and feel with my own hands."

"But—"

"Never spend money you don't actually have. I hate debt. If there's no money, you shouldn't use it. Buy stuff all at once with cash in hand, or don't buy it."

It was a typical one-hundred-square-foot tatami room, the kind you saw all across Japan. In the middle, two men sat facing each other on opposite sides of an old, decrepit *kotatsu* table, the room's only heat source.

On one end, the lecturer. On the other, the lecturee.

The lecturer, taller and thinner than his conversation partner, slowly rose and placed a hand on the door of the newly-purchased refrigerator.

"Your Demonic Highness, let me ask you this."

The "Demonic Highness" being lectured was a man of average build, average height, and dark hair. His lecturer opened the refrigerator door, a twinge of resignation within his otherwise sharp eyes as he shot a stare back at his target.

"How do you plan to survive until your next payday on a block of *konnyaku* gel, a cucumber, and a carton of milk?"

"I...that..."

The "Demonic Highness" being lectured remained seated, unable to formulate a response.

"I-I'm not completely broke yet. There's still some money in my wallet."

The taller man's eyes seemed to say that this was not an adequate response.

"I, uh, I could always grab some extra food from my job..."

"Oh, so you plan to go all *Super Size Me* every meal from now until your next paycheck? Do you think *that* would be the best thing for your health?"

To the side of the refrigerator was a city-provided garbage bag, bulging conspicuously on the floor. It was stuffed with a vast array of boxes and packaging from a certain famous fast-food chain.

"It…it's still young, this body."

"And I would wonder how young it would look after a decade of daily high-calorie, high-cholesterol cuisine! When we finally make our triumphant return, hopefully you won't require a mobility scooter!"

The sarcastic tone continued apace. "Also, you should know that time has different effects on this body from the one before. Ten years as a human being may not *seem* very long, but it is. Your health is a surprisingly fragile thing, Your Demonic Highness. Are you planning for that at all?"

"All right, all right! Lay off me a second! I'm not, all right?! Are you happy now?! And anyway! It's not only *my* fault I'm like this right now!"

"Yes. Of course, my liege. There is no apologizing for the shame that has befallen us. But it was you, as our one and only Devil King, who decided we should bide our time and wait for the moment to rise once more. And in the meantime, you must be diligent in your work *and* in retaining your health. And I fear you are failing at both."

The Devil King fell silent. He turned his head to the side, apparently in regret for his behavior. Then:

"Gah! It's time for work!"

Hopping to his feet, he tore out of the room, as if suddenly remembering he was inside a lion enclosure at the zoo. His lecturer, caught by surprise at this sudden flurry of activity, was left behind by the kitchen counter.

"M-my liege! Wait! We still need to talk…"

"Save it, Alciel! If it's more complaints, I'll listen to it when I get back!"

Just as the man named Alciel caught up to him, he slammed the door in a huff. Mere inches saved himself from smashing his nose against it.

"Your Demonic Highness!"

As Alciel called for his companion, the door opened. The Devil King was there, a tremendous glare on his face as he extended a hand toward Alciel.

"Rain! Umbrella!"

The sky had been clear that morning, but ashen clouds now hung low in the sky. Raindrops had only just begun to fall. Before he could say anything else, Alciel wordlessly handed over the frayed, battle-worn plastic umbrella propped by the side of the front door.

"Thanks! See you!"

The door shut in his face once more, to the sound of the Devil King's feet clanging as he stormed down the stairs.

"Dullahan! My beloved mount! We're off!"

The so-called Devil King, his wardrobe betraying an obvious dedication to the clearance racks at UniClo, the monolithic discount clothing chain, heroically sounded the bell on his bicycle as he climbed aboard. Balancing his umbrella like a knight readying his jousting lance, he scurried down the alley in front of the apartment building.

Alciel, the lecturer who was bedecked in a full UniClo wardrobe himself, craned his body over the stairwell railing as he saw his companion ride off into the rain. A long, deep sigh erupted across his lips.

After a moment, he turned around and ventured back inside the apartment, a plain wooden placard with the household's name written upon it in Magic Marker the only thing decorating the door. It listed the kanji to the left, and the English reading—Maou—to the right, with a dash in between the two. In effect, it read to any passing Japanese as THE TRUTH WITHIN to the left, and DEMON KING to the right.

Closing the door behind him, Alciel shook his head and sighed once more. Why did all of this have to happen? The dark clouds and tinkling rainfall blackened the room, making it as gloomy and shadow-laden as his own heart.

The dim scene was broken only by the somber sound of the doorbell. The doorbell? Oh. Right. This building was far too down-market to offer anything like an intercom to its residents. Alciel opened the door a second time.

"...I'm sorry, we don't own a television here."

The MHK TV-fee collection agent was a familiar presence in his life by now. It was no lie. There was no TV in the place. The Devil King and more-or-less master of the house reasoned that they could use a smartphone for their video-entertainment needs, but such a high-end device was nowhere near within reach of their strained budget.

"Certainly. I just thought I would check. If you do purchase one, please bring this payment slip to the bank, if you could."

The collection agent handed over an envelope just as dull and unadorned as his businesslike tone of voice. Then he left, not bothering with even a perfunctory smile.

※

Vast and sprawling as the yawning continents of Ente Isla were, there was not a soul in their world unaware of Satan, the Devil King. He was the overlord of the demon world and all the creatures that slithered and slavered within, his name all but synonymous with abject terror and cruelty.

His sole motivation in life was to conquer Ente Isla, the divinely protected Land of the Holy Cross, and subjugate the foolish humans within as he transformed the continent into a paradise for his dark legions.

Making the situation even more desperate for the human race were the faithful war generals by the Devil King's side, each as overwhelmingly powerful as the master they served.

They were Alciel, Lucifer, Adramelech, and Malacoda, and together they were called the Four Great Demon Generals.

Ente Isla, the land protected by the gods, was composed of a large central landmass planted within the Ocean of Ignora, itself surrounded by four islands. These islands extended from the sea each to a cardinal direction, thereby forming a rough cross. The Devil King had deployed Alciel's forces on the eastern island, Lucifer's on the western, Adramelech's on the northern, and Malacoda's on the southern. They had deployed far and wide across the land, bringing both the humans and the godly forces that aided them to the very edge of annihilation.

Then, something happened to Lucifer's western forces.

Word arrived from the west that the war-loving general's armies had been routed by a single human being.

This woman, referring to herself as a "Hero," had rallied the few surviving human fighters together to stage a resistance effort.

Lucifer was a former angel that had fallen from the world of the heavens, and the Western Continent was occupied by the resilient forces of the Ente Isla Church, the powerful ecclesiastical institution that was deemed the "closest to heaven" in the land. The Demon King had reasoned that Lucifer, well versed in the ways of the heavens, would be perfect for dispatching the Church and the divine assistance it received. This assumption had been dashed by a single human. A so-called *Hero*, at that.

Of course, every long, drawn-out struggle has its setbacks. Lucifer had had a poor string of luck, perhaps. But, as Satan confidently concluded, the combined forces of his remaining generals would surely make easy work of this Hero.

That was his first mistake.

Satan had thought of humans as little more than grubworms, wriggling in and along the ground he trod upon.

But think about it. Could one ever truly eradicate every single grubworm from the land? Even the mightiest and fiercest of lions could be felled by a single insect bite, if it proved poisonous enough.

Within the space of a single year, first Adramelech, and then Malacoda, followed Lucifer down the path of defeat. Alciel, renowned as the Generals' most gifted strategist, suggested abandoning the Eastern Continent and waging a defensive battle on the Central Continent in order to protect the Devil King's central base. After years of waging war over the fate of Ente Isla, the battle had been turned upside down in twelve short months. Not even Satan could view the situation with optimism any longer.

Soon the humans, on the rebound and campaigning in the name of the Church and their Hero, had pushed their way to the Central Continent, their vast forces descending upon the Devil King's holdings. One had to wonder where all these grubworms had been hiding up to this point.

In the blink of an eye, the central island was overrun. The demonic forces had been brutally crushed, all because he had underestimated the mettle of this single Hero, this mere maggot of a creature.

Satan and Alciel fought back, battling the forces of the Hero and her three stalwart companions at the site of his Devil's Castle on the Central Continent.

The war wore on. Even the Hero faced difficulty against both the Demon King and his sole remaining general. But in terms of manpower and resolve, the Hero's forces far outclassed Satan's and Alciel's.

Eventually, once the Hero's holy sword sliced off one of Satan's horns, Alciel advised his ruler that retreat was in order. Continuing to wage war would lead not only to defeat but threaten their very existence as well.

It was an agonizing decision for Satan to make, but one that even he saw the need for. The demonic forces would, to put it simply, flee Ente Isla. They would escape to another world and wait, rebuilding their strength until they were ready to return.

The look of pained frustration on the Hero's face as Satan plunged through the Gate to another world, just before she could pierce his heart with her holy blade, provided but little comfort to the demonic overlord.

Satan's final scream thundered across Ente Isla, as if he were attempting to address the heavens themselves.

"Hear me, humans! Ente Isla is yours…for now! But I will return… and when I do, both you and this land will be mine!"

But controlling a Gate to another world required a tremendous amount of magical force. Weakened and wounded by the Hero's decisive victory, Satan and Alciel no longer bore the strength needed to fully navigate the portal.

Sucked into the Gate's torrential flow, the two powerful demons were soon astonished to find themselves marooned in a world with an advanced civilization already established upon it.

It was filled with an intense, pulsating energy, the likes of which Satan and Alciel had never seen. Their infernal conquests had never prepared them for the towering structures and seemingly endless stream of shining, dancing lights that surrounded them now.

They were inside a large city, it seemed, one filled with just as many dark, dingy alleys as glorious, massive edifices. They peered into the dim crevices between the buildings, listening in wonder at the unfamiliar, raucous noises that seeped from each one. Who could say what sort of intelligent life-form ruled this land, or what kind of insidious, ferocious monsters might populate it? Still not fully recovered from the shock, the pair of demons decided to find someplace to rest and heal from battle.

Just then, a sharp, intense light shone upon them.

"Hey! What're you doing over there?!"

It was a man's voice, speaking what Satan could tell was a clearly defined, intelligent language. Turning toward the light, he saw someone there—a *human*, just like the ones that infested Ente Isla. The tubelike object in his hand emitted a blinding white light.

"You guys okay? Have you been fighting?"

Apparently the human race ruled this world. Another human was behind him, dressed similarly, eyes turned his way.

Alciel was eager to avoid any further trouble.

"Fall back, foul beasts! Who do you think stands before you?!"

This bold declaration failed to have the intended effect on the man with the light. He furrowed his brows in apparent exasperation.

Even Satan couldn't hide his surprise at this reaction. There was pure, unadulterated magical force bubbling behind the noble cadences of demon speech. It was simply impossible for a human to ignore that domineering essence, treating it like the bleating of some animal.

"Augh, great. Foreigners, huh? Man…"

The first man tilted his head before taking out a small, boxlike object and muttering softly into it.

"Uh, this is Patrolman Sasaki. I'm looking at a possible case of simple assault here. Victims are two non-Japanese Asian nationals. Location is—"

The two humans were dressed in sturdy-looking, well-kept clothing, woven from some manner of leather or cloth. Weapons hung from their waists, their daggerlike hilts visible. The front of their headgear featured a golden emblem modeled after an unknown type of plant foliage. Knights from one of this world's nations, then?

That box must provide some form of long-distance communication. If these *were* knights, perhaps they had just called for reinforcements. A battalion of them could prove dangerous, especially in the demons' current wounded state.

For now, it was two against two. They had their guards down. Seeking to eliminate these possible witnesses, Alciel transformed his remaining magic force into a ball of crackling energy, sending it flying toward the humans. Or he meant to.

"What…?!"

The magic wasn't focusing, somehow, the way he expected. In fact, the more he tried to harness his magic skills, the more it seemed to drain harmlessly out of his body, something he was powerless to stop. He turned toward Satan to explain this anomaly.

"My, my liege… That…that form…!"

Alciel's voice shook as he beheld the ruler of the demon world, bathed in intense white light.

"Hold your magic, Alciel. We must learn of this world first."

Satan appeared serene in demeanor, but his teeth were clenched, as if fighting off some heavy weight acting upon him.

As well he may have been. For the Devil King was standing there in human form—the form of the puny, weak creature he fought, his battle scars still plain to see.

"Okay, so listen, guys… The car'll be here in just a minute, so… If everything checks out, you can go home right afterward. Okay?"

The men seemed blissfully unfazed by Satan's presence. Still reeling from the shock, Alciel looked down upon his own hands. They were *human* hands, hands completely alien to him.

Soon a carriage arrived with no horse driving it, colored black and white and topped with a mysterious device that drizzled red light across the area in dazzling patterns. More men appeared, each wearing the same outfit as the first, and Satan and Alciel were thrown into the carriage.

"Do you speak Japanese? Aren't you hot, wearing that in the summertime?"

The first man spoke slowly to the pair of ex-demons, once noble, proud, with chiseled bodies that would far outclass any normal human's. Now they were human themselves, their clothes as unnatural as a toddler wearing a bedsheet cape, the ominous-looking gilt meant to represent their lordly strength now catching against this or that part of their lanky frames.

Satan and Alciel shared a look, but neither had anything to say to that. Even if they did, it didn't appear the men could understand their speech.

"...Ah, well. Not like they're the only kids dressed up all goofy over there."

The man no longer spoke, apparently satisfied with what he had told them. Soon, Satan and Alciel were taken to a place referred to only as "the station," a building apparently meant for the enforcement of laws in this kingdom.

They were taken to a room within this building for investigation purposes, and there the Devil King and his general were able to recover at least some of their grandeur. Satan unleashed a bout of hypnosis magic upon the investigating officer, seeking to extract as much information about this world as he could. It seemed that, no matter what world one found himself in, the nobility and military men swaggering around the castle were always of far weaker wills than any stalwart man of battle.

As the hypnotized officer revealed, the pair of demons were on a world called "Earth," within an island nation known as "Japan."

They had come to this world near "Harajuku," an outpost on a transport network known as the "railroad" that had been installed around "Tokyo," the nation's capital region.

Things like magic, magical force, Devil Kings, even demons themselves, were all treated as imaginary things in this world, mere flights of fancy that could never actually exist. Magic was something the denizens of the demon world harnessed to exert their wills upon the world, similar to the forces of gravity or magnetism, but there was no way to access this magic if it did not exist in the first place.

"So you're saying we've…lost our magical powers?"

Alciel threw himself upon a chair, unable to wrap his mind around it.

"…Ah, but, Your Demonic Highness, you just…"

"I have a small amount of residual force left. It's proving difficult to keep it from flowing out of me, though…"

The Devil King and his demonic subjects were able to accumulate a vast amount of magical power within their bodies. Even though his stores had been drained in combat with the Hero, Satan still retained several times as much magic as Alciel could ever hope to. It was that residual force which allowed Satan to bend the officer's mind.

"I don't think it will dry up immediately, as long as I strictly regulate the amount I release. But…"

But the problem was, there was no way to recharge the force he used.

His wounds would heal with time, but at this rate, he would never recover his magical skills. Any Gate he could open would be impossible to keep uniform. Not only would he be unlikely to reach Ente Isla; he might uncontrollably blunder into an even more dangerous world.

Instead of taking such risky bets, he reasoned, it would be wiser to find some other method of survival where he already stood.

There may be no concept of demons or magic in this realm, but the concepts of gods and piousness seemed fairly sparse as well, which was a comfort. This nation, Japan, apparently had a vast array of official ceremonies for dispelling evil spirits, but it was all a formality, a façade, at this point. It seemed safe to conclude that none of their practitioners held any actual holy powers within themselves.

As long as they remained in Japan, it seemed unlikely that anyone would attempt to slay these demons. Controlling the officer's mind, Satan ordered him to complete his investigation and release them from the station without any further meddling.

Holing up in a narrow alley the streetlights didn't reach, Satan and Alciel discussed their future plans.

First, they needed a method to recharge their magic in this world. Achieving this would likely require a lengthy stay, something they had to resign themselves to.

Failing to find a method—failing to recharge their magic—was, for a demon, even more a threat to their lives than being wholly robbed of the magic.

The higher-level demons could live without consuming food because they were able to convert magic into bodily energy. A world where magic no longer existed was the same as a barren world with nothing to eat.

But some demons did eat food. Why? Because doing so allowed them to absorb energy in the same way lesser creatures did.

To live in this world without a source of magic, they would need to forage for sustenance. Japan apparently used a currency-based economy. They needed money for food.

But, of course, they lacked any Earth currency.

"Let me ask you this, Alciel. If you had willed it, could you have escaped those officers?"

Alciel shook his head stoically. Satan nodded his convinced agreement.

The two great demons, ones who had set the human race upon their knees, were no longer able to fend for themselves against even a small rabble of them.

And not because the humans of this world were somehow stronger. The only conclusion to be made was that *they* had grown that much weaker. That was how bitter, how bruising, the battle against the Hero had grown.

"So…so we will remain like this…?"

Alciel winced as he beheld his hand, as if observing some strange and hideous being. The soft, thinly stretched skin. The flat face and disheveled hair. The rounded, unsharpened nails. The muscles that formed their bodies, so flabby and pathetic.

"It pains me to say it, but our lack of magical force likely makes it impossible to retain our greater demon forms."

The form a demon took depended on the level of power instilled within it. Foe-slashing claws, powerful legs that propelled it over castle parapets, leathery wings on its back, snakes for hair—every aspect of its ethereal form ran on magical force.

"Amazing to think *this* is how you look when stripped of that power. Perhaps the human form is what lies at the foundation of all life."

"Surely you jest, Your Demonic Highness! I hardly bear to even entertain the idea that we house…*humans* inside of us. It is no doubt some machination placed upon us by this world, or the Gate."

"…Regardless. We have other matters to be concerned about."

They lacked the magic to summon another Gate. They lacked the strength to overwhelm the humans of this world by force. In other words, if they wished to survive, the only choice was to abide by the human race's rules in this…Japan.

Follow *human* rules. For a Devil King and a Great Demon General, the idea was enough to shatter the very foundations of their pride.

But this new reality had been thrust upon them—one where they must eat to live, work to eat.

Shrugging off their unholy demonic robes, the Devil King and the Great Demon General took their first halting steps toward an unknown world.

From what they gleaned at the station, they knew that living in Japan would require at least two things: a "census registration" and an "address." Without those, it seemed, they would be unable to acquire the work needed to earn money.

A "census registration" and "address" were both things one could obtain in a place called a "ward office." They decided this would be their first mission. Pushing their war-battered bodies forward, they plodded toward the "Shibuya Ward Office," the nearest one to them... only to find it would not be open until the following morning.

As miserable as it seemed, Satan and Alciel passed the night in front of the ward office's door, knees tight against their chests.

It was a city where the lights were apparently never extinguished, but things grew more animated once morning arrived. Humans strode around in clothing of a thousand different colors. As more and more of the men passing by began to sport uniformlike outfits colored in blacks and darker blues, the Shibuya Ward Office finally opened for business. Rushing toward the window, Satan commandeered the mind of the worker on the other side, one obviously surprised at the sight of these two men. In a few scant moments, they had successfully created something called a "family register" for themselves.

Their next stop was a "real estate office," a depot that could arrange living quarters for them.

Satan and Alciel had become fluent in the human language of Ente Isla within just three days. Now they resolved to do whatever it took to learn this new language, "Japanese," up to a practical level.

Noticing the pair's broken Japanese and bizarre clothing, the real estate agent, assuming they must be rich businessmen from a foreign country, began to politely bombard them with opulent houses at equally eye-popping prices.

Satan had to explain to the eager agent that they could not live anyplace that required too high of a fee.

Hypnotism did not consume a great deal of magic power if used only once, but since they would naturally be evicted for failure to pay, life in a full-floor penthouse unit without the salary to match would require continual hypnosis of the landlord. So they told the agent they wanted someplace they could easily afford, one that would allow them the barest minimum of a lifestyle. The agent, more than a bit disappointed, showed them one potential location.

"The landlord here is a very...shall we say, *unique* woman."

It was a room in an apartment building located within "Sasa-zuka," apparently a subsection of Shibuya.

The rent was 45,000 yen per month, with no deposit, no advance fees, and no guarantor required. It was Room 201 in the sixty-year-old "Villa Rosa Sasazuka" apartments, approximately one hundred square feet, no bath, one toilet per room.

"The landlord tells me she gives preferential treatment to people like you, who are...if I may say so, unusual? Or from unusual circumstances, I should say."

It was an unorthodox sales approach, but if this was all he had to offer, so be it. After a ride in the agent's "car" (so *that* was what they called these carriages!), they arrived at a two-floor apartment building in a quiet, almost desolate neighborhood. Plaster was peeling off the walls, and the roof was missing more than a few tiles here and there. The rain gutter attached to the roof had given itself in entirely to its brown, rusted doom, and the stairway to the second floor tilted in several different precarious angles at once. There wasn't a soul to be seen; all of the rooms were likely empty.

"This...this is *astounding*."

Alciel groaned to himself.

"Yes. Even I can see that much."

The pair spoke to each other in the demon tongue. As inexperienced as they still were with this world, the utter dilapidation presented to them was still obvious.

These were, bear in mind, the demon elite, two men who had clawed and struggled their way to the top of the underworld. They had fallen far since, yes, but it was hard to accept living in this hovel during their stay. And if every room was empty, this meant not even the lowly humans would stoop so low as to live *here*, would they?

It was simply impossible. Just as Satan turned around to tell the young agent as much, he realized that someone else was standing there instead.

"Is that...a person?"

To their demonic sensibilities, it was an utterly enigmatic, strange creature. It was tall, even approaching the height of Alciel, who towered above most others even in human form. The plump, rounded body—the word *endowed* was not up to the task of describing it—made this creature barely recognizable as a woman.

A colorful hydrangea headdress was perched upon her hair, dyed a silvery purple and towering toward the sky. A violet stole was tossed over her shoulders, covering a shockingly bright purple summer dress. Every finger on her hands had a large amethyst ring on it, and her high heels were coated in a purple enamel. She had on purple rouge, purple eye shadow, and enough thick snow-white foundation that one could imagine it cracking apart if you slapped her. The light dollop of red cheek blush applied over it seemed to shine as brightly as the sun. The image presented was one of an enormous purple potato that had been peeled in random locations.

"Hello there! I understand the two of you wish to move in?"

"It…it talks!"

Alciel's instinctive response was understandable, given the daunting sight before them.

"My name is Miki Shiba, and I'm the owner of Villa Rosa Sasazuka."

Still frozen in place, Satan and Alciel could see the real estate agent's car peel off behind the purple presence in front of them.

"The name *Miki* is made up from the characters for 'beautiful' and 'shine.' Please feel free to call me Mikitty, though."

The demons had thought they were beginning to get the hang of spoken Japanese, but something within their instinct made them reject the words being spoken by this puzzling tsunami of intent, this Shiba, before them that called itself a landlord.

They must keep their distance from her at all costs. They could feel that in their veins, and yet they found themselves being dragged into a room in this beaten-up apartment house, being forced to sign a litany of documents, and receiving a rundown of the nearby facilities.

"Well, then! Starting today, this will be your little sanctuary! I live in the house adjacent to here, so if you have any questions, please, don't be afraid to give a holler. See you later, then!"

The purple hurricane then left. All that remained in the room was the utterly dumbstruck Satan, the equally silent Alciel, and a rental contract onto which a pair of purple lip marks had been pressed.

They had signed the contract, completely unable to mount any sort of protest. The two of them stood there, their minds blank, waiting to regain their composure so they could reflect over these sudden events.

The place was a dump, its landlord a nonhuman behemoth. But what other living space would be willing to accept two homeless, unemployed young men, a concept that would send any sane landlord running at first sight? They resigned themselves to their fate, knowing the answer all too well. At the very least, they wouldn't be rained on.

So, deep in their hearts, the two demons swore to work hard, make the rent each month, and otherwise have as little to do with their landlord as possible.

"'You have to start somewhere,' as they apparently say around here. Perhaps this is exactly what we need."

They were overwhelmed in battle against the Hero, battered by the wild journey across the flows of the Gate, and mentally fatigued by their adventures in an unfamiliar world. Satan, the Devil King, was rapidly expending his magical force, his breathing ragged after only two hypnoses. The sense of extreme exhaustion was like none he had ever tasted.

So the Devil King fell asleep. And he stayed asleep for three days and three nights, healing his scarred body and drained soul.

Then, after sleeping three days straight without eating or drinking, Satan was taken to the hospital for malnutrition. The dehydration and vitamin deficiency had immobilized him.

In order to rescue his master—near death, skin dry and pallid, empty eyes staring aimlessly into space—Alciel had been forced to ask their landlord, Shiba, for help the third day after moving in. He had absolutely no idea what manner of medical facilities to expect in this world.

Using a long-distance communication device known as a "telephone," Shiba summoned an "ambulance," a white car that, again, spat out red light.

Sitting in a hospital room, watching his bedridden master as an IV drip flowed into his arm, Alciel realized they were akin to the humans of this world not just in external appearance, but internally as well. He started to cry, unable to withstand the humiliation.

Reality, however, would prove cruel to them in ways that Alciel had yet to anticipate.

In this world, receiving medical care costs a vast amount of money. There was a public system of sorts, apparently, to reduce individual medical costs, but naturally, neither Satan nor Alciel had enrolled in any such program.

The medical fees presented to them could only be described as brazen profiteering, something Alciel could understand even with his tentative grasp on the value of this nation's currency. Once allowed to leave the hospital, Satan was forced to use hypnosis once again to make the bill go away.

Right now, what they needed over anything else was money. Money earned with methods besides getting arrested or wasting magic.

That, and the national health system. They needed in on that action, too.

For the final usage of Satan's hypnosis, the pair agreed to travel to a "bank" to obtain an account and some monetary resources. Putting the teller under his spell, Satan took ten thousand yen from the employee and used it to open a regular savings account.

It was completely illegal, but no sensible demon would even flinch at the concept of robbery. The thrill at finally obtaining the seed money for their new lives overcame the nagging impression within Satan's mind that they were making some kind of mistake.

The ten thousand yen was used to purchase the food necessary for survival, as well as something called "résumé forms." A "résumé," it turned out, was considered indispensable for obtaining employment.

All they had to do was fill in the required boxes, bring the document to the appropriate place, make an appointment for an "interview," and parrot out the right answers. Then they'd be able to work.

There was just one snag. Neither Satan nor Alciel had any special skills that could be easily applied in this nation. Satan could hardly write "Job History: King of the Demon Realm; Hobbies/Abilities: World domination" on his résumé. Thus, the only option was to focus on jobs that touted "Beginners Welcome!" in their notices.

The two of them sat down and prepared several résumés.

Holding back the frustration and humiliation, dreaming of the day when they would defeat the Hero and regain their grasp upon all that lived and breathed on Ente Isla, they wrote their names down.

"Name…'Sadao Maou.' Perfect."

"Name…'Shiro Ashiya.' That doesn't sound odd, does it?"

"Little point whining about it now. That's what we wrote into the census register, no?"

Thus, Devil King Satan (aka Sadao Maou, the surname of which was written with perfectly ordinary Japanese characters whose pronunciation just happened to be the same as "Devil King") and Great Demon General Alciel (aka Shiro Ashiya) set off on their quest to reconquer Ente Isla, room 201 at the Villa Rosa Sasazuka apartments serving as their Devil Castle for the time being.

The two of them had established a foothold in their drive to find the bare minimum of work for themselves, but they had little time to rest. Money would be needed for other things, too—electricity, water, gas, essentials.

A tear came to Satan's eye as he recalled a time when he could gather the thunderclouds, summon mighty waves, and raze the land with punishing flame, all at the flick of a finger.

Now, Satan and Alciel were just Maou and Ashiya, two slow-looking unemployed young men, neither looking past their early twenties.

The Devil King and his erstwhile Demon General read through every job-listing magazine they could find. Soon they discovered the existence of something called "day labor."

All they had to do was sign up with a given company, and they'd then be assigned short-term work. They would receive payment daily, between five thousand and ten thousand yen depending on the work, perhaps more if they performed well.

Tossing one of their few remaining ten-yen coins into the slot of a public phone, they set up an appointment time for an interview.

Traveling to the office in Shinjuku, they found it was less an interview and more a work-orientation meeting. They signed up at once, found the directors less than picky about qualifications, and work was promised to them before the day was through.

Since they were both inexperienced beginners, they were tasked with assisting a group putting up facilities for an outdoor event, performing their assigned work up to the salary agreed upon.

Staring at the seven thousand yen each of them had earned for the day's work, Satan felt reassured in his convictions.

If they kept this up, they could earn the money they needed for now. And once they saved enough money, they could turn their focus toward finding part-time jobs to keep them working on a more long-term basis.

That mission, however, fell apart in a short two weeks.

They had performed their duties on a consistent basis, to the point where the salaried employees working up front were starting to remember their faces.

Then the company received a stop-work notice from the government, forcing them to leave the work-assignment business. It was a complete bolt out of the blue.

In poor spirits and with no money source, the pair made their way home. Passing by a TV playing the news, they took in more of the story.

The newscast condemned the firm, accusing it of assigning workers to illegal sites and skimming an outrageous amount off the top of their revenue.

Satan focused on the news report, wondering to himself why a great demon as himself had to lose his job because of some silly laws enacted by *humans*, of all things. Suddenly, he came to a realization.

"Hey, Ashiya, wait a sec."

"I would prefer Alciel, please."

"Our mission here is to conquer the human world, right? Not to spend every day of our lives scraping up enough cash to survive."

"Y...yes. As you say."

"Then how about you just focus on finding a way to restore our magic? I can hold down a job instead. I may have more physical and magical strength than you, but *you*—you're the one and only strategist I have. I need you to find a source of magic for me, here, in Japan."

"M-Maou..."

"It's 'Your Demonic Highness.' But anyway, even if it may be more comfortable for us if we both worked, we must never lose sight of our goals. Demons and magic may not exist here, but the *concepts* do. And every concept has an origin. If we can root out the origin, then perhaps..."

"...perhaps we can find a way to regain that magic?"

Satan nodded sagely.

"Far preferable to the both of us stringing part-time jobs together, right? And there is no need to focus on just magic, either. Perhaps we could find some new power, something exclusive to this world. Then we could use that to dominate Ente Isla once more!"

Ashiya...er, Alciel fell to his knees, deeply moved by the first truly motivational speech from his master in many days.

"Absolutely, Your Demonic Highness! I will stake my very life to find a way back to Ente Isla; to find a method to restore my liege's powers!"

"...Will you get up, Alciel? We're in the middle of a crosswalk. You're embarrassing me."

Their fellow pedestrians stared as they walked past, not betraying a hair of emotion at the sight of Alciel suddenly kneeling down and shouting nonsense in the middle of the afternoon.

The Devil King Satan, absorbing himself in the role of Japanese slacker Sadao Maou, gave every inch of strength to his work. He went through a lot of it. Traffic control at a road construction site.

Order picking at a commercial warehouse. Assistant for a moving company. Rush-hour customer management at a train station. The variety, at least, was nothing to complain about.

Meanwhile, as Shiro Ashiya, Alciel devoted himself to maintaining the household, ensuring that Maou remained healthy and able to devote himself to work. In his spare time, he investigated the world's magical possibilities, as well as strictly managing the pair's financial situation.

Exactly six months after the two of them first touched down in Japan, Maou received an offer for his first long-term part-time job— MgRonald, the fast-food giant.

He returned from his first day at work with a pleased look upon his face, the bags in his hands groaning with deep-fried miscellanea. As he put it, "From this day forward, we will never have to worry about our food drying up."

Ashiya, too, was glad to be rid of such concerns. At first. But eating all these burgers, all these French fries, all this fried chicken—all this high-calorie, additive-laden food, day in and day out, wore him out almost immediately. After a week, the heartburn was enough to make him never want to set eyes upon a fast-food container again.

But Maou carried on with this questionable diet, apparently taking a liking to the "cuisine" on offer.

Inevitably, Ashiya had to pay even more attention to their daily food habits in response. The result was that the demon's valiant search for magic was getting absolutely nowhere. If he wanted to avoid a disastrous diet of junk food for every meal, Ashiya had to dash for the supermarkets just before closing time, keeping a careful eye on whatever day-old stuff was discounted the lowest each day.

At least Maou was devoted to his work. Within two months, he had already received a raise.

The day was one Ashiya would likely never forget. The sight of the Devil King, overjoyed at the concept of a one-hundred-yen raise in his hourly wages, was something nobody could bear to behold without their eyes tearing up.

Several more line promotions followed in the ensuing weeks.

And before long, Maou had become an A-level crew member at the MgRonald location in front of the Hatagaya rail station.

His hourly wage was two hundred yen higher than when he joined half a year ago. This was, allegedly, exceptionally kind treatment on MgRonald's part. Using any of his hypnosis magic would weaken him to a point that Ashiya would immediately recognize something was amiss, so everything Maou achieved must have been the result of honest sweat equity.

Eventually, a customer feedback form made its way to MgRonald headquarters, apparently full of praise for Maou's service. That earned him the Crew MVP award for the month.

A marked change in attitude began to settle in. Here was the Devil King after work, talking about how right his boss was to praise him and how talented one of the new hires was proving to be. It was hardly the devious plotting of a would-be conqueror. His qualifications upon the Devil King role gradually shrank, to the point where he began claiming that surpassing his store manager would be the first step to world domination.

For someone like Ashiya, whose sole pleasure in life was to support the Devil King in his illustrious triumphs, the sight was growing increasingly disquieting as of late. It was becoming difficult to think in depth about the future.

Ashiya flung the envelope with the MHK payment slip into the mail holder, not bothering to open it. He willfully bottled up all his concerns and complaints—his oath of fealty rang just as true now as it had when he swore it—and today he had an art gallery and a museum to research.

During his investigations, Ashiya had become convinced that magic either still existed, or had existed, somewhere on planet Earth.

From England's Stonehenge to the Egyptian pyramids and the Nazca Lines in Peru, the world was dotted with cultures and structures that seemed to ooze magic at the core.

This was the result of countless hours spent in libraries, investigating every ruin site and relic the world had to offer. The Devil's

Castle Maou and Ashiya called home had nothing as convenient as the Internet available.

The issue was figuring out the difference between *true* magic and magic-ish-ness.

There was no money to travel overseas, and even if they used Maou's hypnotic powers to make the trip, there was no telling which civilizations were magical unless they actually went to look for themselves.

If a lead wound up going nowhere, he would be too ashamed to even look at his master. That, and who could say there was enough power anywhere in the world to refill his strength in the first place?

Thus, Ashiya decided to start by examining antiquities closer at hand.

The museums and galleries within the city apparently offered rotating displays from foreign museums on a regular basis. He wanted to see if anything on display resonated at the wavelengths of their own demonic magic.

With that, he set off for Shinjuku. His target: the day's special gallery at the National Museum of Western Art in Ueno.

It was still raining outside, so Ashiya grabbed up another plastic umbrella Maou had fished from the side of the road, fumbled with the wobbly cylinder lock on the door to secure a room that offered nothing of value to steal, and set off.

Suddenly, Ashiya was stricken with a gruesome thought. What, he asked himself, if this way of life went on forever? It was enough to make him tremble, even in the late-spring weather.

"Hmm?"

A moment later, he realized he actually *was* being shaken. An earthquake was in progress.

It was nothing to panic about; he learned quickly over the past year that Japan saw quakes on a regular basis. But living in this popsicle-stick apartment that might set the world record for "oldest extant building with no work ever done to it" was enough to make any earthquake seem about 30 percent stronger, sickening him to the core every time.

But nothing happened, again. The shaking ceased after ten seconds or so. In Ente Isla, any earthquake, no matter how strong or widespread, would send the humans into spasms of panic, blathering on about vengeful deities or advancing demon forces. But a quake this size wouldn't even attract the notice of many Japanese. The trains wouldn't even bother to stop for it.

Not that Ashiya needed a train to reach Shinjuku. From Sasazuka, it was only one train stop away on the Keio line. About twenty minutes' walk for any healthy man. Twisting the doorknob again to ensure the lock was still in one piece, he thrust the key into his pocket and gingerly walked down the staircase.

It never dawned on Ashiya that he, himself, had fallen to the point where he gleefully made excuses in order to cheap out on a single stop's worth of train fare.

＊

Sadao Maou, perched atop his trusty steed Dullahan, was on his way to work.

From the Devil's Castle in Sasazuka, it was less than ten minutes' riding to the MgRonald in Hatagaya, assuming no snags. Thanks to the delay from Ashiya's lecturing, however, the rain was now falling at a steady clip.

It was strong enough that his beaten-up umbrella, with its bent ribs, rusting support rod, and clouded plastic that no longer offered full visibility, had no chance of covering for it.

Yet Maou pedaled on, prodding himself forward as quickly as possible.

It was the last day of the month, a Friday, one that always loosened the strings on his wallet a bit. An important day, too. His store was vying for the number one regional sales prize for the current special menu item. It made Maou burn with excitement. This was it. This would be the day when they would set a new record for Black Chili Pepper Fry sales!

"I don't need you yelling at me, Ashiya. I'm thinking about this, too…in my own way!"

The lust was still there. His ultimate ambition, as always, was to conquer Ente Isla. But with no way to return home, there wasn't much to be done about it. Even if he could teleport over right now, he would be cut down and defeated in the blink of an eye without his magic force.

Meanwhile, in Japan, as long as you kept your nose clean, your chances of being slain on the battlefield were on the low side. And if you regarded this current routine as baby steps on the path to reclaiming the Devil King throne, it was even possible to retain one's sense of demonic pride.

For now, this was fine. Maou honestly believed that.

He stopped at a red crosswalk signal, his brakes screeching as his front wheel plowed into a water puddle.

Dullahan was a bargain, but its brakes, like the scream of an enraged mandragora, were one sticking point.

At this intersection, cutting through a residential area a block away from the Koshu-Kaido road, there was a small park and a trendy restaurant, its walls covered with glass from floor to ceiling.

Across the street, toward the direction he came from, Maou spotted a woman nestled beneath the restaurant's rain canopy.

The street was filled with passersby in search of lunch, but this woman caught his eye. She apparently had no umbrella with her. Even from afar, he could see her make a face as she wiped down her hair and shoulders with a small handkerchief in her hand.

Her annoyed stare was pointed toward the sky as the light remained steadily red. She likely wasn't expecting the rain. Even when the light finally turned green, she remained under the canopy, seemingly at a loss.

Maou, ever mindful of traffic laws, dismounted his bike and walked it across the street. Once across, the woman noticed him for the first time, eyes turned toward his. He nodded lightly at her, then ducked under the restaurant's canopy next to her, taking care to place Dullahan in between them to dispel any suspicions.

"Um, if you like…"

Folding up his plastic umbrella, he presented it to her, handle first.

"Huh?"

Her clear, refreshing voice sounded confused at first. She looked around her surroundings, unsure how to proceed.

"Oh, I… It just started so suddenly, so I thought you might need it."

She had seemed like a mature woman, judging by how she looked and acted from across the street, but up close, she looked younger, perhaps even high school age. She was, at least, younger than Maou's external appearance.

Her flower-print, tunic-length top and tight, skinny denim jeans were a good match for her natural beauty. The rain in her long hair, slightly curled at the ends, gave it a sheen that made it all the more attractive. A pity she didn't think to pack a folding umbrella inside the small purse hanging from her shoulder.

Her strong, willful eyes were now clearly focused upon Maou, a whiff of anxiety on her face.

"But…are you sure? I can't just take this from you…"

He had no spare on him, of course. This one had been plucked off the ground; actually spending money on one was an exotic concept to him.

"Oh, no, I work right nearby here, so… It's only about two or three minutes by bike. We've got more umbrellas over there."

Nervously, the woman took up the handle offered to her. As she did, Maou swiftly remounted his bike, not wishing to make her feel any more indebted.

"Um, thank you very much! I'd like to repay you somehow…"

However, the woman turned out to be more insistent than Maou was expecting. He held his hand upward in response.

"Forget about it. It's kind of junky anyway. You can go ahead and toss it once you're done with it."

"Oh, I couldn't just…"

Maou turned toward the woman, who was still acting a tad hesitant about the whole thing.

"Well, how about this? I work at the MgRonald right nearby here, so why don't you stop by for a bite to eat sometime?"

"Right nearby…? You mean the one by Hatagaya station?"

She nodded her understanding as Maou pointed out the direction.

"Yeah. I'll give you an upsize on the special fries we got right now, if I'm there."

It was this sort of grassroots marketing that Maou specialized in around the neighborhood. He saw himself as a MgRonald employee everywhere he went in public, and anyone could be a potential customer. The way he saw it, this extra effort was what led to his job promotions.

"All right. I'll be sure to do that. Umm…"

The woman stood up straight, looking right into Maou's eyes.

"Thanks again."

With that, she bowed lightly.

Her smile was like a beautiful ray of sunshine peeking through the distressing rainclouds of his heart.

"Sure thing. Be careful."

Maou turned around, attempting to hide his pangs of awkwardness. Waving his hand, he plunged back into the rain, never turning back.

"Brrrr! Cold!"

Perhaps that exchange was too knightly for his own good. But it was all for a better tomorrow, better sales figures, and—let one not forget—a better chance at brutally dominating the world.

Also, losing one's umbrella for a valid reason should make Ashiya release his iron grip on their finances enough that he could purchase a new one, right? If not, he could always take his pick from the umbrella rack in front of the store.

Back at the intersection, the light long since back to red, the woman remained motionless, until Maou was no longer in sight.

In the end, Maou's location failed to top the Black Chili Pepper Fry charts for the region. One of the fryers stopped working after the lunch rush.

It took two hours for the repairman to show up, and those two hours made all the difference.

A frustrating ordeal for Maou, to say the least, and one he dwelled upon as he lugged yet another bag full of junk food home with him.

The heavy rainstorm was a thing of the past by the time evening rolled around. That kept him from needing to "borrow" an umbrella from the store, but there was no doubt the foul weather kept customers home.

But was there anything else? Yes, there was the fryer and the rain, but did they go wrong elsewhere at all? The question was all Maou could think about on the way home, as he reached the intersection where he had lent his umbrella out earlier.

"...Huh?"

It was now late night. The restaurant at the intersection had long closed, looking completely dark inside. The only light illuminating the deserted crossing was a lone streetlamp and the blinking traffic signals.

There was someone lurking beneath the restaurant's canopy.

He hadn't noticed in the darkness at first, but it was the girl he encountered on the way to work.

"Hey, are you the...?"

Maou stopped himself midsentence. Something was off about this.

The woman was silent as she fixed her gaze upon him. There was something cold, almost hostile in her eyes.

Her smile from before was like a rainbow arcing across the drizzly sky, and now her expression was like an Arctic iceberg, frigid enough to crystallize the sun itself.

She was glaring at him, there was no doubt about that. Maou swallowed nervously, almost cowering at the sensation of her eyes upon him.

Unable to take the woman's silent leering any longer, Maou mustered up the courage to speak.

"Um...did it work out okay? You didn't get wet, did you?"

"No, it did not work out okay."

"Uh?"

Her voice was like a polar vortex in the middle of winter.

"I went to your MgRonald today."

"Oh? Um. W-well, thank you."

Now seemed like an unsuitable time to take up the sales pitch. He didn't remember seeing her while manning the register.

The woman took a step toward Maou, almost making him lose his balance and fall to the ground. Flustered, he jumped off his bike and—for completely different reasons from before—positioned it between the two of them.

"I was watching you. From the place across the street."

"Watching me?… You mean, the restaurant?"

There was a bookstore that overlooked MgRonald from the other side. She was watching them from over there? Was she one of those mystery diners they kept hearing about?

"No. You."

"M-me?"

Now Maou was even more confused. She came to the store…but not to return the umbrella, at least? They had barely brushed against each other, and now she was *stalking* him? There was only one—

"…You looked so different from before, I thought my mind was playing tricks on me. But after a while, I realized."

—only one woman who would—

"At first, I doubted my five senses. I knew you were somewhere near, but not *this* near."

—who would be *looking* for him!

"You can try to hide what little magic you have left, but you can't fool me!"

Impossible!

"Devil King Satan! Why are you working part-time at the MgRonald in Hatagaya?!"

The flowing jet-black hair; the beautiful, unblemished skin; the keen, magic-detecting eyes. She had to be—

"Y-you…! Emilia, the Hero!"

She was Emilia Justina, the Hero who snatched Ente Isla from the Devil King's gnarled hands. The Hero glorified as the holy savior of her native land. Why was *she* in Sasazuka?

"Yes! It is I, Emilia! And surely you must know why I am here!"

"Y-you couldn't be…!"

"You and Alciel, your sole remaining general, may have just barely escaped us. But I have traveled across worlds in the pursuit! If I let you escape, our world will be enveloped in darkness once again! And before that can happen, I will *destroy you!*"

"W-wait! Wait a sec, Emilia! We can talk this out!"

"Never, Devil King! Prepare to die!"

Suddenly, the Hero Emilia took out a knife and lunged for Maou, slashing at the air. Maou leaped backward, dodging the blade as it zipped past his bike. The once-proud Dullahan clanked to the ground, loudly protesting the unexpectedly rough treatment the entire way.

"Whoa! Watch it!"

"Enough of your cowardly evasion! Stand still and let me kill you!"

"You gotta be kidding me!"

He barely avoided the knife's second swipe past Dullahan as it coursed just past the pit of his stomach.

Maou took a moment to collect himself. He was weaponless. The trip home from the fast-food joint rarely called for any. That clearly put him on the defensive, but a sense of supreme confidence still filled Maou's mind. One look at Emilia's weapon was all he needed to know how this confrontation would end.

"Uh...Emilia?"

"Hmm? Begging for your life, is it? I shall never negotiate with my sworn enemy!"

The forcefulness of her declaration did throw him slightly, but he still managed to croak out an observation—one that had a surprising effect on his opponent.

"Where's your holy sword?"

"...!"

It was enough to make her visibly gasp.

"You bought that knife at the hundred-yen store in Sasazuka, right? I have that same one."

"H-how did you...!"

Now Emilia was visibly shaken. The knife in her hand shone dully in the light of the red traffic signal.

"You...you lost all of your holy force, didn't you? Or even if you didn't, you can't afford to waste any, huh?"

"Nnngh…!"

The way Emilia gnashed her teeth in response was all the confirmation Maou needed.

He had expected, to some extent, pursuers from Ente Isla would be forthcoming. But not the Hero herself from the outset. And yet here she was, across the Gate just like himself, sniffing out the trail of his magical force.

"B-but…but you're in the same situation, aren't you? Your power feels so weak…so fragile! It's nothing compared to before!"

"Well…yeah, but…"

Maou winced internally. But there was no point pretending otherwise.

"With or without my holy blade, I have nothing to fear from a Devil King who's a powerless fry cook! Die!"

Emilia held the knife aloft in the air.

Light flooded over the two of them.

Ashiya, fresh from an ultimately disappointing trip to the National Museum of Western Art's special exhibit wing, tossed the museum pamphlet into the mail holder. Snapping a four-hundred-gram block of expired discount *udon* in half, he began to boil the noodles in a pot as he waited for Maou's return.

There was no way either of them could survive only with the food left in the refrigerator. Ashiya had been saving his own money as well, in part to raise the funds for his museum investigations, so he was still able to perform a bare minimum of shopping. He kept this stash a secret from his liege.

"Ugh. He's bound to bring back more of those chili-pepper fries, I just know it…"

Swatting away the bugs flitting inside from the open window, Ashiya took a glance at the clock.

"Hmm…His Demonic Highness is late."

"So you're Sadao Maou, and you're Emi Yusa? Right. So could you tell me why you were arguing at that intersection?"

"I was there to *slay* this man!"

The Devil King and Emilia were seated on folding chairs at the Hatagaya police substation, a wizened officer in front of them.

"Listen, ma'am, I don't know what your friend here did to deserve this, but there's no excuse for going around flailing a knife at him. You need to just calm down and talk things over, all right?"

The officer's advice was enough to send Emi Yusa, aka the Hero Emilia, into a rage.

"I... Who do you think he *is* to me...?!"

"Right now," Maou interjected, an angry scowl on his face, "I bet he thinks we're having a lovers' spat or something."

"Well, if I'm wrong, I apologize. You see that sort of thing a lot lately, you know? So just talk it over and... You know, if you're gonna break up, try to be a tad more quiet about it, okay?"

"I'm *telling* you, it's not *like* that between us!"

A local resident had called the police at the confrontation. Now the Devil King and his rival, Hero, were at the station, getting the riot act read to them.

It took an hour or so of lecturing about the perils of domestic violence before the two of them were finally released.

Emilia plodded wearily forward as they exited. The ordeal had apparently caused her some measure of emotional pain.

"...I'm letting you go today. But next time...that'll be *it*."

"Oh, what, you planning to bring a rolling pin next time?"

Emilia chose to ignore the jab.

"Hmph. I hope you're happy you've been granted an extension to your life. And this evening hasn't been a waste at all. I memorized your home address, I'll have you know. Hope you weren't expecting to get a full night's sleep for the rest of your life."

"You're sounding more like a mob boss than a Hero." Even as Maou winced at her brazen threat, a question suddenly popped into his mind. "Oh, by the way, what about my umbrella?"

For a moment, Emilia's face betrayed her inability to comprehend the question. Then, she let out a haughty, nasal laugh.

"You said I could toss it out once I was done. So I did! I made sure to thoroughly mutilate it before I did, too."

"Oh, that's just *mean*!"

The anguish was sincere, from the bottom of his heart. Thanks to all the neighborhood cleanup efforts around Shibuya ward, it was growing difficult to find abandoned umbrellas lying around.

"And why would a Hero such as myself gleefully accept an umbrella from the Devil King himself? May my family be cursed for generations if I did! I'd never keep such a putrid, tainted cancer near me for even a *second*!"

To prove the point, Emilia took out a handkerchief, one in a strangely cutesy pink color, and began to wipe her hands.

"I am the sworn enemy of the demon race and all that take comfort with it. Starting tomorrow, you'd best watch yourself on the streets at night!"

With this final, rather unheroic flourish, she disappeared into the Hatagaya night, her footing still a bit unsteady.

"...Well, *that's* all I need." The Hero had pursued the Devil King across multiple worlds. But why? It hardly seemed like anything important had happened at all. His even still had work tomorrow.

The day was already starting to break as he muttered to himself on the way back home.

"Man, Ashiya's gonna be *pissed* if he hears that girl is here. Maybe I should keep it under my hat for a while."

He found out the next morning.

Since Maou's shift began in the afternoon, this meant the secret was revealed as they were eating the plain omelet—no filling, no ketchup, no nothing—Ashiya made from the slightly distressed medium-sized eggs he'd purchased at discount last night.

The two of them exchanged glances as the doorbell rang. MHK had just visited the previous day. The assorted newspaper salesmen had long since given up on the place.

The rent and phone bill were deducted straight from their account. Which meant that it had to be some new door-to-door solicitor.

Neither bothered to even entertain the possibility of any mail or packages addressed to them. That was reality for you.

"Yes? Who is it?" Ashiya called out from behind the door. They couldn't pretend to be out; the kitchen's ventilation fan was running.

"'Who is it?' Well, thank you *very* much for such a polite greeting! I've found you, Alciel! Last of the Four Great Demon Generals!"

Maou choked in response. Scrambled eggs flowed down his windpipe, throwing him into a coughing fit that sprayed bits of egg up into his nose. It was both an agonizing and rather nonthreatening response.

"Wh-who're you?!"

In an instant, Ashiya jumped away from the door, ready for battle.

"Who? I believe the last time you asked me that, we were battling each other in Devil's Castle. You haven't forgotten, have you? The name of the Hero, Emilia Justina?"

"The Hero Emilia!"

Panicked, Ashiya turned toward Maou, who was tearing up as he tried to unclog egg fragments from his own nostrils.

"Now, come! Open this door and prepare for your destined fate!"

It was difficult to believe, but there was no one in Japan besides Maou who would know the name Alciel. He had had concerns about being pursued by potential Devil King assassins, but who could have expected the Hero herself to reach them first?

The reality of the situation threw him at first, but even now, Alciel was the most gifted of the demon forces' strategists. He had an insider's knowledge of every one of Emilia's moves, and he already boasted a full grasp of his enemy's weaknesses.

Checking the lock on the door, Ashiya slid the chain into place, shut all the windows that looked into the outside corridor, and turned off the ventilation fan. "Your Demonic Highness! It's the Hero! The Hero is here!"

"Ah...! Wait! Alciel, wait! I'm telling you, open up!"

There was a tone of panic to the Hero's voice, as she realized the nature of his tactic.

"Yeah, I know, Ashiya. Hey, get me a tissue."

"The Devil King! You're in there, too, are you? Give it up and open this door!"

The doorbell rang incessantly, beating a predictable rhythm. Ashiya paid it no mind.

"What should we do, Your Demonic Highness?! The Hero is right at our doorstep!"

"Ugh, I can't get this bit out of my nose. Yeah, we met yesterday. Sorry I didn't tell you."

"Wh-what?!"

Maou's distracted remark as he pinched a nostril shut was enough to stun Ashiya into silence.

"She attacked me over at that intersection on the way from work. Then someone reported us, so we got taken in by the cops. That's why I was late last night."

"The most humiliating moment of my life! They...they thought I was the Devil King's *girlfriend*!"

They could feel the waves of anger radiating from behind the door. Ashiya's eyes shot toward it for a moment, but quickly turned back at Maou as he half-shouted his response.

"Why, my liege?! Why did you not tell me sooner?!"

"Well, I mean...like, no one got hurt, so... Besides, she's kind of in the same boat we are."

"The same boat...? Meaning?"

Maou inserted a probing finger into his nose to clear out any rogue egg bits remaining.

"She recognized me as the Devil King Satan yesterday, but she couldn't bring out her sword. That's made out of Holy Silver, right? The heaven-born metal that's imbued with holy power? She couldn't summon it. You know what that means?"

"...It means she cannot afford to waste her holy power? So she's lost the ability to recharge her own powers as well!"

"Yeah. Not that she'd mind using up all her holy force to defeat the Devil King, though. However, we've got one decisive advantage on our side."

"Her...life span, right?"

The ball of anger on the other side of the door began stamping her feet in disgust. It was loud enough to raise serious concerns about the cheap wooden floor giving in on her.

"Even if she killed both of us, there's no guarantee she'll regain enough holy force to get out of this world before she dies. The humans on Ente Isla, they're lucky if they reach fifty. Of course, women in Japan average a lot higher than that, so *maybe* her mideighties or so. But she'll be old and frail by that time."

"So the Hero would lack the strength to control the Gate as well, then."

"Basically, yeah. Here, you mind letting her in? She's starting to cry out there."

The sniffling was loud enough to be audible from beyond the door.

"What a *dump*!"

Emilia's first reaction upon entering was as heroic sounding as she could muster with a beet-red face and bloodshot eyes.

Ashiya was ready to launch into an angry response, but Maou stopped him, knowing full well she wasn't exaggerating.

"Hey, at least it isn't cluttered, right? We can't even afford any stuff to clutter it up with."

"I find it hard to believe that two men could truly bear to live here…"

"I like my Devil Castles more functional than comfortable."

Maou, nasal passages finally cleared, had returned to his omelet.

"Not much of a breakfast there, either."

"Dude, Ashiya's a genius at this. He makes breakfasts out of practically nothing. Like magic."

"I thank you for your praise, Your Demonic Highness."

Ashiya knelt meekly behind Maou as his liege sat cross-legged at the table, running his chopsticks against the plate to wipe up the crumbs. Emilia rolled her eyes in exasperation. What kind of ridiculous charade was this? The Devil King and his faithful general, savoring this meager slop?

"Are you crazy? The Devil King, eating eggs and nothing else for breakfast? You could at *least* buy some bread to go with it."

"We're poor, all right? Is that bad?"

Maou's defense was sorely lacking.

"Yes! Yes, it is! I clawed my way over to a completely different world just so I could kill these two dirty hobos? This is horrible...!"

The sight of Maou sitting cross-legged in front of his beat-up *kotatsu* table, enjoying breakfast in his boxers and sweat-stained running shirt, finally made Emilia break down in tears.

Six tatami mats lined the floor of the apartment, bronzed over time by the rays of the sun. Against one wall, a cheap-looking three-level particle-board shelf, sitting on top of some cardboard to keep from damaging the tatami mats. On the other wall, a closet, the sliding doors similarly discolored by the sun.

There was no balcony, no screens over the windows; just a few rusted iron bars welded to the other side. Bits of laundry—mostly shapeless, solid-color T-shirts, threadbare underwear, and socks—were draped over the window frame, taking every available inch of space. The washer that cleaned them was outside in the corridor, too large to actually install in the apartment. Looking around, Emilia spotted a single lonely door, the paint peeling off of it. A plastic plate reading "Toilet" hung from it, as if the occupants had trouble remembering where it was. The john was the old Japanese-style floor model, no doubt.

The kitchen counter boasted an array of thin, dull, flimsy-looking plastic accessories, all likely purchased from the hundred-yen store, as well as a few stacks of ceramic bowls and such, none of their designs customized for the season or anything. A garbage bag was thrown into one corner, crammed to the brim with MgRonald packaging, ready for disposal whenever anyone gave enough of a damn to take out the trash.

There was also a stainless-steel trash bin with a funky flower motif, another garbage bag lining the inside. The dents and old packing-tape markings one could spot here and there suggested the bin was a relic from the local thrift shop.

The refrigerator that made the already cramped kitchen even more constrained was a medium-sized model, likely meant for a single-person household. A MgRonald desk calendar with "Monthly Shifts" written on it was tacked to the door with broken bits of old kitchen magnets.

"I…I live by myself, and I *still* live better than this. You've got two of you holding jobs, and *this* is the best you can do?"

Emilia was trying to condemn Maou's pathetic lifestyle, but Maou's interest was laid upon a completely different subject.

"By yourself? You don't have any friends?"

"Shut *up!*"

Without skipping a beat, Emilia threw the nearby tissue box at him. Maou nimbly dodged it, and it harmlessly bounced off a stack of free newspapers and job-search magazines, tied up with plastic twine, before falling with a thud upon the tatami mats.

"The…the archbishop was supposed to join me! We were going to head right back home after you were defeated! And…and *now* look what happened!"

Emilia was the one who decided to pursue the fleeing Devil King through the Gate at once.

She had taken the lead position and plunged inside, but once it swallowed her up, it had suddenly shut itself off, leaving the rest behind.

Her last glimpse of Ente Isla as she looked behind her was the strained face of Olba Meiyer, her friend and one of the six archbishops of the Church, seemingly unable to comprehend what had happened.

"Hmm…"

"What?"

Emi shot a glare at Maou. He shook his head to indicate it was nothing, motioning her to continue.

Once she touched down in Japan, Emilia went through the same ordeal Maou and Ashiya did—conserve what remained of her powers while attempting to build a life in this new world.

The main difference was that her part-time work paid a lot more by the hour than Maou's, enough to let her afford a fairly decent condo-sized apartment.

"You got a phone?"

"Yeah. Dokodemo."

She took out a sharp-looking touchscreen device, a high-end one, advertised as offering the power of a modern laptop in the palm of your hand.

"...Well, you win."

"I win what?"

Maou and Ashiya's phone was an old, unpopular model that was a pain to navigate and sported a camera that would have been hot stuff thirteen years ago. They had concluded that when it came to a phone, talk and text would be good enough.

"So how long have you been here in Japan?"

"It...uh, hasn't been a year yet."

"How old are you this year?"

"Seventeen! So?"

Most seventeen-year-olds in Japan would still be under parental care. They'd be attending high school.

So how could *this* one be living a better, more relaxed life than Maou? It honestly puzzled Maou inside, but he opted not to dwell upon it. It wasn't like knowing the answer would improve life at all.

"Well, no matter what happens, we're gonna need to find a way out of this world before we use up our natural life span. I know you found us and all, but we don't exactly have the cash to move out of here. So, welcome to the new Devil's Castle. This one-room apartment is all we need to open the first chapter in our new quest for world domination."

Maou attempted to affect as much bluster as he could, using his chopsticks to point at her as he did. Her expression as she looked around the room was part doubt, part sympathetic compassion, and part natural wariness.

"Do you think you can back up all that junk, though? A Devil King living day to day off menial part-time work?"

"I am not your typical demon, Hero. I know I cannot solve every problem with force alone. If you think I'm willing to live out my life in Japan, rolling along with my comfortable job, you are deadly wrong."

"Huh?"

It was Ashiya, unexpectedly, expressing doubt at this statement. Maou ignored him as he himself laughed heartily at Emilia.

"I fully intend to have Japan in my grasp before long."

Emilia tensed up as the Devil King started to sound the part, for a change. Noticing this, Ashiya steeled himself, preparing for whatever might happen. A single word from Maou was all it would take. After a pause, his master spoke.

"So listen. At MgRonald, if you work hard enough as a part-timer, they have a system where you can become a full salaried employee."

"...Uh?"

Another word was all it took to immediately break the tension. The quizzical looks on faces of Emilia and Ashiya told the whole story. What did the violent takeover of Japan and the human resources department at MgRonald have to do with each other?

"You should know as well as I do, Emilia, how much your schooling and past experience affect your social position here in Japan."

"Yeah. So? That's 'Emilia the Hero,' by the way!"

"Look, try to use your brain a little, all right? In Japan, we're magicless. Powerless. The only power we *can* get our hands on is the title of a salaried employee!"

Maou belted out a howling laugh, the laugh that once sowed seeds of terror across Ente Isla.

"So heed my words, Emilia the Hero. My ultimate goal is to become a full-time employee in this world!"

"I...don't see how that affects me."

Emilia was frozen on the spot, unsure how to react to this unexpected declaration.

"Soon, the day will come when I outclass even my store manager. Then, as a full-timer, I will build up my stores of cash and social currency. Before long, I will wield enormous powers, forcing massive armies of people in Japan to grovel before me! Then I will use this power as a weapon to invade Ente Isla once more! Well, Emilia? Think you have what it takes to stop me?"

Ashiya could only stand to the side, unable to speak as he listened to the speech unfolding in terrifying fashion.

Chopsticks still in hand, Maou stared proudly at the plainly dumbfounded Emilia.

"...You are *so* stupid."

After a moment, Emilia averted her eyes. Maou, noting this, puffed up his chest in glorious victory.

"Hah! I thought so! A mere human could never comprehend the extent of my glorious spiritual strength!"

"If I may," interjected Ashiya, "I think she said that precisely *because* she comprehended it."

After a sigh, Emilia continued, obviously crestfallen at this anti-climax.

"This is just exhausting me... I don't know if it even matters anymore. I'm going home."

She wiped her reddened eyes before shooting Maou another glare.

"But I hope you don't have the wrong idea. I don't understand you at all, and I am definitely *not* going to let you run free. I still have some of my power left. I could kill you anytime I want. But if I do that, I won't have any way back home. So if I want to get back home, then I won't be able to kill you. And that's how it is."

What did she hope to accomplish, admitting up to her own predicament? It puzzled Maou as Emilia laid it bare for all the world to see, as if nothing could be more natural.

"It wouldn't be fair if you told me about yourself and I didn't return the favor, would it?"

This threw both Maou and Ashiya for a loop.

"Well, how wonderfully thoughtful of you."

"So...until I find a way to procure both your defeat and my pathway back home, I'm not going to take your life. But don't let your guard down yet!...Ugh."

The fatigue was written upon Emilia's face as she walked toward the door.

"Also, my name here in Japan is Emi Yusa, all right? Try not to mess it up."

"Yeah, sure thing."

Emilia opened the door, then turned back toward the two men.

"Also, what kind of name is 'Sadao'? That's, like, a grandpa's name."

Then she slammed the door shut behind her, kicking up dust apartment-wide. Ashiya stared at the door, still reeling. They could hear her tramping down the stairway, and then all was silent.

The Devil King spat at the unseen "Emi's" back.

"All the Sadaos in Japan are gonna make you beg for mercy!"

✳

"Hi there! Are you dining in today?"

"I want to talk to you. Outside."

The MgRonald in front of Hatagaya station was staying fairly busy today. Enough so that Emi, dressed in a gray business suit instead of the morning's casual outfit, didn't even bother hiding her peeved annoyance as she stood in front of Maou's cash register.

"To go, then? Okay, what would you like to order?"

"I want you where we were last night once you get out of work. I'm not taking no for an answer."

"Can I make that into a value meal for you today?"

"Come alone."

"Just the sandwich? Certainly! If I could just have you wait one moment by the side here… One Big Mag, please!"

"You better show up. This isn't so I can fight you."

"Thank you very much! Come back soon!"

Emi briskly paid for the current seasonal burger, accepted the bag, and left.

All Maou could think, the businesslike smile never leaving his face, was *Dammit dammit DAMMIT* repeatedly. There was no way this little "talk" was going to go smoothly.

"Maou?"

A voice called for him from behind.

"What's up, Chi?"

It was Chiho Sasaki, one of the new part-timers. She was a second-year high-school student whom Maou had mentored during her training period. Even now, as a full crew member, she still turned to Maou whenever something came up.

She put her medium-length hair up during her shift, and her natural-born brightness and guileless smile made her a hit with the customers. Maou appreciated how quickly she soaked in all the knowledge she needed for the job.

"That was kind of a weird customer, wasn't it?"

"You mean the...woman just now?"

"Right. Kind of creepy, huh? And she kept on muttering, too."

"Yeah, well, we get all kinds in here."

"Do you know her? It sounded like you were having a conversation."

Yes, he knew Emi. No denying that. Thinking about it, he realized that Emi, at age seventeen, could be just as old as Chiho. It was funny how they made the exact opposite impression on people. Emi seemed far more mature than her years betrayed...or, more likely, she had a childhood that forced her to grow up fast.

"Mmm, yeah, a little."

Maou hoped to drop the subject as quickly as possible, but Chiho's sense of curiosity was unlikely to let that ambiguous response pass without comment.

"Ooh! Something's *up*!"

"What?"

Chiho peered at him from below, hands clasped together behind her back.

"And she *was* kinda pretty, too, huh? Huh? Huh, Maou?"

"You don't have to say 'huh' three times, Chi! Like, what makes you think her and me are—*Hello* there!"

By this point, the instinct to loudly greet every customer who passed through the entrance was embedded into his brain stem.

"Will this be for here, ma'am?"

This time, Chiho took up the register. They were out of the rush, so anyone was free to take the front counter as long as they knew the job. Chiho was still new here, but whenever there was a spare moment, she readily sought out and accepted new duties. Maou was impressed enough that he willingly took a step back and let her take over.

The customer was a kindly-looking mother with baby in hand, a boy who might or might not have been old enough for school yet was clinging to her side. It was a pretty common sight to see at the semiresidential Hatagaya restaurant, once the lunch period ended and the herds of office flacks cleared out.

The mother's eyes darted between Chiho and the menu as she placed her order. Suddenly, Chiho's fingers came to a halt over the register keys. "Just one moment, please," she said before turning to Maou.

"Um…Maou?"

"Yep?"

It was generally frowned upon for full employees to whisper at trainees in front of customers. Instead, requiring crew members to discuss issues with customers and solve them together helped train the staff and gave customers a better impression of the place. Chiho pointed out the family with her eyes as she continued.

"This customer's son has issues with allergies."

"Allergies? Certainly. Do you know which types of food trigger these allergies?"

It was still Chiho's duty to attend to the customer. Maou worked through her to address the customer's concerns as politely as possible.

"It looks like shrimp, crab, and some fruits, too."

Maou nodded and provided a colorful menu to the mother as he explained her options.

"Well, products that include shrimp are required by law to be specifically mentioned on food menus, so as you can see here, it's used in all of our seafood products."

"Oh!"

The mother, as well as Chiho, seemed oddly impressed by this presentation.

"Regarding fruit, the government recommends informational displays for kiwifruit, oranges, peaches, and apples. Out of those, apples are the only type used in certain types of seasonings that we use. This includes the sauce on the Teriyaki Burger, for example, as well as some salad dressings. Over on our side offerings, it would also be best to avoid our seasonal fruit-flavored ice cream selection, as well as the vegetable juice."

Both the mother and Chiho were held enrapt by this lecture, as Maou pointed out the menu items to be avoided. Satisfied by this, the mother made her choices.

"By the way, ma'am, would you like to use our microwave?"

"Hmm?"

"Huh?"

Chiho and the mother responded in almost identical fashion. Maou motioned toward the mother's infant as he continued.

"If you have any baby food or other products meant for microwave preparation, we'd be happy to assist you with that. If you don't mind my intrusiveness, I thought you might like your youngest to enjoy lunch with you and your son."

The mother glanced at the baby in her arms, a wide grin on her face, before nodding.

"Well, thank you very much! Here... This should take about forty seconds to cook."

She took a vacuum-packed pouch out from her shoulder bag as she spoke. Maou accepted it, then handed it over to Chiho.

"Here, Sasaki, put this in for twenty seconds. Make sure it's ready alongside the rest of the order."

Employees in Japanese restaurants were expected to refer to each other by last name in front of their customers. Chiho took the vacuum pack and was about to trot toward the kitchen when she stopped herself.

"Didn't she say forty seconds?"

"That's for a household microwave. We've got an industrial one here that's at least twice as strong, so twenty ought to be enough."

"Oh! All right!"

Chiho nodded respectfully toward Maou before disappearing into the rear kitchen.

Maou took up the reins from there, accepting payment, arranging the order on the tray, and handing it to the customer. He wound up being thanked multiple times by the grateful mother. Just another small step on the path to a full-time position. And, from there, to conquering Japan. He could physically feel the steadily forward progress on his skin today.

"Mmm? What is it, Chi?"

Chiho, who had reappeared by his side at some point, looked up toward him, practically in awe.

"That was *amazing*, Maou!"

"Huh?"

"I mean, look at you! Did you memorize all that stuff about allergies and what kind of ingredient goes in what?"

"Well, it's all in the training manual, isn't it?"

Maou replied as if nothing could be less unexpected. Chiho's excitement continued apace.

"But that's still amazing! And you even thought about the baby food, too!"

"Yeah… Well, that kind of thing's tougher during the rush, but when you have the time for it, it's nice if you can be flexible with customer needs. It helps make a better long-term impression."

To Chiho, young and chock-full of desire to perform her job well, this was enough to make her sigh in rapt admiration.

"That's just so…so *cool*, Maou! So grown-up and responsible!"

"Ha-ha… Still just a part-timer, though."

The only thing that could have intensified Chiho's look of awed respect was if the background behind her were literally spewing rose petals in all directions. Suddenly, though, she snapped out of it, her face serious once more.

"Oh! Speaking of which, Maou, were you okay after the earthquake yesterday?"

"Um…"

It was always difficult—as difficult as trying to control the Gate to another world—to predict what kind of sudden new directions a teenage girl would take a conversation. It was astonishing to Maou, and something he had been introduced to only once he had Chiho for a coworker, but he was well used to it by now.

"Yeah, no real problems. I live in a junky apartment, so I guess my roommate thought it was a pretty big one, but it didn't shake *that* much, you know? I didn't even feel anything."

"Oh? Uh… Oh! I guess so, huh?"

Chiho, judging by her reaction, wasn't expecting this response. She had this very unnatural way of acting surprised that was in itself surprising.

"That's what all my classmates said at school when I asked them, but for me, it was, like, so awful!"

"Really?"

Spotting Maou's apparent interest, Chiho began to gesticulate wildly to emphasize her harrowing experience.

"My mom said there was this really loud noise, like something exploded, and it shook really bad, too! When I got back home, all the CDs and stuff had fallen off my bookshelf! It was the worst!"

"Wow. That bad?"

"Oh, you don't think I'm lying, too, do you, Maou?"

Chiho puffed up her cheeks in protest, eliciting a laugh from him.

"Oh, I'm not, I'm not. So then what happened?"

"Well, then we had to clean up all the dishes and stuff that had broken! My dad was calling around all over the place!"

"Calling who?"

"Oh! My dad's a police officer, but he was home yesterday because he was off duty. But he used to be a regional director and one of the emergency contact points for the town assembly, so he made a bunch of calls to all his contacts. The ward's disaster management office told him that it wasn't a big earthquake at all. It was a real bummer!"

"Huh."

"Maou?"

" ......"

"Hey! Maou!"

"Mm? Oh. Sorry. I just thought that sounded kinda weird, you know? Like, only your house getting affected."

"Yeah, isn't it?... Oh, uh, by the way?"

"Hmm?"

She had been excited up to now, darting from word to word, but now Chiho's voice was toned down a notch as she expectantly looked at her coworker.

"You said you had a roommate just now?"

Something about her eyes made Maou want to avert his own.

Yeah. An old general of mine. *Friend*. Friend of mine, from way back."

The "living on a shoestring with my old friend" cover was something he had decided upon with Ashiya in advance. It had the side benefit of being almost 100 percent true. Maou sighed to himself.

"Is-is it your...g-girl—"

"He's a guy, Chi. Just the two of us, slumming it in our ancient apartment building."

"Eh? Oh? Ohhhh. I...see. Yeah...I get it. Good!"

"What's good?"

"N-nothing! Are...are you on the first floor, Maou?"

"Nah. Second. My friend didn't feel anything on the second floor, so I guess that's why I didn't think it was anything big. The place definitely woulda been shaking if it was. What about you? Do you live in a condo or something?"

"No, it's...um, it's a house. Uh..."

"Hmm?"

"If...if you'd like, we could—"

"Come on, kids."

The conversation was interrupted by Mayumi Kisaki, head manager of the Hatagaya restaurant. She had the body proportions of a model and stood a good head taller than Maou. Her long black hair, easily sleek and shiny enough for her to star in shampoo ads, was tied back, the colorful MgRonald uniform doing wonders to accentuate her body.

"Oh! Ms. Kisaki!"

"No personal conversations while you're on duty, please. Have you completed the evening floor check yet, Chi?"

"Oh! I'm sorry! I'll go do it right now!"

Every two hours, someone had to go around the store to ensure everything was clean and in the proper place. Chiho hurriedly took a checksheet from the shelf beneath her register and flew away from the counter.

"You try not to spoil Chi too much either, okay, Marko?"

Kisaki's eyebrows were furrowed, but Maou knew she wasn't truly angry. Unless someone from the executive office was lurking around, she preferred to keep things relaxed on the floor, referring to every employee by a nickname and refusing to let anyone call her "Manager."

She was one of MgRonald's most well-known managers. More than a few male regulars stopped by just for a chance to chat with her, and she had appeared several times in the ads they printed on the paper place mats. Why an intelligent, attractive woman with such a perfectly shaped body was content with running a fast-food joint was a mystery. The only secrets she guarded more closely were her age, height, and weight.

"But didn't you tell me not to be so harsh on her, Ms. Kisaki? She's probably gonna be the first student in a while to settle into a regular shift schedule."

Just as Maou finished the sentence, they heard the sound of assorted objects falling to the ground beyond the door in the staff room next to the customer seating, where the crew stored cleaning equipment and other accessories. She must have knocked some of it over by accident. Chiho's frantic "Sorry about that!" could be heard above the noise.

"Well, yes, but the home office is starting to send people in unannounced to check up on things. If we let the private chat go too far, it might come back to bite us later on."

Fair enough. Even weirdos like Emi were spying on this place. There was no telling who else might have their eyes on it.

Of course, Maou had yet to see Kisaki have to apologize to anyone from the main headquarters. It seemed more like they actively tried to avoid her, in fact.

"Anyway, Marko, you mind doing an afternoon stat check for me?"

Maou tapped away at the register, printing out a receipt listing customer and sales figures for the slow afternoon period between the lunch and dinner rushes. Kisaki took a glance at the receipt and nodded, apparently satisfied.

"Nice! We're gonna make our daily sales target easy today. Great job, people! You all get one free drink on me. Let's keep it going through the dinner rush, all right? Oh, and Marko, that was a perfect ten, how you treated that customer just now. Keep setting a good example for the new guys, okay?"

Besides meeting her daily sales goals and keeping things positive and upbeat with the crew, Kisaki was a woman of few motivations. Hence why she was so ready to give Maou raises. Everything he did to improve his output and drive sales was exactly what she wanted to see.

Maou firmly believed that surpassing her would be the first concrete step along the path to world supremacy.

"Oh, by the way, did the earthquake yesterday affect you at all, Ms. Kisaki?"

"Earthquake? Was there one?"

That was about all the attention Kisaki paid the query as she pored over the sales figures. She had a condo somewhere nearby, but if that was her reaction, it was doubtful she felt anything at all.

"Ah, nothing worth worrying about at this point, I guess."

He felt a twinge of guilt about Chiho, but for now, he knew his primary concern should likely be his upcoming late-night conference after work. Maou was on duty until closing time at midnight, so it would likely come at the same time as yesterday. The more he thought about it, the more it plunged his mind into a state of depression.

❋

"So, what did you want to talk about?"

Emi, drawn up to her full height, was waiting for Maou at the darkened residential intersection. Since their last encounter, she had changed into a blouse and a trim pair of jeans. There was nothing in her hands, but there was no telling what kind of hidden weapon she might whip out and fling at him.

Kisaki's free drink—MgRonald's signature Platinum Roast Ice Coffee—was safely ensconced in Maou's right hand, ready to be thrown at a moment's notice.

"I just wanted to ask you something."

His hips were firmly planted upon the saddle of Dullahan, allowing him the option of escape if times called for it.

"Do you even *have* any intention of returning to Ente Isla?"

"Huh? What're you talking about?" Maou honestly failed to grasp her point. "Of course I do."

"So you don't want to spend the rest of your life in this world?"

"What, are you kidding me? What's this all about, anyway?"

"I was watching you work earlier."

"Wha—Where?! Not the bookstore again!"

Emi ignored the question.

"Your smile. Your snappy responses to questions. The trust the manager and the other employees put in you. That flexible approach you took with customers—that takes real *talent*. You're, like, the ideal Maggie's employee."

"What, are you from Osaka?"

The battle over how to correctly abbreviate the name "MgRonald" was intense and heated, cleanly splitting the nation of Japan in half vertically, with both sides doggedly sticking to their preferred version. Maou knew that, and as a resident of eastern Japan, he knew that "Ronald's" was the only correct—the only *sane*—version.

"When we talked this morning, I thought you were just spouting nonsense to me on purpose. But watching you work today...you were really telling the truth, weren't you?"

Emi shrugged. "And, you know, if you're *willing* to live out life as a bright, happy young man in this world, I'm perfectly willing to not kill you. That girl you worked with—you know, the cute one? It looked like she's got a thing for you."

"Yeah. I was pretty much the guy who gave Chi all her training. She's only been a full crew member for a coupla days, but she learns quick, and she's really good at being polite with customers...so..."

The Devil King was boasting about some rather unexpected feats.

"Think about it. If you live out your life here, everything's going to be fine. Peaceful! You can make the area around Hatagaya station happy for everyone. And I wouldn't have to fight anyone I don't have to. Would you consider it, at least? You, and Alciel, living here until you're dead and buried?"

"Alciel is a valued assistant of mine, I'll grant you that. But why would I want to live all the way to old age with him?"

"Well, you know, I heard that sort of thing is getting popular these days."

Maou scrunched up his face at the concept.

"Look, Emi, are you...*suggesting* something, when you're ordering me to live with another man my whole life?"

"No! Of course not! I just wanted to...bring up the idea, all right?"

Emi took a breath. "I just want you to give up Ente Isla for me. I want you to give it up, and find a new life for yourself here. On Earth."

Maou was quick to respond.

"Not happening. I'm gonna make my way back to Ente Isla...and it *will* be mine."

He meant every word of it. He had lost a great many things, but the strength behind his avowal still rang true.

That much was clear to Emi as well.

"...All right."

"Is that all?"

"Yes. That's it. Now it's been decided. I will chase you down for all time, until you are dead by my hand."

"So the same as before. Great."

Maou placed his feet upon Dullahan's trusty pedals. He pumped them once, defiantly, hoping to place a final exclamation point on their conversation, when:

"Yagh!"

He felt a dull force thunk against his front wheel. Losing his balance, he fell lamely to the ground.

Even Emi, who was about to briskly walk away from the scene, was surprised at the sheer artistic grandeur behind the wipeout. If he were a little closer to the side of the street, he might have cracked his head open on the curb.

The cup of iced coffee in his hand arced through the air, the liquid and ice splattering across the pavement.

"What was *that*?"

Without thinking, Emi ran back to Maou, helping him back up.

"Oww… Man, that came out of nowhere. Did I run over something?"

"Hah! And you call yourself Devil King! Get it together, won't you?"

"Shut up."

Emi inspected the bike as he supported Maou's side. His eyes had teared up a bit from the shocked surprise.

"That's a new bike, too, isn't it? Oooh, too bad." She pointed at the front wheel as he brought the kickstand down.

"Aw, man, it's flat!"

Falling to one knee, Maou groaned in pain as he realized the enormity of it all.

For a moment, Emi reveled in the sight.

"Come on, Dullahan! You can pull through this! It's just a flesh wound! I've only just purchased you!"

But seeing Maou whine emphatically at a cheap fixie made her feel a twinge of empathy instead.

"You don't have to act like that. It's just a flat. Just bring it to the bicycle shop tomorrow. It's only a thousand yen or so to patch up the tube. Replacing a tire costs more, but…"

"R-really?!"

Maou's hands still tightly embraced Dullahan as his head turned toward Emi, who edged backward in response.

"Um… Yeah. Really. But get away from me! You're all dirty! It's disgusting!"

"I am *not* disgusting! But…okay. I'll go get it fixed first thing in the morning. Thanks for the help."

"You're welcome… No! Wait! I don't need your petty compliments! You were just acting so pathetic over a stupid bicycle flat, it threw me off guard, so…"

Emi failed to finish the sentence.

"Huh? Earthquake?"

The ground palpably shook underneath them for a moment. Before she could check up on Maou, they heard a faint bursting sound emanate from somewhere. This time, the rear wheel had blown.

"Whoa!"

"Agh!"

Just when they had a spare moment to shout, the signal light above them shattered into a million pieces. The Hero and the Devil King covered their heads at the sound of shards scattering across the ground.

"Are we…"

"…being shot at?"

They were answered by a cracking sound at their feet.

"Whoa, whoa, what the hell?!"

"We need to get out of here!"

The two of them flung themselves into a nearby alley. The sparks and bursting noises followed them.

In the darkness of Sasazuka, a silent sniper had bared its fangs at the Devil King and the Hero.

"What is going *on* here—Ahh!"

"Stop screaming! And stop tripping over the bollards, too!"

They had made their way into Koshu-Kaido road, hiding behind the cars in a coin-operated parking lot as they evaded the sniper. No one was walking by, but the car traffic was incessant.

The Shuto Expressway above them blocked off the night sky. The two of them caught their breath in front of a shuttered office building.

"What just happened?"

Emi's voice was higher than usual. Maou's was equally strained.

"The Devil King and the Hero are together. And someone is attacking them. It's got *something* to do with Ente Isla. Even if it didn't, what kind of criminal's shooting *that* kind of thing in Japan? You know how crazy strict the weapons laws are."

"I *know*! So was some street gang firing an air gun at us…?"

"They don't make street gangs like *that* around here anymore! Get down!"

Maou forced Emi's head downward.

At the exact height of Emi's head, there was now a small hole in the metal shutter.

"…You can't shoot a BB through a steel door, either."

"Get *off*! Stop messing with my hair!"

Emi brushed Maou's hand away. Maou obliged, staring at his hand as he asked a question.

"So you're about as strong as the average Japanese person, too?"

"…Strong or not, you're still gonna cut yourself in the kitchen! It's still gonna hurt if you stub your toe against a lamppost!"

Maou took that to mean Emi no longer enjoyed her Ente Isla–era strength. As a demon, he had taken it for granted that his physical, defensive, and spiritual strength would always outclass his foes. Now, every trait of his strength was on an even keel with the Japanese national adult average—a fact that became all too clear to him over the past year of life in Japan.

"That last one came from in front of us."

"Don't be so sure. You hear any gunshots yet?"

"Nothing like that, no… Ah!"

Just as she spoke, she lunged toward Maou. They both spun in the air together before hitting the ground. If she had been a moment slower, they both would have been perforated. The sad, suddenly-very-well-ventilated shutter told them as much.

"Nice one."

"I'm not an idiot, you know. I'm a Hero."

"Yeah, sorry. You mind getting off me? I can't dodge sniper fire like this."

"That's *your* fault for landing first! I'd be only too happy to extract myself from your putrid hide!"

They were being less than polite to each other, but their quarrel was with another foe. Quickly, they rose to their feet and composed themselves, backs against each other as they watched their surroundings, ready for attack from any direction.

"Can we make it to the station?"

"Good idea. The *izakaya*s will still be open around Sasazuka station; there'll be a bunch of people there. It'll be risky, but it's up to whoever's shooting us to react. Can you run?"

"Better than you can. You had it easy all this time with that bike."

"Okay. Go!"

Could the sniper keep up with the two of them running? There were no bystanders up to now, but the closer they came to the station, the more they encountered. The *izakaya* bars near the station were lit in a dazzling array of colors, herds of salarymen roaming the streets around them, wondering which to hit next.

The two of them warily eyed the area, the station wall behind their backs. A pair of middle-aged men in business attire hollered at them, but they didn't have the spare time to play around with drunk office grunts at the moment.

They must have remained frozen where they were for ten minutes or so. By the time they finally concluded there were no snipers in well-lit, populated areas, they were both physically and mentally exhausted.

"So what...*was* that?"

Emi heaved a sigh of relief, brushing the sweat-heavy hair off her brow as she asked no one in particular. Maou struggled to catch his breath as he responded.

"I don't know...but that wasn't just some random sniper. Those were bolts of magic energy."

"Magic...?"

Emi's eyes opened wide.

"That shot aimed at your head near the building? It came from the angle we ran in from. It had to change direction to aim for us, that much I'm sure of."

"You mean..."

"Whoever's behind it, he's got a lot of power behind him. That, and he knows who both of us really are."

"Both of us? There's someone like that *here*? Besides Alciel?"

"Guess so. Don't know who, though. I didn't even feel anyone else nearby."

Maou stretched his body. The tension had finally started to drain away.

"Man. Look at all this trouble you've gotten me into."

Emi fired back at Maou's accusatory tone.

"Me?! You think this is *my* fault?!"

"This wouldn't have happened if you chose a more normal time and place, would it?"

"I chose that because that's when you got off work!"

"Morning would've been just fine. Better, even."

"I *work* in the morning! *And* the afternoon!"

"Not my problem."

"Hey! Where're you going?!"

Emi stopped Maou as he attempted to walk off, a hangdog look on his face.

"Home."

"You're leaving by yourself?!"

"Well, yeah. You should go home, too. I'm sure it's nearby if this is where you're hanging out all the time. Later."

"Hey...!"

Maou set off, leaving Emi's frantic shouting to dissolve into the background murmur of the Sasazuka night. He hated to abandon his bike so soon after purchasing it, but there might be more attackers stationed nearby. His faithful Dullahan would have to wait for morning to be reunited with its master.

He hadn't mentioned it to Emi just now, but this attack had kindled a small sense of hope within Maou's mind.

The fact that their enemy had the freedom to wield magical power to a certain extent was an immense discovery. Regardless of who he was fighting, he was still Devil King—lord of the underworld, the demon who was within moments of conquering all of Ente Isla. If it appeared to be worth the exertion, he would gladly call upon his own magical reserve to fight and claim his enemy's force.

That, after all, was how he gained such vast magical strength in the demon realm.

Tomorrow was his regular day off. He was ready to scour the neighborhood for clues. There was a spring in his step as he dwelled on it, walking briskly through the dark residential neighborhood toward his apartment.

Suddenly, he realized someone was following him.

An attacker? Perhaps, but there was no sense of magical force, no murderous intent with this pursuer. Probably some drunk staggering home in the same direction as he was. Still, whoever it was seemed to be paying an unusual amount of attention to Maou, making sure to keep a prudent distance away.

The apartment building was in sight, but with Ashiya's magical force long depleted, Maou wanted to avoid involving him in a fight.

Ashiya was too valuable a resource to squander—for the subjugation of Ente Isla, and for life in Sasazuka as well.

Quickly, Maou ducked into a side alley that ran across the neighborhood, into an area unlit by streetlamps. If the person behind him lived nearby, he'd probably walk right past—and if he didn't, he'd be too spooked to continue the pursuit.

The footsteps continued unabated. The figure proceeded onward, not noticing Maou in the darkness. Maou raised his head a little, wondering if he had made a mistake.

What he saw instead was the figure heading straight for Villa Rosa Sasazuka, the apartment Maou called home. He seemed to hesitate for a moment in front of the stairway, but quickly made his way upstairs.

The figure stopped in front of room 201, by the door with the "Maou" sign on it.

"Ugh...I know I said 'come for me anytime you want,' but *now*?"

Maou called toward the late-night visitor. She turned around, startled, not expecting a voice from behind.

"Look, I've already gone through one ambush tonight. You're going to wake up all the neighbors. The landlord lives right next to us, too, and I *really* don't want to deal with her if I can."

"...I'm not here to attack you."

Emi stood there, the bravado from before notably absent. Her face was white as a sheet, her breathing quick and shallow. She looked intensely nervous. Perhaps she had fallen ill; perhaps she had been hit with a magical bolt when he wasn't looking.

"H-hey...what's wrong?"

Maou drew closer, concerned. Her response was stronger than he expected.

"It utterly disgusts me to ask you this... In fact, it feels like I'm betraying my world and everyone in it..."

"If you came here to rile me up, it's working."

· This doorstop encounter was the last thing he wanted before bedtime.

"I...if you don't mind...could I...I..."

"You?"

Her pale complexion had now turned a bright shade of red as she turned her head downward.

"Could I...stay here tonight? I...I kind of dropped my purse."

Maou opened his mouth wide, almost dislocating his jaw in the process. It took a while for him to close it again.

\* \* \*

"What?! The Hero Emilia?!"

Ashiya, patiently awaiting Maou's arrival, tensed as he noticed Emi cowering behind him. Maou lifted his hands, placating.

"No, no, it's okay. She hasn't got enough energy to fight right now, anyway."

"Your Demonic Highness, how could you be so reckless?! You, the Devil King, staying out partying all night with the Hero?!"

"You don't have to put it like *that*! It's still two a.m.!"

"The wee hours of the *night*, my liege!"

Emi stood solemnly in front of the door.

"We both got attacked just now. By someone we couldn't see. He was flinging magic at us."

Maou's explanation was almost too straightforward, but Emi lacked the mental fortitude to add anything else.

"And while we were fleeing, apparently she dropped her purse."

Emi seemed to go even smaller as he continued, almost disappearing entirely.

"So, you know, she can't catch a taxi, she can't spend the night at an Internet café... She doesn't have any friends nearby, either, she claims. Turns out she lives over by Eifukucho, so that's kinda far to walk."

"But, Your Demonic Highness... If you remember where it was dropped, I'm sure nobody's touched it at this time of night..."

"Yeah, I know, but we just got written up by the cops yesterday, you know? I don't know who was targeting us, but if she winds up getting killed out there, we're both gonna be the prime suspects. It wouldn't hurt to let her sleep in the corner, would it? As long as she takes the first train outta here."

Ashiya brought a frustrated hand to his temple.

"Here, c'mon in. Have a seat wherever you like. Hope you're not expecting a futon or any other luxury goods."

"...I get it, all right?" Emi grumbled softly.

"Emilia! After the gracious pity the Devil King has bestowed upon you, is *that* how you repay him?!"

"Pipe down, Ashiya. The landlord's gonna hear us. Hey, Emi."

"What do you wa—oomph!"

Maou had thrown a bath towel over Emi's face. "You can use that if you want. If you need a pillow, go ahead and use those towels over there. I'll spot you a thousand yen, so get out of here before the trains start up, all right?"

Gritting her teeth, Emi reluctantly accepted the wadded-up bill, which Maou plucked from a plastic change purse he had clearly purchased from the hundred-yen store.

"Emilia! That is a royal donation from the Devil King's personal meager resources! I order you to treat it with the respect it deserves!"

"Shut up, I know that! I didn't ask for any of this, okay? Thank you for the money!"

"You little…!" Ashiya seemed angry enough that steam would be blowing out his ears at any moment, but Maou paid it no mind as he took his own bath sheet out of the closet.

Watching him, Emi wrapped her own towel around herself and took a seat on the floor. They may all be normal Japanese people now, but even so, she wasn't so careless as to lie down defenselessly in the den of the Devil King. Pulling the towel close for protection, she found it to be freshly washed, with a surprisingly pleasant scent to it.

"…This is the same detergent I use."

"Don't start whining about how stiff it is. Ashiya refuses to buy any fabric softener." Maou turned over on the floor as he spoke, his ears having picked up on Emi's quiet mutterings.

"I-I was just saying… It didn't need a response." And thinking she wasn't going to get another, Emi turned her back to Maou, balling herself up even more tightly.

"Yeah, yeah. You go to bed, too, Ashiya. Hey, Emi, don't worry about locking the door behind you, okay? Night, people."

Within moments, Maou was sound asleep. For a moment, Emi was astounded at how fast he went under.

Ashiya, however, sized up the unlikely couple in front of him.

"Do note that I have not dropped my guard yet. Try anything

underhanded, and it will be you who pays the price. A good night to you!"

With that rather bizarre farewell, he laid himself down and quickly fell asleep himself, one of the few ways the servant resembled the master. They had acted so cautious around her, and now they had left themselves wide open in their slumber.

She watched them sleep for a moment, but soon found the idea of remaining vigilant in front of these senseless, comatose corpses too silly to consider. Soon, she had lain down as well.

"I'm gonna have to cancel my Kakui credit card... My bank card, too. Oh, and how many rides did I have left on my pass?"

Recalling all the life necessities she held in that purse made her feel even gloomier.

"Why am I even doing this...?"

Only she could hear herself whispering this final statement before her fatigue and emotions drove her to the land of dreams.

Around the time that Emi's breathing grew slower and more rhythmic, Maou spoke up, his eyes still closed.

"We're a team of two, but it seems she's alone, huh?"

"Indeed."

"We were pretty miserable at first, too, weren't we? And she had to deal with all of that by herself. You think about it that way...I'm not gonna be her friend, no, but I do feel bad for her."

"You've grown complacent, Your Demonic Highness."

"Just for the moment, Ashiya. I made her promise not to hang around me any further."

"Well, so be it, then."

"Exactly. So...huh?"

From the corner of his eye, Maou noticed something glinting in the air.

"What is it?"

"We got a text." Maou scooped the phone up from where it was last tossed on the floor. The screen showed two new messages. "Huh. One's from Chi... Hey, stop looking."

Maou wriggled away from Ashiya, who was also trying to peer into the screen. "The other one's from an unknown number. Weird."

It was from an unregistered source, a mail address that seemed to be a random mishmash of letters and numbers. Either spam or the wrong number, Maou figured...at first.

"Your Demonic Highness?"

Ashiya was moved to speak as he watched Maou's eyes suddenly grow pointed, serious.

"Hey, Ashiya? This is kind of nuts, isn't it? I got pretty much the same text at the same time...from someone I know and someone I don't."

The texts from Chiho and the unknown sender seemed almost to dovetail with each other.

*The earthquakes will continue. Be careful.*

*Maou, there's gonna be another earthquake. What should I do? Chiho*

THE DEVIL
GOES ON
A DATE IN
SHINJUKU
WITH THIS
GIRL FROM
WORK

By the time Maou and Ashiya woke up the next morning, Emi was already gone.

Her bath towel was neatly folded up and placed on top of the washer. The key to the front door was on the floor beneath a window, and next to the kitchen sink...

"What's that?"

"Some kind of pickled dish?"

It was a small bowl of chopped-up *konnyaku* gel and cucumber, tossed with vinegar and miso paste. Ashiya had no memory of preparing it.

"Her way of repaying us for the lodging, perhaps? Here, allow me to test it for poison."

Removing the plastic wrap over the bowl, Ashiya flicked a slice of cucumber into his mouth.

"Hmm... She is our foe, yes, but she's also a gifted cook."

"It's good?"

"I do not find it wanting, my liege."

"Huh. I don't usually eat anything vinegary like that." As he spoke, Maou tried a pinch for himself.

"I do wonder what the key is doing on the floor, however..."

"If I had to guess, she opened the window, locked the door, then tossed it back in through the window. The bars over the windows facing the corridor would've kept anyone from getting inside anyway."

"Impressive. The Hero is a woman of high morals." Ashiya sniffed derisively as he picked the key up off the floor.

"And what would you have done if you were her?"

"Simple. I would have locked the door and taken the key with me."

"Devilish."

"Your point being?"

✳

Emi was safe in Room 501, the Urban Heights Eifukucho condominiums, seven minutes from Eifukucho station on the Keio Inokashira rail line. And Emi was still kicking herself over falling asleep before the trains began running again.

It may have been just a crummy apartment, "Villa Rosa" in name only, but it was still the Devil's Castle, a dark domain of ultimate evil. She had been blatantly reckless in her behavior. What's more, it was the Devil King's own filthy lucre that paid for train fare. She gritted her teeth in frustration.

"I feel so *unclean*..."

But she needed the remaining cash for the fare to Shinjuku. Today was another workday.

She could withdraw money easily enough with her passbook and seal, but Emi's bank didn't have any manned branches near Eifukucho.

Hurriedly, she made a bum rush for the shower, eager to wash away the stink of the ancient tatami mats that lined Devil's Castle.

She had ample time to take it easy this morning, but the thought of demonic corruption writhing its way through her pores made her blood freeze.

Savoring the hot, cleansing water, Emi suddenly put a hand to her head, right where Maou touched her as they were dodging magical blasts. She recalled, a shiver of disgust crossing her spine, how Maou had virtually palmed her head like a basketball.

Lucky thing she'd thought to purchase a new bottle of shampoo. Spending twice the usual time lathering up her hair, she ran the conditioner deep into her scalp, following it up with a thorough hair pack treatment.

Methodically, she rubbed a freshly purchased bar of medical moisturizing beauty soap repeatedly against each area where Maou's fingers touched her, as if they were contaminated by some hideous disease. Soon, nearly half the bar was gone.

Walking from the shower to the living room as she wrung the excess water out of her hair with a towel, she picked up a remote control from a low table covered with a flower-print cloth and turned on the TV.

Japan, as a nation, was always overly sensitive to gun-related crimes, no matter how far out in the sticks they took place. Their "gunshots" were magical in nature, of course, but they had still made holes in the asphalt, broken a traffic signal, and ripped apart a protective shutter. If something like that took place in the middle of Tokyo, it was only natural that it was the top story once the morning news programs went live.

MHK was airing a traffic report for the train and highway systems. The JR and private train lines were all running on schedule, so Emi shouldn't have much difficulty riding the Keio Inokashira line to work.

After a moment, the program shifted to the morning's news. As expected, the shooting dominated. They began with a shot of the intersection at which Emi had spoken with Maou the night before, now lined with cameras and TV reporters.

The police had shut the intersection down, lining it with yellow Do Not Cross tape. Images of the innocent building shutter, now twisted into an unrecognizable shape, were inserted into the coverage here and there. The reporter used the term "shots fired," but said that no further details were uncovered as of yet.

Switching through the channels, Emi found largely the same story elsewhere. Then:

"Whoa! It's them!"

Maou and Ashiya were clearly visible among the crowd of onlookers in one of the camera shots.

Emi resisted the instinctive urge to shut off the TV. They were on-screen for only a moment, but it seemed like they were discussing something with each other, somber looks on their faces. Perhaps Maou was explaining the scene to Ashiya.

"...and a bicycle with two flat tires was abandoned in the middle of the intersection. Police detectives are in the midst of determining the bicycle's owner, since they believe it may have something to do with the case."

Emi's eyes opened wide at the on-scene reporter's script.

"You...*idiot*..."

*That* was why they looked so somber! Presumably they didn't think anyone would care much about any of this. He must have thought it'd be fine and dandy to stroll on over early in the morning and pick up the bike then. And *now* look at him.

It wouldn't be long before the police seized the bike and figured out who owned it. And from there, it wouldn't be long before they rooted out Sadao Maou, lurking within Villa Rosa Sasazuka.

"...Well, not *my* problem."

With that conclusion, she returned to the bathroom to dry her hair, leaving the TV on.

Maou was the victim here, after all. It didn't bother Emi much if the police thought he was related to the shooting. In fact, him getting arrested would be nothing but good news for her.

After a few minutes, the news switched over to a report about a string of late-night convenience-store robberies and muggings of women and the elderly, apparently carried out by a crazed maniac wearing bizarre clothing. Listening to the lurid details was enough to darken Emi's mood all over again.

Some days, it just felt like one depressing thing piling on top of another.

Emi was a part-time contractual employee for a call center.

Her office was in a branch of Dokodemo, a nationwide cell phone provider, located in a business district about ten minutes from Shin-juku station's east exit. Her department chiefly handled complaint processing and customer service.

Very few people, even the kind of people who willingly worked at call centers, actively volunteered for the complaints department. That was why she landed that for her first job in the world, and why she still held it down now.

Being constantly short on staff, the department paid handsomely. Someone like Emi, with an attractive voice and a chip on her shoulder, was an invaluable resource.

What was more, Emi was gifted with the ability to grasp every language spoken in the world.

Even when greeted in a language she'd never heard before, her brain had a sort of telepathic ability to understand at least the general outline. All she had to do was reply with her own general emotions, and the caller understood. To an impartial observer, this would apparently be interpreted as her fluently speaking English, French, Korean, Chinese, anything.

Walking into the office locker room, Emi changed into her uniform: a gray vest, a tight skirt, a blouse, and a bow-tie-shaped ribbon. She then clocked herself into the company system and sat down at her assigned cube. Not being a full-time employee, she had yet to be granted her own exclusive desk, but given the department's chronic staff shortage, she usually found herself among the same island of cubes.

"Morning, Emi!"

"Oh, hey, Rika."

Rika Suzuki had called out from the adjacent seat. Her employee number was only one removed from Emi's, so they would always find themselves seated next to each other when both were on duty. Her short brown hair was a smart match for the gray uniform.

"Hey, did you hear about that crazy shootout? That was right near you, wasn't it?"

Emi's heartbeat accelerated for a moment, but she was never the kind of girl to wear her emotions on her sleeve.

"Well, three train stops away, but…yeah."

"Oh? Well, still, a gun battle right in the middle of Tokyo! Nuts, isn't it? Japan's gonna go down the tubes before too long if *that* keeps up."

The morning news simply reported that shots were fired, but in Rika's mind, it had already escalated into an action-film bloodbath.

"And, you know, there's been all these earthquakes lately, there's some weirdo robbing people on the street… It's outrageous! The whole world's going crazy, and it's draggin' all of us down with it. Oh! There's a new curry place opening up today, did you hear about that?"

Emi was already used to the unexpected new directions in which the women of this world could suddenly take a conversation.

"No, I didn't."

"One of the big joints in Shimo-Kitazawa opened up a new location. Wanna join me there for lunch, maybe?"

"Ooh, but if it's popular, won't there be a line and stuff?"

"It'll be worth it!"

Ever since she arrived in Japan, Emi had been repeatedly floored by the vast variety its kitchens offered. Curry, in particular, was a revolution for her senses and her taste buds when she first tried it, exceeding all expectations she ever had for a decent lunch. That astonishment remained today, long after she had grown accustomed to other aspects of the Japanese lifestyle. Rika's invitation sorely tempted her, but for today, with painful reluctance, she found herself shaking her head.

"Well, sad to say, I don't have time to stand in line today. I lost my purse."

"Oh, no *way*! Really?!"

Rika's reaction was so grandiose, Emi was concerned she would tip over her office chair.

"Yeah, and it had everything in it, too. Train ticket, bank card, credit card… So I have to go visit my bank to deal with all that and withdraw some money."

"Ooh, yeah, no waiting around for lunch today, then."

"Sorry about that!"

"Oh, no problem, no problem. So you wanna just hit up Maggie's or whatever instead?"

"Ooh, *anything* but Maggie's."

To Emi, Rika was more than just a coworker—she was the first friend she'd found in this world. Her influence was part of the reason Emi had fallen into the habit of saying "Maggie's" instead of "MgRonald," for one.

Maou had picked on her for not having any friends, but the only thing she lacked for on Earth were friends from Ente Isla. A pity that no acquaintances lived nearby the Hatagaya neighborhood in Sasazuka. Then maybe she wouldn't have gone through all that anguish overnight.

"You better cancel all those cards real soon, though, right?"

"I already put a temporary stop on them, yeah. That much you can do over the phone."

"Oh, I see. Well, you just name the place, Emi! It's on me today! Don't want to leave you heartbroken, after all."

"Ah, you don't have to do that…"

They continued on in this fashion until the starting bell rang.

Emi checked the interoffice mail on her assigned PC, where the day's special issues to watch out for would be waiting.

The first call signal had already sounded off from one cube or another.

Being a subsidiary of Dokodemo, the calls were naturally all about issues related to cell phones. The morning report mentioned that phone service had been knocked out for a period last night in part of the city's center due to electrical issues.

If anyone was itching to complain today, that would be the main reason. Emi could hear Rika sigh in the next booth over. Plainly she thought the same thing.

Emi received her first call practically the moment she set her terminal to standby mode. An elderly woman, having trouble understanding the jargon in the instruction manual. After politely walking her through the problem, she received another call five minutes afterward. It was a transfer from another station with a "foreign language" code attached.

The department would be loath to admit it, but the staff relied almost wholly upon Emi for all non-Japanese support.

Apparently it was a Chinese man who couldn't read the Japanese manual and decided to just try the phone number printed on the back.

And so the flow of inquiries continued, Emi handling each one efficiently and effectively. By the time she noticed the clock, it was already near her lunch break. The call load always tended to slow down a bit once the afternoon rolled around.

"Ugh! There's just so many complaints today!"

Rika was groaning in the adjacent cube.

"Like, try to at least make an *effort* to figure it out yourself, Grandpa!"

Rika, after spending over an hour battling it out with a middle-aged man accusing the manual of excess crypticness, still had a tightly stretched smile on her face as she banged her fist against the desk several times.

"So are you going anywhere besides the bank today, Emi?"

"Umm..."

In recent days, she had been turning down lunch offers from her coworkers so she could spend time spying on Maou. The mere idea of continuing the surveillance filled her with indignant rage.

"Nope! Just the bank!"

"But Kakui, too, right? Since you need to cancel that card. So how 'bout we check out that new *okonomiyaki* place next to Kakui? The crowds there have probably thinned out a little bit by now."

"Sounds good. Give me one sec, okay? I need to check where the nearest bank branch is... Hmm?"

Another foreign-language call transfer popped up on Emi's terminal.

"Ooooh, you hate to see *that* before lunch!"

"Hey, it's a living."

The individual timing behind lunch breaks depended on how

many people were on staff each day. A call-center staffer unlucky enough to field a particularly talkative customer could wind up seeing their break pushed to later in the afternoon.

Flashing a reassuring smile to the obviously peeved Rika, Emi adjusted her headset and prepared her standard English-language greeting.

"Thank you for your patience! This is Emi Yusa from the Dokodemo customer support team. How can I—"

"...Yusa?"

"Huh? Um, yes?"

The soft, muffled voice that recited Emi's last name was plainly speaking native Japanese, something obvious enough even with two short syllables.

"Yes, this is Yusa. How can I help you?"

"Yusa...is it? You're a full-fledged Japanese woman by now, aren't you, Emilia the Hero?"

"Ah!"

Emi gasped. She tried to keep Rika in the adjacent booth from noticing her shock, but a shiver still ran down and across her throat.

"May I ask who's calling, please?"

"Someone who knows of the Hero, and the Devil King. And someone who is driven to destroy the both of you."

Emi had no recollection of this voice.

"So you were trying to utilize the network late last night?"

"It was unexpected to see the Hero and Devil King engaged in tandem operations."

"Yes. It was a very regrettable situation for us as well."

"Heh-heh-heh... I could imagine. You may consider me an assassin, one sent from Ente Isla. And you may consider our encounter last night as a method of introducing myself."

"......"

It was difficult to make any bold moves. She had no idea who the person on the other end of the line was. Then, he made an even more confounding statement:

"I am here to eliminate Satan, the Devil King, and Emilia the

Hero, in the world they have traveled to. It is both my mission and the will of Ente Isla."

"What?!"

Emi—Emilia—could no longer hide the shock.

Why would Ente Isla, the land returned to peace and stability by human hands, want her dead?

"I…I'm afraid that we will be unable to provide an answer to that without further consideration…"

"Heh-heh… Consideration, is it? I am keenly interested to see what the Hero and Devil King have left to consider, judging by the way they tucked their tails and fled from such a simple attack."

The voice seemed to echo ominously, as if rattling up from the depths of darkness. Emi recognized that tone. It could only come from the demon world. Suddenly her mind was cool, serene, as she regained her Heroic composure.

"None of Satan's generals survived apart from Alciel. What part of the demon realm are *you* from?"

"……"

"You can try to shock me into submission with your lofty words about the 'will of Ente Isla.' But it will *never* faze me! I have no time for the prattlings of a monster."

"I see. A pity you choose not to believe me. We will meet again, soon."

The conversation ended earlier than she expected.

With a heavy sigh, Emi removed her headset.

Rika, in the adjacent seat, looked on incredulously, having little clue what Emi was talking about or what kind of conversation they were having. Emi turned back to her.

"It takes all kinds in this world, doesn't it?"

"I…guess so."

Rika still looked skeptical, but apparently decided the topic wasn't worth dwelling upon.

Soon, their lunch break arrived. Rika smiled at Emi, her eyes still betraying her curiosity a bit.

"Hey, sorry. So what did you want to do? Wanna eat lunch first? The bank's gonna be busy right now anyway."

"Sure, Emi. If that works for you."

Heading for the locker room, she placed her phone, passbook, and seal inside a small tote. Just as she was about to leave, her phone began to vibrate.

Her heart skipped a beat. She had put on a strong face, but that mystery call from earlier had unquestionably cast a pall upon her life in Japan.

"Is that your phone?"

"Yeah…"

Checking the screen, it was from an unknown fixed-line number within Tokyo.

"You gonna answer it?"

"I dunno… I got a bad feeling about it."

The phone continued to ring. There was nothing else to do.

"…Hello?"

"Hello! Is this Emi Yusa's cell phone?"

Emi's nerves loosened themselves a bit. It was a different voice, a friendly-sounding middle-aged man.

"Yes! Can I ask who this is?"

The man had unexpected news for her.

"I apologize for bothering you. This is the Yoyogi Police Department calling."

"Huh?"

Emi simmered silently inside the waiting room into which she had been led. Her eyebrows furrowed deeply into her forehead, as if chiseled on.

The ill temper so plain in Emi's eyes was enough to make even the female officer manning the front desk of the Yoyogi Police Department choose to keep her distance.

"Sorry to keep you."

Eventually, a uniformed officer entered the waiting room and greeted Emi, who lacked the psychological peace of mind to return the favor at the moment.

"I really appreciate you taking the time to come here. There's a whole process we have to go through, you understand."

"Yeah…"

"Um, first off, if I could check your ID… Thank you. Now, if you could just write your name and address on this paper and place your seal right here…"

She was starting to wonder why she bothered to bring her insurance card and seal with her today. They were *supposed* to help her obtain another bank card, but now here she was, waiting and waiting and waiting.

Emi signed the document, almost applying enough pressure to rip the paper apart, then smashed her seal into the inkpad before practically stamping it through the sheet and into the desk.

Slightly put off by this display, but not realizing what was causing it, the officer continued to smile as sincerely as he could at this law-abiding citizen.

"Right. That should take care of the transfer documentation. Mr. Maou and Mr. Ashiya are waiting in another room, so you can go ahead and leave together. We might need you back here later on if we find out anything, though."

"I am *not* leaving with them!"

Emi snarled at the officer like a caged tiger.

"Yeahhh, sorry about that. We couldn't think of anyone else, so…"

"We truly, *truly* wished to avoid relying upon you for this, but…"

Maou and Ashiya tried their best to keep it cool near the police station entrance.

"When that detective showed up at the door, man, we were freaking out. I had no idea they could track down our address from my bike! That's some pretty killer police work."

"And the Hero truly *was* faking her age, too."

"Yeah, just like I said, right? You can't do something like rent a condo if you're underage—not unless you get some guarantors and your parents' approval. I don't know what kind of trick she pulled off, but I figured she *had* to be registered as an adult, at least twenty years of age. Funny, huh? Usually people round their age *downward* if they want to lie about it."

"Indeed. Unless she wanted to buy some beer. Could that be the main motivation, perhaps?"

*"It doesn't matter!"*

Emi's sudden shrill scream made Maou and Ashiya cower before her, covering their ears.

"Why...? Why does it have to be me...?"

She was shaking with anger at this point.

"Why do I, the Hero of Ente Isla, have to serve as a personal ID reference for a bunch of demons?!"

"Sh-Shut up! You're being too loud!"

Smiling distractingly at the people staring at them, Maou pushed Emi outside of the station.

"What do you want from us? I told you, we couldn't think of anyone else!"

"I had thought about Ms. Kisaki at MgRonald...but even if my liege *was* the victim here, I feared she would fire him for his issues with the law."

"Ahh, I doubt Kisaki's that kind of manager...but, no, I don't want to bother her, either."

But Emi was singularly uninterested in their excuses. Besides, lending an ear to a demon's malicious lies would make her a very unworthy Hero.

"What?! So it's okay to bother *me*, then?!"

"Well, hey, it's the Devil King's job to bother the Hero, isn't it?"

Emi ran a frustrated hand through her hair. He didn't have to look so *smug* about it!

"How did you even get my phone number?! You didn't go snooping through my phone last night, did you?"

"Of course not! You had to write it down when we got taken to the station last time, remember?"

"Okay, but...but why did you have to name *me*?!"

"There was nobody else! What do you want from us? We don't have any friends, either! Besides, c'mon, we let you sleep over last night."

"Nnnnnghhhh!!"

"Hey, is that your work uniform, by the way? The Hero's a secretary or something? That's pretty cool."

"Who asked *you*?!"

Emi ripped the bow tie off her neck, then hung her head in abject shame.

"Look, calm yourself, Emilia. What kind of Hero acts like that?"

"I don't need *you* lecturing me, Alciel! Look at you guys! It's the start of the month, and your refrigerator's absolutely barren! They called *you* the greatest strategist of the demon forces! Hah! Don't you idiots have a budget or anything?!"

"Urrgh!"

Alciel fell to the ground, apparently suffering mortal injuries from this brutally accurate verbal strike, groaning something about it not being his fault as he did so.

"Will you people just take care of yourselves a little more, please?! I had someone making death threats to me over the phone today! And *you're* being targeted, too, Devil King! Better be careful, you got that?!"

"What?"

Ignoring Maou's question, Emi placed a hand on her hip, puffed up her chest, and pointed a finger straight at him.

"You *got* that?! I'm warning you, all right?! But don't you forget this! *I'm* the Hero, and *I'm* going to slay the Devil King and guide Ente Isla into a bold era of peace! Okay?!"

"I appreciate your enthusiasm, but please, try not to forget we're in public."

Maou looked frantic. Ashiya was rolling around on the floor, crying. And Emi continued jabbing her finger at Maou, ranting on with the stentorian voice of a natural-born ranter.

Suddenly, Emi noticed the officers and visitors staring at her. In an instant, the entire region between her neck and the ends of her ears glowed bright red.

"I...I...uh... Look, just be careful, all right?! That's all I want to say!"

"Thanks for the warning..."

Emi, ignoring Maou's listless response, swung her small tote bag around and quickly strode off, making her escape.

"Me...*and* her. They're after us both. And yet they called, huh?"

Maou took a moment to pick the fatally wounded Ashiya off the floor.

"Get a grip on yourself, Ashiya."

"It...it wasn't my fault... I kept a perfect accounting ledger..."

"Snap out of it! Look, let's go home. I need to meet up with Chi later."

"Dammit! Those cops made me waste so much of my off day."

"But it worked out well in the end, did it not? They even fixed your flat tires for you."

It wasn't enough to keep Maou from groaning as he wheeled his returned bicycle back home.

He *was* questioned by the police, yes, but was treated strictly as the victim of a passing thief, not a shooting suspect.

The reason he gave for the abandoned bike in the intersection was not exactly his most eloquent moment as Devil King.

"I, uh, I was scared... I didn't know what was going on, so I ditched it and ran."

The officer questioning them accepted it without an ounce of suspicion. He even said he felt *sorry* for them. An utter humiliation.

Back in their apartment, the Devil King and his aide-de-camp discussed their current pressing issues.

The texts they received the previous night from Chiho and an unknown number both discussed earthquakes.

Maou had replied to both, but the mystery texter fell silent after that. Meanwhile, Chiho wrote:

*I'm not playing around and it's not a joke. I think an earthquake's coming. —Chiho*

It was a little difficult to decipher the meaning behind such a clipped response. For one, why did she sign her name at the end of every text? In emoji, no less?

After a few more texts, Chiho clarified that she believed an earthquake had a chance of occurring sometime soon. She went on to explain why, but Maou offered to meet her this evening anyway, since it seemed like direct conversation was the easiest way to get to the bottom of this.

"What did Sasaki tell you?"

"Something about hearing a voice."

"Huh?"

"A man's voice. She said it was giving her some kind of weird warning or something."

"That doesn't make sense. This isn't a movie or an anime. You don't see high school girls suddenly get telepathic messages out of nowhere."

"Yeah, I thought she was just having weird teenage delusions, too. At first."

Maou smiled grimly.

"The thing is, I figured she'd have a more grandiose story behind it, but apparently Chi started having strange experiences once she got hired at MgRonald."

"Once she made contact with you, my liege? That's when it began?"

"'Made contact' isn't exactly the term I'd use, but you could say that, yeah. She started to have ringing in her ears, and whenever there was an earthquake, it'd be huge only in the area around Chi. You know, I may not look it, but I'm still king of the demon realm, right?"

"Absolutely. And you do not, my liege."

"...*Meaning*, it wouldn't be strange at all if even my mere presence was having an effect on the people and things around me. I *am* Devil King, after all."

An unaware observer could be excused for thinking Maou was the one with weird teenage delusions at this point.

"But in that case, why aren't you affecting anyone else on the MgRonald staff?"

"Who knows? Maybe they just haven't noticed. Or, it's entirely possible that Chi's just imagining things. But we *did* just kinda get attacked with bolts of magic, and Emi got that death threat, too, right? I don't know who we're fighting, but it's possible they figured out who we are so they could put more pressure on us. And in the worst case…"

"In the worst case, you think Chiho might be the enemy's advance party?"

"I don't want to think that, but…yeah. Anyway, we have to explore every possibility, no matter how remote."

"I understand, Your Demonic Highness. But…in that case, I wish to accompany you. If whoever attacked you last night is involved in this, it would be best to have as many eyes out on the street as possible."

"Ah, you just want to see Chi, don't you?"

Maou needled Ashiya, a mischievous look on his face. Ashiya responded with a defiant sneer.

"If I may, Your Demonic Highness… If I were not holding watch over it, I have little doubt you'd forget about how your bank account is empty and treat Sasaki to all sorts of things in a crass attempt to show off. And if our enemy *does* appear, if we do not discover and dispatch him quickly, you will become the laughingstock of the demon realm. 'Oh, look, there's the Devil King flirting with a teenage girl!'"

Even the mighty Devil King fell to silence against such infallible logic.

"So where and when are you planning to meet her, and how long will you be out?"

"What are you, my mother?! She said she had some kind of club activity after school, so we're meeting at the Shinjuku station east exit at five."

"Ah, so we have time. Shall we go, Your Demonic Highness?"

"Huh?"

Maou watched, puzzled, as Ashiya began to leave anew, just a few minutes after they reached home.

"We must go shopping, and then to the barber shop. Surely, Your Demonic Highness, you did not intend to go out on a date with your messy hair and head-to-toe UniClo wardrobe?"

"Who *cares* about my clothes and stuff? We're just gonna have some coffee, talk for a bit, and then sayonara! We don't have to make it a—"

"*If* a young girl is facing trouble, she would never deign to discuss it with anyone but her closest of friends. Not even her parents. Surely, Your Demonic Highness, you understand the meaning behind confiding such close, intimate secrets to another person."

Having it thrust upon him like this, he could see the logic.

"All...all right. Sure."

"Wonderful. And I would hate to think that a human girl would think that my lofty master cares naught about how he looks on his day off. You must strike a lasting presence at all times! Clothes, my liege, make the man!"

Maou finally found something to fire back while Ashiya strode briskly out the door.

"I will make you rue the day you berated my clothing!... And berated UniClo, the fastest-growing apparel franchise in all of Japan!"

The Dokodemo call center was open for business until five p.m. on weekends and holidays. Emi herself left the office half an hour later.

Thanks to Maou and Ashiya wasting the entirety of her lunch break in extravagant fashion, her job performance through the afternoon severely lacked in enthusiasm. She had grown pale enough that Rika, in the adjacent cube, grew concerned for her health.

"Hey, why don't you take off a little early today?"

"Yeah...I think I should."

"I don't know if something happened, but...try to feel better, okay?"

"Thanks..."

Emi smiled limply.

As Rika saw her off, Emi plunged into the hustle and bustle of

Shinjuku, bobbing against the constant waves of people as she walked on.

What great crime had she committed, which she could only repay by serving as the personal reference for her sworn enemies? She had been floating helplessly amid the punishing currents of modern society, and the next thing she knew, there were now multiple official, signed government documents claiming she was a close relation to the Devil King.

It was the ultimate humiliation.

The Keio-line entrance Emi used was near the west exit of Shinjuku station. From the east exit, she preferred to use an underground corridor that kept her going forward without being cut off by traffic signals and excess crowds. Today, though, the steep stairway that led to the corridor seemed like nothing less than the descent into a pit of darkness.

"…I can't stand it."

That was why, as she descended the steps, she hoped to write off the figure she had noticed for just a moment, passing by her amid the shops and restaurants to one side, as a figment of her exhaustion. But she reconsidered, feeling that her pride as the Hero was now at stake. Drumming up all the courage that remained in her heart, she approached the figure from behind and pulled at his shoulder.

"What are you doing here, Ashiya?"

"Aghh!"

Seeing Ashiya in the city center like this, it was even clearer how much taller than average he was.

"E-E-Emili—"

"Emi. Emi Yusa. Don't you think you should be more careful with calling people by their real names in front of everyone, Ashiya?"

"Ngh…hh…"

Ashiya groaned, a twisted look on his face.

"You're acting weird right now. I can tell. I even thought you were stalking someone."

"Gahh!"

Ashiya's face grew even more contorted.

"Oh, bingo, huh? I'm impressed security hasn't stopped to question you."

Emi had noticed Ashiya because he was hiding behind a station support column, sticking his head out into the corridor like he was playing hide-and-seek with the rest of the world. Actually, forget that. Real hide-and-seek players would've been far less conspicuous than that.

"It...it's nothing to do with you! Begone!"

Judging by that panicked response, she had caught him at a pretty bad time. Something in Emi's mind kept her from dropping the subject.

"Oh, is *that* how you treat the woman who sprung you from custody, Ashiya?"

"Yooou! That was just a small favor! Don't go bandying it about like some great, hallowed treasure!"

"You demons certainly are ungrateful, aren't you? And besides, did you think a Hero would simply let you go unchecked after she discovered you?"

"I did not, but...please, just let it go for now!"

"I never let you go during your demon days. Why should I start now?"

Opting to ignore Ashiya for the moment, Emi scanned the area he was standing guard over.

"Ah! Wait! No!"

Pushing the flailing Ashiya back, Emi realized that the demon's previous guard post was directly facing a small café. It was your typical chain café, like any of a million others, but over there, on one of the tables lining the front glass...

"Whoa..."

Emi gasped.

"Ahhhh! Forgive me, my liege...!"

Ashiya began to moan loudly behind her.

"Ow! Alci—*Ashiya*! What's *that* all about?"

"I'll never breathe a word! Figure it out yourself!"

"Figure it out? Figure it out *how*?!"

She had been greeted with a startling image.

It was Maou and that teen from MgRonald he called "Chi"—chatting with each other like best friends! No matter how one looked at it, they were a couple in the middle of a date. Maou had even transformed himself in the meantime, looking like he jumped right out of a "Modern Sassy Studs" feature in a fashion magazine. The before-and-after juxtaposition was more incredulous than weight-loss infomercials.

"*You!*"

"Wh-what?!"

The look of sheer spite on Emi's face as she turned around made Ashiya instinctively take a step back.

"What are you two going to *do* to that girl, you bastard?!"

"Gah…!"

Ashiya stood motionless, stunned by the sudden, shocking accusation lodged by this woman—this Hero, no less.

"Here you are, you two demons—the Devil King parading this cute little high schooler around, and you watching in the shadow—you *degenerates!*"

"Degen…! E-Emi—no, Emi! Please, just listen to—"

"And I honestly thought you two were trying to live decent lives in Japan! Boy, was *I* wrong!"

"Y-you have it all wrong! I-I don't know what you're thinking of, but my liege has not a single perverse thought in his mind when he—"

"How could a Devil King *not* be perverse?!"

Emi's logic was undeniably sound.

"Please, just listen to me!"

Driven halfway to tears, Ashiya tried his best to explain the story to the highly irritated Emi.

The girl was Chiho Sasaki, an employee at Maou's workplace, and she was first to voice her desire to talk things over with him. Maou had agreed in hopes of gaining clues to restoring his magical force, and he would never, *ever* harm her in the process. Ashiya tried to seem as sincere as possible (by demon standards) as he told the tale.

Emi had no intention of taking Ashiya's words at face value, but they were still enough to keep her from immediately rushing in to slay the Devil King where he sat.

"Do...do you see now?"

Gingerly, Ashiya asked for a response.

"I can see that my sworn enemy is looking absolutely ridiculous, yes."

"Nnghh... I am sorry..."

"You should be. But why does he have to go on a date with her? Couldn't they just call or text each other?"

"I thought so as well. But she wanted to meet him directly, so here we are. Judging by what I've seen, I think this girl Chiho has at least a passing interest in my master."

"I can see that."

"And that does not bother you at all?"

Ashiya, who had just made what (at the very least) his demon mind thought was an epoch-making revelation to Emi, was expecting far more of a reaction than that. Instead, Emi returned his glance, brows high and eyes full of doubt.

"What, are you disappointed I don't care about him in particular?"

"N-no, I just... A simple human girl, having amorous feelings for the Devil King... I had considered it the pinnacle of folly, myself."

"Me, I'm wondering what that girl sees in him. She could do a lot better."

"How *dare* you insult His Demonic Highness!"

"I'm the Hero, remember? But, yeah, any girl can see that she's into him. It's hard to tell from this far, but that kind of dress is the 'in' style this summer. Her hair's all done up, like she just went to the beauty salon, and those shoes are brand-new, too."

"R-really? They are?"

Thirty minutes of tailing the couple, and Ashiya had been completely oblivious.

"Ah, most men probably wouldn't even notice. She used her

wardrobe to come up with a fresh, summery look, and she's wearing a close-fitting outfit to emphasize her curves…"

Suddenly, Emi stopped. She strained at Chiho across the storefront glass, then muttered to herself.

"What is it, Yusa?"

"…Those are *big*."

Without thinking, Emi brought a hand to her chest.

"What are?"

Ashiya's quizzical voice made her snap out of it.

"Huh? N-no… Nothing! Being big doesn't make you a better fighter!"

"Pardon?"

"Being smaller makes it cheaper to have your own custom breastplates made up. They don't get in the way so much when you're moving, either."

"…What are you talking about?"

"Nothing! B-but, you know, the Devil King's gotten a lot more, uh, presentable, too, hasn't he? He's actually got some decent clothes on, too. Not that UniClo junk!"

Emi forced the change of subject, in part to keep her own mind from dwelling upon certain hang-ups. Ashiya, meanwhile, looked on proudly. He was still having trouble deciphering Emi's behavior, but hearing this sudden praise for his master provided an instant rush of self-satisfaction.

"I flipped through some magazines to come up with that outfit. It wouldn't do for some human girl to think my master dressed like a slob, after all. I've been performing odd jobs here and there to save up for a time like this."

Emi nearly lost hold of her bag as she pictured the concept.

"…So, what? What're you expecting out of her?"

"How should I know? I was merely shadowing them to ensure no one suspicious approached."

"You're the most suspicious guy here right now, Ashiya. Can you hear what they're saying with your demon hearing or anything?"

Alciel, despite his current deviant behavior, was still the Devil

King's right-hand man, his sole remaining Great Demon General. It was a natural question for Emi to ask, given what she knew of his true identity.

"Nonsense. We demons wield superpowers because of our magic! And now that my magic is gone, I could hardly pull superhearing out of my hat or whatnot."

Emi was lost in thought, ignoring the majority of the oddly boastful explanation the Great Demon General had provided.

It would be bad, very bad, for her if the demons found a way to restore their magic. If they gained access to a massive store of power before she could recover her own holy force—it was difficult to picture Emi having a way to cope with that.

At the same time, even if she moved to dispatch Maou right now, she couldn't tell if she would retain enough holy power to return to Ente Isla, to say nothing of dealing with the authorities afterward…

After all, unlike Ashiya, Emi could still detect magical force within Maou—enough to confirm his identity as Devil King. For all she knew, he could still be concealing the full extent of his remaining power.

In which case, there was only one option.

If the Devil King and his minion—the chief danger she faced right now—discovered a source of magic, she would have to destroy it before they could harness it. A stopgap measure, perhaps, but it beat sitting around and twiddling her thumbs.

"Ashiya?"

"Wh-what?"

"You know there's no point standing here watching them. Follow me."

"Follow you? Where?"

"Into that café, of course. If you aren't sure you can trust that girl yet, then you have to get closer. Listen to her while you scope out the surroundings. Otherwise, how can you call that 'shadowing' them?"

"I-I wouldn't dare! What would His Demonic Highness say if I performed such a bold—*Ahh!* Wait a minute!"

Her tenuous line of logic laid out, Emi grabbed the scruff of the reluctant Ashiya and dragged him straight into the café.

Half an hour before Emi spotted Ashiya, the great Devil King Satan met with Chiho Sasaki, new part-timer at his MgRonald location, in front of the Shinjuku Alita big-screen display.

"Oh! Hey, did you cut your hair, Chi?"

"Yes! I thought I'd take the plunge and go short for a while! Do you like it?"

It was a minute difference from before, one Maou could spot only because he spent hours by Chiho's side during her training period, and it was difficult to tell how much of a "plunge" it honestly was. However, given that he normally saw her in either her school uniform or her MgRonald uniform, the untied, free-flowing hair and well-defined lines of her blouse seemed graciously fresh to him.

"Yeah. It suits you really well."

"Aw, great!"

Chiho gleefully pumped her fist in the air at Maou's honest response.

"I thought you were gonna show up in your school uniform, though. Didn't you have some kind of after-school club or something?"

Maou had no particular motive behind the question, but it was enough to put Chiho straight off her *I did it!* gesture.

"Oh, I'd *never* show up in that! No way would I wear *that* lame outfit to the café with you, Maou! Besides, if you were walking around Shinjuku with a girl in a school uniform, people might start jumping to conclusions, you know?"

Chiho seemed oddly riled up as she defended her choice of clothing. He had seen Chiho in her school clothes before, whenever she came to work straight from class, but the uniform didn't seem *that* bad on her. The response was a tad surprising.

"Oh, but look at *you*! I thought you never shopped anywhere except for UniClo, but you're going upscale today, huh?"

She wasn't trying to be mean, presumably, but Maou still had to chuckle at the meaning beneath the words.

"Yeah, my roomie said there was no way he'd let me out on a date in UniClo stuff."

"Not that there's anything bad about UniClo, but if you want to go head-to-toe with it, you gotta be careful how you coordinate it, or else it'll turn out all weird. But, wow, you saw this as a date, huh? That's awesome!"

*What's* awesome? What's so bad about UniClo? Is this *really* a date? Maou nodded vaguely, a thousand questions popping into his mind.

"You gotta get home before dinner, though, right?"

"Well, yeah, but…"

Chiho nodded sullenly. That much was unavoidable; she had family waiting. Maou knew by now that the sort of teenage girls who partied in Shibuya or Harajuku until the wee hours were only a tiny handful of the entire population.

"So what do you wanna do? We can't just stand out here on the street. I don't go out to eat much, so I can't really think of any place to sit down and relax except Ronald's."

Chiho, apparently anticipating this, thought in silence for a moment.

"Why don't we go to the Barluxe café? It's cheap, and it's usually pretty laid back."

Maou knew about Barluxe. The name, at least.

"Oh, and don't worry about paying! I can cover all of that, if you don't mind listening to me."

She must have said that out of concern for Maou, who emitted a palpable "working poor" aura at all hours of the day. But even Maou boasted the pride of a young adult male—to say nothing of the pride of a Devil King.

"Nah, nah. I'm the guy here. I can cover that much for the two of us."

Ashiya's prediction was spot-on. It figured.

"Ready to go?"

The nearest Barluxe was a short ways down Yasukuni street, at the near end of a food court within an underground commuter-rail corridor.

"Oh…uh, Maou?"

"Hmm?"

Chiho stopped Maou, just as he began to walk off.

"Um…"

"What? What is it?"

"Your, uh, hand?"

"Hand…?"

Chiho turned her eyes downward a bit, teeth clenched, her face a little red for some strange reason. Maou thought she was going to cry out for a moment, but what came out instead was even more surprising.

"Do you mind if we…uh, hold hands?"

She was a grinning ball of energy earlier, but all of a sudden her voice was as soft as a buzzing mosquito. Maou looked on, confused.

"Sure, whatever."

He casually picked up Chiho's right hand. Chiho, surprised, tensed her body for a moment.

"What?"

"Oh, uh…no! Awesome! Uh, it's nothing! Thank you very—"

"Sure, sure. It's a crowded street anyway. Wouldn't want to get separated from you."

"Ngh…!"

Chiho's whirling carousel of mood changes made it difficult for Maou to figure out what she wanted. She seemed to flip between each one like a deck of cards, from surprise to happiness to blankness to some weird sense of capitulation.

"…You're right, aren't you? I kinda see that now."

Maou took another close look at Chiho's face. Chiho, eyes wide open, tried to maintain a certain distance from him in response. She was less than successful, given how they were holding hands, and thus simply twisted her body a little instead.

"You're acting kinda weird today, Chi."

"Oh? Oh. Well, I guess it's probably because of all this stuff that's been happening to me!" Averting her eyes in an odd fashion, Chiho started to walk, dragging Maou's hand behind.

"Yeah… Guess so."

Maou had little choice but to accept the excuse, but…

"Mmm..." He peered at Chiho, as she let out what sounded like a very torn sort of sigh.

At first glance, she appeared not to be manifesting any sort of magical phenomena. There were no unusual deviations from the typical human body, and even as they made contact with each other, she neither showed any noticeable changes nor demonstrated any reaction to the remnant magical power she might have absorbed from Maou.

The only notable deviation from the norm was that Chiho's palm seemed warmer than his, her pulse oddly fast.

Which meant that Maou had to consider the idea of someone externally interfering with Chiho's psyche. Perhaps the enemy that attacked Emi and him, or perhaps some unrelated magical force, was acting upon her at the moment.

And all of that assumed Chiho was telling the truth...

Regardless, there was nothing unusual about her right now. It was time to hear the full story.

The eastern exit from Shinjuku station was home to a large underground shopping mall built around the JR Shinjuku entrance. They walked down a nearby stairwell to find the food court largely uncrowded, it being the lull between early afternoon and evening.

Barluxe, luckily, was fairly empty as well. He chose a table next to the front window, figuring it'd be easier for Ashiya to see him there, but then realized it could be difficult for anyone to observe them undetected from outside a food-court café.

Taking a glance back, he spotted Ashiya hiding behind a pillar a distance away.

"So anyway, Chi, how about we start with you going over the whole story again for me?"

"Okay."

Maou kicked things off, a regular-sized blended coffee in his hand, a seasonal frozen latte in hers.

"So I told you how my ears have started ringing a lot more since I started working at MgRonald, right? At first, I thought it was stress—like, trying new things I wasn't comfortable with, and stuff.

But you and Ms. Kisaki and everyone were so nice to me and we never have to deal with any weirdo customers or anything...and I don't have any problems at school, either, so I thought maybe I just wasn't feeling well."

Maou nodded politely as she continued, taking equal care to keep a perceptive eye on both their surroundings and Chiho herself.

"So then there was that really big earthquake I told you about, right? The one that hit our house, and nobody else's. I thought, wow, *that* was kind of weird, but last night, I was alone in my room, and all of a sudden I heard this voice talking into my ear."

"Yeah, about that voice. What did it sound like? Different from you and me talking right now?"

Chiho placed an index finger on her chin, thinking for a moment.

"Mmm... Well, do you ever watch movies or anime or anything, Maou?"

"...Sometimes."

Almost never, actually, considering the lack of a TV in his apartment. He glossed over that to keep the conversation going.

"Well, you know how they depict telepathy and stuff, right? Like, a really echo-y voice? It wasn't like that at all."

"No?"

Chiho's pace accelerated, as if she just remembered something.

"It was, like, this very dignified male voice, and it sounded really frantic. I could hear it okay, but it kind of sounded like a radio that wasn't tuned quite right."

"Really?!"

"Y-yeah..."

Chiho nodded, a tad surprised at Maou's sudden burst of life.

"And everything he said was, like, really basic. Things like 'Uh, can you hear me?' and so on."

Hearing a strange man's voice in your ear would be enough in itself to make anyone panic, but apparently Chiho sat quietly and listened.

"I ended up talking out loud to reply to him, but he just kept on saying 'Can you hear me' and stuff, so I guess he couldn't hear anything from my end. So I sat around waiting for him to say something, and then I heard, like, 'Ah, whatever. This is only comin' out to a limited number of people, so I'm just gonna say it. Your world's got all kinds of weird natural events happening right now. There's gonna be a really big one before too long, so watch out. And we'll be over there, too, once the time is right, so...'"

With that, Chiho fell silent and took a sip from her frozen latte.

"...That's it?"

"That's it. And I don't know what that means at all, so I figured it was, like, a wrong number or something. It definitely wasn't for me. So I tried saying and thinking, like, *That's not for me, you got the wrong girl,* but then the tuning got worse and the voice went away. My ears haven't rung at all since."

"So you thought the 'natural events' he mentioned must have been the earthquakes you've been feeling."

"It took a little bit to figure that out, but yeah. I was so surprised to hear that voice, I couldn't think about anything for a while."

Chiho laughed a little to herself and sipped at her latte, which was starting to melt a bit as she lost herself in telling the tale.

Maou, meanwhile, pondered over this, not overly concerned about his increasingly lukewarm coffee.

The voice Chiho heard was probably a type of mental maneuver known as an "idea link." It involved synchronizing the internal psyches of two people from different worlds and with differing languages, converting (for example) the speaker's Japanese into a concept the receiver could natively understand.

In a world advanced enough to develop Gates that opened to other planets, sonar technology had been well-established for ages. Launching this "sonar" triggered invisible explosions of magic, the shock waves from which could be analyzed to determine the state of things in a Gate's destination. These magical explosions could take on different forms wherever they took place.

It was entirely likely that one of these sonar blasts was directed at Earth—at Japan, to be exact—and manifested as the "natural event" of an earthquake.

A cadre of assassins launched it, no doubt, to destroy the Devil

King. The possibility of the sonar blast just happening to fall on Chiho's home was dizzyingly low, but it wasn't zero. That would explain why the quake was felt only in that immediate space and nowhere else.

They could have aimed that sonar blast at a fairly specific position as well, assuming they followed the tracks in Gate-space made by the Devil King, Alciel, and the Hero pursuing them.

And come to think of it, wasn't there a little bit of shaking the night he and Emi were attacked? Maybe the attacker was hiding nearby, firing off a short-range sonar to gauge the Devil King's potential magical response.

Something was going to happen, and much sooner than he expected.

Maou and Ashiya's external appearance had assimilated fully to the Japanese norm, but in essence, they were still full-fledged demons. Demons who, just the previous night, had allowed an unseen foe to slink right up to them.

As Chiho put it, "There's gonna be a really big one before too long"—which likely meant someone with a similar level of magical energy was about to take action.

The enemy was seated right next to him, waiting for the just right opportunity.

"Ahh… I'm really glad I could get this off my chest, Maou."

"Huh?"

He snapped back to reality at the sound of Chiho's voice.

"Thanks a lot. I knew you'd believe in me."

"Oh, no, no, it was nothing…"

"No, it is! Most people wouldn't give the time of day to a story like that. To be honest, I was a little scared to text you. I thought you'd just laugh at me."

"You think so? Have you told your parents or your friends?"

"Oh, no *way* I could do that. I'm in my late teens. If I came out with a story like this, they wouldn't just laugh—they'd be seriously worried about me. Like, why can't this girl tell the difference between fantasy and reality?"

"Huh… Yeah, I guess so."

Maou tried his best to reassure the downtrodden Chiho.

"Well, you know, if you ever need anyone to talk to, I can *grnghghff*!!"

"Uh, are you okay? What happened?!"

Chiho, concerned at Maou's sudden and intense choking, offered him a glass of water. Gulping it down, his eyes tried to get a handle on his situation, but the image in the corner of his eye made it impossible to think rationally.

*Why? Why are Emi and Ashiya entering the café together?!*

"Maou?"

"Ahem! Sorry, I'm fine. Guess something went down the wrong pipe. I didn't do anything wrong!"

"Huh?"

"Forget it. It's perfectly normal for someone to discuss matters with their coworker, and there's nothing at all dark or sinister about it, so I am definitely *not* here for any malevolent reason."

"Um, are you all right, Maou?"

"Mm? Oh, sorry, Chi. Don't worry about it. Just had kind of a seizure there."

"A…seizure?"

"Fossa Magna."

"Maou?!"

"No, no, I'm sorry. I'm all right, so…"

His befuddled, unresponsive mind had taken seven trips around the globe at light speed in the course of a second. Realizing he had stopped himself on the other side of the world, he took one more semicircle around to reach the café.

"Uh…anyway! Putting everything you said together, I don't think that voice or the ringing in your ears is any kind of direct problem for you. What really matters is whether anything really bad *is* going to happen, that 'really big one' you mentioned. Will it, or won't it? *That's* the key here!"

Chiho was wonder-stuck at Maou's extremely bizarre behavior over the past two minutes, but nodded nonetheless. He appeared to be treating her seriously, at least.

"Luckily, it doesn't sound like that man had any kind of malicious intent when he reached out to you. If anything *does* come up, just let people around you know. That could make a big difference."

"I…guess so, yeah."

"That's about all I can say for now. Sorry it's not really any kind of real solution."

Maou took another gulp of water, attempting to prop himself back on track.

Chiho, hands still clasped around her glass of now-completely-melted latte, thought over something for a moment before bringing her head back upward.

"Thank you very much, Maou. This really feels like a weight's been lifted from my shoulders."

"Oh? Well, great."

*Take that, Emi! Maybe it's a far cry from a Devil King's normal behavior, but I've done nothing weird with her at all! No matter how you look at it, I'm just another nice guy, helping out the new girl at work!*

"By the way…what made you think to talk to me about this?" Internally, Maou felt he had every right to be proud, but some nagging doubt in his mind made him ask Chiho the question. He *had* been Chiho's training supervisor at work, yes, but it was less than two months since their first encounter. He knew full well that "veteran burger flipper" was not a particularly coveted position in modern Japanese society.

"Um…"

Chiho's eyes darted around the café. The question seemed to embarrass her.

"You know…I don't know. I guess I just thought you'd believe me, Maou. You've always been real nice to me, and…I dunno, you're kind of different from other people."

Maou chewed this over. "Nice" was never a compliment a demon appreciated. He did accept, however, that he, as a Devil King, was a marked deviation from the norm.

"Yeah, I guess I'm a little weird, huh?"

"Oh, no! I mean, I didn't mean that in a bad way or anything."

Chiho seemed oddly frantic as she tried to explain herself. Maou had to smile at her predictability.

"I know, I know. Hey, try not to gesture all frantic like that. You're gonna spill your drink."

"Aw, you're really mean sometimes, Maou!"

Chiho let out a cough, her expression somewhere between concern and anger.

"But, I don't mind if you're weird. It was fun getting to have some coffee and talk with you like this."

"Mm?"

The words emerged from Chiho's light smile. It was hard to say if she directed them to Maou or herself, but either way, there was some serious portent behind them. Even Maou could see that.

"So...uh, Maou?"

The voice Chiho drummed up was shaky and weak. She was looking right at Maou, eyes full of concern, cheeks blushing a healthy shade of red.

"I...I think I..."

"Stop right there!"

Chiho's furtive opening was blocked by a loud voice from the side.

Maou froze. Chiho, unsure what was happening, turned and looked up quizzically at the defiant woman glaring down at them.

"Nothing good's gonna happen if you hang out with this guy."

"E-Emi! What're—"

"I just want to give you some advice. This guy's going to be away from Japan before too long. You better just keep things where they are now, or else it's gonna hurt you later on."

Surprised at Emi's sudden intrusion, Maou found his brain shutting down on him once again. Ashiya, who was sitting with her, was half crouched behind, having failed to stop her in time.

Chiho, for her part, responded rapidly.

"I'm sorry, but do you know Maou at all, ma'am?"

Her previously lost and forlorn expression was fortified into a strong one the instant she stood up. Meeting Emi's stare, her words, to Maou's surprise, were full of hostility.

It was something Emi must have felt on her skin. Her face remained stern, but her voice switched to more of an advisory tone.

"Listen, I'm telling you this for your sake, all right? This man isn't what he looks like. He's a lot sharper...and a lot more brutal inside."

"You can't just come out of the blue and say those horrible things about him! How do you know Maou, anyway?"

Maou was shocked to see Chiho fire an equally powerful volley of reproach back toward Emi. He knew she was a bright young woman, but had no idea there was such dynamic passion lurking below.

Ashiya, meanwhile, could do little more than look on from behind Emi as he nervously swayed from side to side.

"I am this man's enemy. Nothing more than that, and nothing less. Listen to me, Chiho Sasaki. I've given you my warning. Hang around with Maou, and you're not gonna come out of it happy."

"Y-Yusa, knock it off!"

Finally, Ashiya stepped up from behind to stop her.

"Here, calm down a little, Chi."

Maou, for his part, tried his best to appease Chiho, but—

"Don't tell me what to do!"

"Please stay silent, Maou."

The quiet battle between the two women continued unabated, the sparks almost visibly flying as they stared each other down.

"No, I mean...I don't want to cause any trouble for the café, so... How about we just go outside, okay?"

The rest of the staff and customers had picked up on the conflict between Chiho and Emi, but strangely, only Maou and Ashiya—the demons—found themselves cringing at the attention. Sadao tried his best to defuse the situation—

"Oh! Now I remember. You came to our restaurant the other day, didn't you, lady?"

"...What of it?"

—but they refused to listen!

"You were talking to Maou then, too, as I recall. Are you his ex or something?"

One didn't even have to see how the edges of Emi's lips tensed painfully tight for a moment to understand how much force the term was infused with.

"Nngh! *What* did you say?!"

The exasperated growl was Emi's way of expressing the rage and humiliation having that accusation leveled at her caused the first time the police hauled her and Maou off. But Chiho interpreted it as a sign that she was right on the money.

"I thought you might be. Well, how I approach Maou shouldn't be of any concern of yours anymore, should it?"

"Can you stop talking stupid for a moment? He and I don't have that kind of—"

"You don't? So why are you always lurking around wherever Maou is?"

"Look, our relationship can't really be summed up that easily, okay?"

"Oh, so you were *that* close with him? Is that what you're telling me?"

"What would *ever* make you think that?"

"What other way *is* there to see it?"

Whether they were listening to each other or not, the accusations and ranting had gradually ratcheted up. Feeling the intense, cold stares from the other customers on his back, Maou spoke up, a cold sweat pouring down his twitching face.

"Can the two of you just calm—"

He never managed to add the word *down* to the end.

A loud rumble coursed across the café, accompanied by a sound that was impossible to describe.

At first, no one could figure out what was going on—neither Maou, nor Chiho, nor Emi, nor Ashiya, nor any of the other witnesses watching their no-holds-barred battle royale with bated breath.

The next moment, someone shouted out:

"Earthquake!"

Someone else chimed in:

"It's a big one!"

The next scream was drowned out, along with every other sound in the underground corridor, by a massive, stomach-churning groan as the shaking began.

They were underground, but the up-and-down motion was so intense that it was impossible to remain standing. Utensils and furnishings fell to the floor as the lighting and window glass shattered.

"Look out!"

Whoever said that, and whoever heard it, were greeted by a crack in the ceiling that opened up in the blink of an eye.

The rumbling and shaking was incessant, as the crack spread its ominous tentacles toward the support columns and the floor.

"It's gonna fall…"

The ceiling began to buckle, all but pulverizing the table Maou and Chiho were sitting around.

"Maou!"

Chiho screamed, but her voice failed to reach him. He could see the ceiling crumble above them, but his feet were frozen to the ground, unable to flee amid the shaking.

The entire corridor began to collapse. Through the rain of debris, Chiho's fear reached critical mass, her consciousness melting into the darkness.

She could feel her eyes opening, but there was nothing but darkness to greet her. Confused, Chiho jerked involuntarily.

It was the first time she had ever lost consciousness like that, but her memories of a moment before brought her fear right back to center stage. Gingerly, she tried moving her tensed-up limbs, making contact with countless pebbles and small rocklike objects on the ground.

"Wh-what's going on?" she whispered to no one in particular.

"Oh, good, you're awake."

A woman's voice was right nearby.

"Wh-Who's that?"

"It's me."

The voice rang out in the darkness, slightly unclear through all the obstacles.

"You…"

The face she could faintly see floating up through the dimness was the woman who'd so rudely interrupted her little date with Maou.

The sight of the woman made Chiho recall their conversation before all of this happened. Then she noticed her face in the meager light. It was marred by something black flowing down from her forehead.

"Are…are you all right?!"

"Oh, this?"

It continued to flow as she absentmindedly wiped her face. A scream erupted from deep within Chiho's throat.

"This is nothing big."

"But…but all that blood…"

"It's not as bad as it looks. It'll clot up in a little bit."

The woman, acting like she had just scraped herself slicing an onion, clutched a cell phone in her hand. It was their current light source, all the light Chiho needed to stare at the blood streaming down the woman's forehead.

"This is bad news, though. We're completely shut in."

The woman flashed the cell phone's light around the area. Rubble from the underground corridor loomed around them on all sides. There was just enough space for Chiho and the woman to stand upright.

"From…from the earthquake?"

"Yeah. I guess the corridor collapsed. There's probably a ton of people buried alive in here."

"H-how long was I…?"

"It's been less than half an hour since the quake. It looks like we're breathing okay, so there must be some path for air to get through."

Chiho tested out her body. Nothing hurt in particular. And, perhaps because of the woman's blissful calmness, she was gradually overcoming her fear of the darkness. She took a deep breath. "You're acting pretty calm about this."

"Yeah, well. A little while ago, things like this were an everyday occurrence. You seem like you've gotten used to theatrical fights, though, so aren't you acting a little calm right now, yourself?"

"It's because I have an older sister who's probably crying alone right now."

Despite their circumstances, at that, the woman smiled. "I'm Emi Yusa. And just to be clear, there's absolutely nothing between me and Maou."

"My name is Chiho Sasaki. Let's just leave it at that for now."

United by a common crisis, they shook hands. Chiho was surprised at her own serenity amid this disaster. She wasn't alone, which was a major factor, but that alone wouldn't explain how undisturbed she felt.

"Maou…?"

"Nowhere near us, that much is for sure. He can't be that far away, though."

"No, I mean…"

They were all circling the same table, and now he was gone. Which meant…

"Oh, you're wondering if he got crushed by rubble?"

Chiho's mind was boggled at how easily Emi was able to suggest such a horrible fate.

"Well, it'd make me more than happy if he died right here…"

The follow-up was even worse, but her tone of voice indicated that Emi thought little of it.

"…but he's definitely alive. No way am I gonna let him die now. I want to kill him by my own hand. Dying by accident in a disaster like this… That's just pathetic. I'm not letting him off *that* easy."

She sounded incredibly confident. The resolve behind her voice even coaxed a strange sense of courage out of Chiho's mind.

"Yeah… You're right. I'm sure he's safe."

"Of course he is."

Having said her fill, Emi sat down next to Chiho. They both had a grasp of each other's positions within this confined space, so Emi powered off her cell phone to conserve battery time. Darkness dominated once again.

"This is kind of weird, though, isn't it?"

"Weird? How so?"

"Like, having this perfect little space here, just big enough for the two of us."

"...Oh."

Chiho herself had watched disaster-relief news reports at least once or twice in her life. Considering how often they involved survivors spending days trapped inside rubble, completely immobilized, before finding rescue, being safe and able to move inside this space was beyond a miracle. It was an unnatural phenomenon.

"There are probably little pockets like this all across the rubble. I think I can feel miniature-sized magic barriers nearby. Lots of them, too. Maou must have done something or other."

"Magic...barriers?"

Chiho repeated the unfamiliar words back, but Emi continued, wholly unfazed.

"If I had to bet, I'd say that nobody's dead in here. In fact, the farthest barrier isn't even fifty meters away. This might not be as widespread as it looks."

Emi was half-talking to herself by this point, showing no signs of waiting for Chiho's reply.

"I suppose we all need to thank him...but what would drive the Devil King to do this? Just deciding to save all these people's lives spur-of-the-moment?"

"Um...you mean Maou?"

Emi's apparent nickname for her ex sounded a bit contrived to Chiho's ears.

"If he had enough magic force left to create this many barriers in the space of a few seconds...he's more of a potential menace than I thought. He probably created this pocket for us, too."

"Here? Maou…made this?"

"Yeah. So he could save us. This pisses me off *so* much! Why would a demon go around rescuing heroes? I mean, it's like *I'm* some kind of egocentric villain here now, just because I couldn't create a protective wall with my holy force!"

Emi spat out the words, chiding herself in the darkness.

"Um…I'm not really sure what you mean, Yusa…"

"Don't worry about it. I'm just talking to myself."

A soft, bitter chuckle coursed across the space.

"Look, what do you even see in Maou?"

"Huh?!"

The unexpected question made Chiho lean back, startled, in the darkness.

"What…what…what're you talking about?!"

Chiho wildly flailed her hand in front of her face in a "no" motion, despite the total darkness.

"You were mouthing off at me because you like him and didn't like what I was telling you. Weren't you?"

"L-like? I-I'm not, I don't like…"

This threw Chiho into a state of frustrated confusion. She thrashed her arms and legs around for a moment, looking around the completely black landscape as she whined in frustration. It continued for another minute before she responded, her voice cracking.

"Y-you…you can't just *tell*, so easy, like that!"

There was another bitter chuckle in the air.

"The girl herself is always the last to know. Anyone watching you, it's totally obvious. I'm not too sure if Maou himself knows yet, though."

"Nngh…"

Chiho could feel the blood rushing toward her face.

"Wh-wh-what do you think of him, Y-Yusa?"

"Me?"

"You seem like his total enemy or whatever you said, but you're always hanging around him… It *seems* like you were kind of close, anyway."

"…I'd absolutely hate to use the word *close* to describe it. I'll admit that we've kind of known each other for a while, but…"

"How long?"

"Well, I knew about him first, but I guess he started paying attention to me around two years ago."

"Did you both graduate from the same middle school or something?"

"No. If we did, maybe we would've had a more stable relationship, though."

Emi chuckled to herself.

"But I'm telling you the truth here. If you start liking him, it's gonna be tough for you. That's why I tried to stop you, at least."

"Well…yeah, but I still don't really understand."

"You will soon enough…or maybe it's better if you didn't. For now, anyway."

As she said this, Emi raised her hand and placed her finger on Chiho's forehead in the darkness.

"You'd better sleep for a bit. The Devil King's been acting really self-conscious around other people lately."

It was over in an instant. The tip of Emi's finger glowed softly as it pressed against Chiho's head. When the glow disappeared, Chiho was already lost in a deep sleep.

As she breathed softly, her body slowly, gently laid itself down.

"Sorry you had to listen to all that complaining. You'll forget all about it by the time you wake up."

Emi placed her finger on Chiho's forehead once again. The glow returned for a moment, then quickly disappeared.

"You're right nearby, aren't you? I just put Chiho to sleep!"

As if in reply, a large magical force ballooned up nearby, beyond the rubble. For a moment, Emi's eyes opened wide at the unexpected size of it.

"Yeah, thanks for *that* conversation."

Maou's voice chimed through the sound of falling rubble, followed by several small rocks crumbling to the floor. Then, there was another presence in the darkness.

"You putting it that way, though…I guess our relationship's pretty complicated, huh?"

"Gee, you think? It's not like either of us *wanted* to be near each other. It's a pain in the ass, mostly."

"You said it."

Maou's voice sounded like he was standing on top of something. Emi squinted her eyes. There was some sort of ambiguous, unknown power lurking within his words.

"You help Chi out, okay? We're getting out of here. I don't think anyone's seriously hurt, but we can't all just sit here and wait for rescue."

A light flickered in the darkness, an ominous, bloodred glow that summoned horrifying memories in Emi's mind.

"D-Devil King!"

"What?"

The reply was strictly matter-of-fact.

"You…you look… What *happened* to you?!"

"Dunno. Just kind of happened."

His face, at least, was unmistakably Sadao Maou. But there were horns, the classic symbol of the demon race, poking out of his black hair. One of them was cut off halfway—exactly where Emi's sword sliced through it, not long ago.

The magical force, strong enough to visibly shimmer in the darkness, made the twisted sight all the more plain.

Maou's voice seemed higher up than usual because his legs had transformed into a demon's, more gnarled and twisted than any animal in this world.

The transformation ended there, but it was clear to see that Maou was in the process of regaining his Devil King form.

"So I have the barriers up, and it'll be easy to get this rubble out of the way. But this still isn't enough power to control the Gate, so don't worry about that, okay?"

It was difficult to keep from worrying when faced with a sight like this. Emi had no idea why, but Maou was able to regain the magical power necessary to become the Devil King, all in the short, fleeting moments after the corridor collapsed.

"I'll have to find a way to keep the barriers going while I get the rubble out of the way. Who knows how I'm going to explain this new look, though."

Little by little, Maou infused his bright red magical power into the rubble around him.

Satan, the Devil King, wielding his untold force to rescue Emi, rescue Chiho, rescue Ashiya, rescue any number of Japanese people he didn't even know the names of. If "the Hero Emilia" were here, face-to-face with the Devil King, his back wide open, there was no doubt she would be lunging at him, holy sword glinting in the light. But this was Emi Yusa, and all Emi could do was stare at the defenseless back of her sworn enemy.

In her heart, she feared that demon's wings would shoot out from his back, pushed to the surface by this dreadful magic. If she threw all caution into the wind and drummed up the final bit of holy force left within her, she would be able to summon a holy sword with enough power to defeat the Devil King, right here, right now.

"Mmm..."

Chiho's half groan, half dreamlike whisper in her sleep quickly quashed the microscopically tiny candle of murderous rage that had kindled itself within Emi's body.

If she killed the Devil King here, she would fulfill her mission. But it would also snuff out the lives of so many others, crushed in an instant by the rubble instead of surviving by the grace of that infernal demonic force. Emi and Chiho would be no exception.

"Why?"

Deep within her throat, imperceptible to anyone else, Emi cursed herself.

"Why is the Devil King *saving* people?"

✳

As far back as Emilia Justina could remember, the land of Ente Isla lay in a delicate balance between the Devil King's forces and those of the human race, which were led by Ente Isla's Church armies.

She was an only child, daughter of Nordo Justina, a humble farmer who tended a small wheat field in the countryside of the Western Continent. They were a father-daughter household, with no other relatives; she had no recollection of her mother.

When Emilia was ten years old, the Northern Continent and the kingdom to the east fell, destroyed by a demonic force that fanned outward from the Central Continent like a tsunami.

The Western Continent was well protected by the royal forces' generals. Its armies centered themselves around the troops provided by the Church, a seemingly omnipotent presence whose powers were connected directly to heaven itself. But the advance of the western invasion forces, led by the Great Demon General Lucifer, had plunged the island into total war.

Nordo Justina, a devout member of the Church, made sure to visit the local chapter with her daughter on a daily basis. The young Emilia didn't know what the words of prayer sung by the parishioners meant, but even she could tell something serious was happening. Copying her father's motions, she clasped her small hands together and prayed with all her might.

But all the prayers were for naught, as the western forces slowly began to crack under the pressure of the demons' advance.

Emilia passed her days listening to the criers that brought the latest ill-boding news to the village. Her nights were passed in fear, constantly wondering when the demons would come to burn the crops she and her father had raised.

Her father was a simple man of the field. He knew nothing of battle, for he had devoted his entire life to the cultivation and production of wheat.

Whenever Emilia would lie in bed at night, crying to herself out of fear, he would always seem to appear, stroking her hair with his thick hands until she fell asleep.

Emilia loved her father. She respected him, adored him, and relied on him more than anyone else in the world. He was the greatest hero she had.

Then, in the year Emilia turned twelve, the fateful moment came.

The message arrived that the land owned by the local nobility, right next to the province where Emilia lived, had fallen.

And then, almost as if on cue, the bishops came from the Church.

At first, Emilia thought the Church Guard had swooped in to save the village.

But she then found herself being loaded into a Church wagon, alone, her father telling her he would stay here.

At first, Emilia had no idea what her father was saying. She begged the bishops, and the village elder who had come to see her off, to convince her father to come along. *I can't live alone. I am who I am because of Father, because of the villagers.*

"Let's go, Father! Let's go together!"

Emilia screamed as loudly as she could, but the response her father gave was nothing short of unbelievable.

"Emilia, please, go."

Emilia doubted her own ears.

"Father! Father, what are you...!"

"This is all for the sake of a day I hoped would never come. For twelve years, I have protected you. I have been the father of an angel's child, one I had no right to receive."

"I don't understand! What are you saying, Father?!"

"You are the child of an angel. You have inherited the blood of heaven, the blood that will wipe away the darkness covering Ente Isla. You are the only one in this land with the power to defeat the Devil King."

"Me? No! No, Father, I'm your daughter! The daughter of a village farmer!"

"Yes. You are. But you are also your mother's daughter. The daughter of an angel."

"My...my mother? An angel?"

Her mother was dead. Her father had said as much for years.

"You will understand someday, Emilia. Please, let the bishops take you. Your mother is still alive, somewhere. I know she looks down upon you now."

"But...but Father—"

"I made a promise to your mother. I promised we would all be together, the three of us, here in this village, someday. And if I want to keep that promise, I have to fight for it."

Nordo gave another, stronger hug to Emilia, who clung to him like a toddler, then knelt down to her eye level. A large, rough hand reassuringly patted her on the head.

"It'll be all right. Everyone in the Church army is fighting alongside us to protect this village, this province. The day will surely come when we all live together again."

"...Really?"

"Of course. I never lie to my girl. Have I ever broken a promise before?"

"...No."

Sniffling, Emilia used a fist to wipe away the tears as she shook her head.

"There's a good girl."

Her father laughed, his laugh as warm as a fresh bushel of wheat.

"I'll be praying for you. Praying for a world where evil is driven away, where you can live your life bathed in holy light. Emilia...my daughter, I love you from the bottom of my heart."

The rest was all a cloud in her memory. Her father, blurred in her teary eyes, and the arm of the bishop trying to separate them. The village, and the only parent she knew, growing smaller and smaller through the carriage's thick portholes.

She must have cried herself to sleep, because the next thing she knew, she was in an ornate, luxurious, and wholly unfamiliar bedroom.

The bishop serving as her steward explained that this was Sankt Ignoreido, the Church's headquarters on the Western Continent. It was the day after she was separated from her father. The same day news arrived that her homeland, her village, had been razed to the ground, the Church's exertions proving to be all for naught.

After this, the young bishop told Emilia a great number of things.

The revelations flowed like a stream. Her mother was actually one of the great archangels; only a cross between human and angel could wield the heaven-gifted holy sword known as the "Better Half." To Emilia, hearing all this provided neither solace nor pain.

Having all of these bizarre tales spun before you, then being told all of it was the unadorned truth, would have been hard to accept for anyone. But Emilia had no desire for a holy sword, nor for whatever dubious stories they had about her mother. All she wanted was power. Power to gain revenge against the Devil King forces that destroyed her small, peaceful village.

From the day after she arrived in Sankt Ignoreido, she begged to be taught in the ways of the sword. Even now, she remembered her surprise at the weight of the iron weapon that the grown knights seemed to brandish with such ease. By the time she was ready for routine training, her body was already scarred, her hands deeply calloused.

Her first journey to battle came a year later. She was to join a defense line mounted in a rural frontier. The demon side was composed of strictly the lowest level of monsters, just common goblins and imps, and yet the sight of her first battlefield, the smell of blood, made her legs fall out from under her. She failed to defeat a single demon; the Church knights were forced to safeguard her from start to finish.

Her own weakness, and how far advanced and deathly terrifying the foe she was attempting to challenge truly was, was now revealed in graphic clarity. The tears she swore she would never shed again after losing her father poured out all too easily.

But time continued to pass, and Emilia gained more battlefield experience. Before she knew it, she stood upon the front lines, leading the Church knights as they captured Devil King citadels and command posts.

The name of Emilia Justina, knight of the Church Guard, spread among not just the Church forces, but also through the knights and mercenaries serving the armies of all the land's kingdoms. She bore a great shield, her armor composed of silver plate with the Church's seal etched in gold and scarlet; her knightly sword featured the Cross of Ignora, the symbol of the Ente Isla Church. Those who witnessed her slaying the throngs of demons that dared to challenge Emilia called her the Virgin of the Battlefield, the Holy Knight; and soon, Emilia was known across the human race as the leader of the Guard fighting the Devil King's hordes.

A vast, wide group of trustworthy friends gathered behind Emilia's lead.

Olba Meiyer, one of the six archbishops of the Church, the highest figures in the Church bureaucracy. Emeralda Etuva, alchemist and member of the court of Saint Aile, an empire on the Western Continent that had been captured by Lucifer's forces. Albert Ende, a martial artist who toiled as a woodcutter deep in the mountains of the Northern Continent.

Sometimes they fought as a quartet. Other times, each captained their own force against the Devil King's armies.

By the time Emilia's sixteenth birthday tolled, she had matured to the point where she was a warrior capable of wielding the holy sword. The Better Half was instilled into her body, granting her, in both name and ability, the power to destroy the Devil King himself.

News of the birth of Emilia the Hero, the woman who wielded the sword from heaven, spread across the land, galvanizing the spirits of all who heard it. The day the Hero was born was also the day when the humans of Ente Isla launched the first truly unified resistance against the Devil King.

Emilia's response was subdued. She felt no pride at the adulation; there was no sense of holding a great mandate for the people. To her, the day held no special meaning, apart that she now held the power to challenge the demon overlord at his own game.

Within Emilia's heart dwelt two things: the eternal, unflagging image of her father, and a dark desire for revenge against the demons. Her companions stood silently, all too aware of this, ready to become her sword and her shield as they united together for a common cause.

With seemingly unstoppable momentum, they defeated three of the Great Demon Generals. After pitched, bloody combat, they had stormed the Devil's Castle, the edifice that would serve as the site of the final battle. The dark joy Emilia felt as her sword sliced through one of the Devil King's horns nearly shook her to the roots, so sublime it was. And the dull blue rage she felt as the Devil King escaped through the Gate, robbing her of the final blow, was cataclysmic.

From the moment she began training, she had dreamed of the single moment when the Demon King would be dead by her hand.

✳

Aboveground, the scene was chaotic, as if someone had dropped a hornet's nest right in the middle of downtown.

Yasukuni Street was shut off to traffic, the site of the collapse ringed from far away by several dozen rescue vehicles. A starry field of red and blue lights disrupted the nightscape, and a herd of media vehicles were lodged just outside of the ring.

By the time rescuers made it to the underground corridor, Maou had already extracted all the victims from the rubble. None had any obvious injuries. The teams had arrived nervously expecting a grisly scene; now they were beyond surprise and into a sense of near-panicked disbelief.

The Devil King reverted back to Sadao Maou before the rescue was completed. The effort had understandably exhausted him; he was lying facedown on the ground with the other victims. But, given the circumstances of the scene, no one paid him special suspicion.

Maou, of course, was not about to report his single-handed rescue to the authorities. Once the victims came to, almost all of them rose back to their feet. It was to the point where Emi, with that superficial cut to her forehead, was the most severely injured of them all.

Chiho, put to sleep by Emi, immediately opened her eyes after a light slap on the cheek. Realizing she was back aboveground, she looked at Maou sitting next to her. She moved forward, about to say something, but then closed her mouth.

"Well, at least we're okay."

"Y-yeah…"

Chiho looked confused as Maou patted her head, but smiled weakly nonetheless. Paramedics and police officers ran to and fro around them as they corralled the "victims" inside a secure zone.

Seeing Emi Yusa being treated for her injuries inside a nearby ambulance, Chiho tried to recall their conversation before she lost consciousness. For some reason, it was all a foggy blur.

"Excuse me, are you both victims?"

A uniformed police officer sidled up to them, some kind of ledger in his hand.

"You're both pretty lucky you weren't seriously hurt. I apologize for intruding, but we need to confirm the identities of all the victims, so would you be able to write down your contact information here? We can use the information to provide compensation and any personal effects we recover later on."

Several names and addresses were already jotted down on the ledger he handed them.

Maou obediently added his own contact to the list, then gave the book to Chiho, who followed suit.

"Hmm? Say, you aren't Lieutenant Sasaki's daughter, are you?" Chiho's written address had apparently rung a bell in the officer's mind.

"Um, if you mean Sen'ichi Sasaki from the Harajuku department, then yes."

The police officer nodded at Chiho's startled response. "Ah, I thought so. Lieutenant Sasaki's somewhere out here on the scene right now, too. We're having parents or guardians pick up the minors here, so I'll go get him on the radio. Better if the lieutenant knew you were safe first, before he learned you were caught up in this."

"Oh! Sure!"

As Chiho nodded her approval, the officer took out his radio and started speaking, no doubt calling for her father. Watching him, Chiho began to fidget restlessly.

"Um, Maou…?"

Maou, realizing what Chiho was about to say, gave her a smile, in part to calm her nerves.

"Your dad, right? Yeah, I can imagine. Even if nothing bad happened, I bet he wouldn't be a fan of you getting involved in this because you were on a date with some guy, huh?"

"…I'm sorry." Chiho sounded it, from every vein in her body.

"No, no, it's all right! We're both okay; that's the important thing. I'll see you at work, okay? Next time I'll teach you how to maintain the ice cream machine. See you!"

His hand waving in the air, Maou walked away from Chiho as she bowed toward him. He turned around after a distance, just in time to see another uniformed officer in front of him, hurriedly jostling his way through the crowd. The man leaped toward Chiho.

"Whoa."

The officer surprised him into reacting out loud. He knew that face.

Who could have guessed that the officer who discovered Alciel and the wounded Devil King as they wandered down a Yoyogi back road, fresh from escaping Ente Isla and falling into Japan, the man who drove them to the Harajuku police department for voluntary questioning, was Chiho's father?

"'Patrolman Sasaki,' huh? That's no coincidence. If that guy was responding at all to our magical force back then…"

"Devil King!"

"Gah!"

Maou, lost in thought and recollection, found himself pulled back to reality by Emi's shout. She stood right behind his back.

"So you're back to Sadao Maou now, hmm?"

Even with the bandage placed on her forehead, Emi's sharp eyes were still focused squarely upon Maou. The horns were gone, the demonic legs that ripped through his denim pants now just a pair of pale, hairy legs visible through the rags.

"What do I look like, some kind of wild boar?"

"I'm not here to joke around with you, Maou."

"I don't know. It was a total coincidence that I reverted just now. I don't know what caused it, and that little bit of exertion was all it took to turn back to this form, too."

Maou found himself replying honestly. Not only was his joke a total failure, but Emi was still staring at him with those deadly serious eyes.

"It's not gonna help you if you hide anything from me."

His good-faith effort was meagerly rewarded.

"Man, you're sounding less and less like a Hero every day. You can keep on stalking me if you want, but I don't think I'll be transforming again anytime soon. Though I *might* want to try taking action based on today's events, you know."

"...What do you mean?"

"Oh, you know, go out to eat in more underground food courts, wait around for another collapse."

"Don't be stupid with me."

"Ah, lay off. I'm gonna go home and sleep. I'm tired."

"Wait!"

"Quit it, would you! Nothing else is gonna happen today, okay? Whether it was a coincidence or not, I had my magic power back, but *your* attack was a total failure."

Maou unenthusiastically waved Emi off, trying to bring an end to the conversation. But Emi was unwilling to let that final jab go unanswered.

"My attack? What do you mean?"

"You were listening in on me and Chi, right? Like, starting halfway through?" Maou shrugged, exasperated. "No way is what she's going through normal. All this happened when you and I were here. Someone hatched it on us. I don't know if it was a sonar pulse or magical interference or whatever, but what I *do* know is, our cover's been blown."

Emi's eyes burst open.

"So our enemy..."

"He's right nearby, yeah. We just never noticed before. And I bet he didn't attempt a second stab because I was about to return to my full Devil body."

"B-but…but what *was* that? We're in Japan. You can't refill your strength; I can't refill mine. How could they unleash this kind of force?"

Maou flashed a wry smile.

"Oh, I have my ideas."

"What? Oh, come *on*!"

Maou's expression remained firm, almost cold, against the agitated Emi.

"Not that I've got any duty to tell you. It's not like you could do anything about it."

Emi contemplated firing back for an instant, but resisted the urge. In his own way, Maou was right.

"But I'll give you a hint, anyway. Don't want you getting all panicked whenever things go down."

"…A hint?"

"Sure. First off, whether it's indirect or not, our opponent's throwing around his powers like crazy, whenever he wants to. Think about who could do that in Ente Isla right now, huh? Someone who's apparently confident that he can kill the both of us?"

Emi had deduced that much by herself. But who? She drew a total blank. Watching Emi lost in thought, a cynical smile grew on Maou's face.

"Got it yet? I'm going home. I need to think about how to counter him. Plus, I'm tired."

"W-wait! Wait a minute. I still need—"

"You still need to talk? Great. But how 'bout we take a rain check for today? You got company."

Maou pointed over Emi's shoulder. There, they found a figure stretching her body past the police tape behind the ambulances, excitedly waving toward them.

"Rika…"

"Oh, is that your coworker or something? She keeps calling your name, did you notice that?"

Rika Suzuki, still in her work outfit, began waving even more fervently when she noticed Emi's look of recognition.

"So you *do* have some friends."

"That's none of your business! Stop bothering me!"

Emi spat out the words as she turned her back to him.

"Hey, I'm just being jealous. Here, go say hello to her."

"But…you think they're going to strike again once things settle down?"

This question came from the heart, the personification of her anxieties. This collapse wasn't like the flurry of magical blasts from earlier; it had endangered a large number of innocent bystanders. If a third attack was forthcoming, it might get Rika involved next time. But Maou just laughed haughtily, voice full of confidence.

"Doubt it. He declared that both you and I were his targets. If he attacks one of us, that's gonna set off alarms for the other guy, right? Trust me. I know how an evil villain thinks. I'm the best one out there."

It wasn't necessarily something to be proud of, but Maou still puffed up his chest as he spoke.

"Well? C'mon. Don't keep her waiting."

He gave Emi a push. It was a less than pleasant experience.

She took a step forward, then whipped her head around.

"Just for today, got it?"

"Yeah, yeah. 'Don't try anything funny,' right? Sure thing."

He doubted that she believed such an airy reply, and likewise Emi twisted up her face a bit before quickly jogging away. Her coworker behind the tape embraced her, tears running down her face. Her uniform was typical secretary gear, her sandals plain and unadorned. She must have thrown on whatever was handy when she heard the news.

Maou chuckled wistfully to himself. "If she's trying to demotivate me, she's damn well succeeding."

He turned on his heels, preparing to walk away from the scene.

"Your Demonic Hiiiiighness…"

"Agh! Ashiya!"

He nearly collided with Ashiya, not noticing him lurking behind like some vengeful ghost.

"I-I'm so sorry, my liege!"

"What's *that* from all of a sudden? For that matter, where *were* you?"

Ashiya sniffled pathetically in front of him, wailing as he pointed out an ambulance in the distance.

"I allowed Emilia to approach us... I failed to notice our advancing foe... And you even saved my *life*, my liege! How could I ever... ever *repaaaaaay* you?!"

Maou wearily pushed the dusty, blubbering Ashiya to the side.

"Look, will you shut up? Stop sobbing like that in public. You look terrible. C'mon, let's go home. You aren't hurt, are you?"

"N-n-no... No, nooo! Th-thank you for...for *caring*...!"

They were stopped three times by other officers to check their identities as they left; two of the officers gave them information about reparations and nearby hospitals. They then fled, nearly getting caught by the media covering the scene, but nonetheless cheaping out on train fare and walking the entire way from Shinjuku to Sasazuka. It was two hours later by the time they arrived home.

"Oh my *goodness*, what a surprise! You, like, always go down to that food court, right, Emi? I thought maybe you got caught up in all that, and... You know, I was just beside myself!"

Rika, after confirming Emi was fine, broke down in tears, as if the tragedy happened to her instead.

"I couldn't get you on the phone, you didn't respond to any of my texts... So I was like 'oh, no', so I ran over here, but no way would they let me in... I'm telling you, I was in a *panic*!"

"Sorry to make you worry."

"No! No, it's not your fault, Emi! I mean, if anything, it was just bad luck! Or maybe *good* luck, I guess, since you're okay now! Were you hurt really bad?"

Rika had finally gained enough of her wits to notice the bandage.

"I cut my forehead a little bit. Enough to draw blood. But it's nothing big. I didn't need stitches or anything."

In Emi's mind it really was a tiny scrape, but to the standards of the average Japanese person, it was worryingly serious.

"So can you go home now?"

"Well, I gave the police my contact info, and the paramedics told me about hospitals and compensation and stuff. They said they'd take me to the hospital once things settle down, but this is really the only injury I have, so…"

"Ooh, well, you better not run off home yet, then! Better at least get a medical note from the hospital. Do you have your phone and some money?"

Emi, amazed by Rika's utter zeal to help, thought it over.

"I have my phone, but everything else is in my bag, under the rubble. Ahh! My insurance card, my passport…my seal…"

She could feel her blood pressure drop. She just *had* to be carrying all her valuables in one place today.

"Okay, take this. Lemme know once you're out of the hospital. I'll meet you over there."

Seeing her friend in need, Rika quickly took three 10,000-yen bills out of her wallet, pushing them into Emi's hand.

"R-Rika?"

"Hey, you never know when you're gonna need it at a time like this! Plus, you don't want the media catching you, so call me, all right?"

With that, she pushed Emi back behind the tape, making shooing motions with her hands. Emi humored her, looking back once there was enough distance between them. She found a man, presumably media, confronting her, hoping to get a story from someone who spoke with a victim.

Rika was too far away to be audible, but she chased the man away, looking plainly annoyed, before disappearing into the crowd.

Once she was gone, Emi returned to the ambulance that bandaged her and meekly traveled with several other victims to the nearest hospital.

After a thorough examination, her injury was officially classified as "light." Nonetheless, the doctor went ahead and exaggerated a bit on his official report, smiling at Emi as he did.

"If I were a young woman like you, if something scratched *me* on the forehead, I'd hope to get some compensation from it."

Emi let out a bitter laugh.

It was already past nine p.m. by the time everything was settled and she left the examination room.

"Hello, Rika?"

Being in a hospital, she used a green public phone, an endangered species in the urban landscape, to call Rika. Her friend answered on the first ring.

"Emi? Hello! How'd it go?"

"Well, the doctor examined me all over, but they said it was nothing big. He disinfected my scratch and gave me some medication just in case, but he said I didn't have to take it unless it hurt."

"Oh! Okay, I'm so glad it's nothing serious! Where's your hospital?"

"Shinjuku. The university hospital."

"Got it. I'll be right over, so hang tight, okay?"

"Oh, that's all right. I don't need to bother you."

"Oh? Is your family there or something?"

A sensible enough question to ask in the midst of this catastrophe, but for Emi, it required a lie to settle.

"No, uh, my parents aren't in Japan, so…"

"Oh, really? Like, overseas?!"

The surprise was evident in Rika's voice. Judging by the background noise, she was already preparing to go.

"Yeaaah, that sort of thing."

"Well, all the more reason I better keep an eye on you! I'll go take a taxi there right now. It'll be about ten minutes, all right? See you then!"

"Whoa, Rika, wait a—!"

Emi stared at the green handset, stunned at how briskly Rika had hung up on her.

There was nothing to be done. She sat in the waiting room for a few minutes before the receptionist called her name.

The way it was explained to her, the fees for her examination and its certificate would be compensated for once she paid the fees in her name, and then sent an invoice, plus any other necessary documentation, to the appropriate location.

As she paid the receptionist, Emi recalled that her new purse was underneath the rubble alongside her commuter bag. That, and she remembered Rika's monetary support: "You never know when you're gonna need it at a time like this!"

She could bring her insurance card in before the end of the month to take care of everything, but even then, the assorted fees she racked up this evening were on the pricey side.

Just as she accepted her receipt and the prescription for her medication, she noticed a taxi stopped outside the lobby and Rika walking inside. She immediately ran over to Emi once she saw her.

"Are you okay, Emi?!"

"Uh, yeah. Thanks a lot. You're being a big help."

Emi brought the receipt and prescription up to Rika's eyes.

"See? Told you."

Rika smiled.

"I'm just happy it was nothing serious. Here, how about you stay at my place tonight? I've got the taxi waiting."

"S-sure, but is it really okay?"

"Oh, of course! No need to worry about anything, okay? C'mon!"

"All right!"

Unable to protest Rika's vigorous invitation, Emi was taken outside and thrown into the taxi. The next thing she knew, she was standing in front of Rika's condo in the neighborhood of Takadanobaba.

Rika's condo was around the same size as Emi's, but the smell of fresh building materials, wallpaper, and paint belied its very recent construction.

"So, anyway, if you aren't hurt anywhere else, you should go take a shower and get changed first. I can lend you my sweats for today; you'll be more comfortable in those."

Rika handed her a sweatshirt and pants, both neatly folded, along with a hanging wardrobe bag.

"And put your old clothes in here. Better not throw them away, even if they're ripped or whatever."

"Why not?"

Emi meekly removed her clothes as ordered. The gray suit she had worn for work wasn't particularly damaged, but her blouse was stained with blood from her forehead.

"Because you might get whatever company manages that food court to pay for it, is why! No harm keeping the evidence safe until it's all over."

"Oh. Makes sense."

The concept of individual compensation provided by large firms, public or private, was unimaginable in Ente Isla. Even now, Emi still lacked a full grasp of the idea.

The prevailing system back in her homeland was still largely feudal. If a citizen summoned for some public construction project was hurt by an accident or a disaster, the common expectation was that he'd be given a pittance of a consolation payment and tossed by the side of the road.

"I'm impressed, though, Rika. You sure know a lot about this kind of thing."

"Well, you know, I've been through a thing or two in my life. Oh, the bathroom's that way. I've got some brand-new underwear you can take home, too. I'm pretty sure we got the same bra size."

"Smaller than Chiho's, probably."

"Huh?"

"...Oh, uh, never mind."

She sighed, not quite managing to stop the complaint before it crossed her lips. Checking the size of what she was given, it was indeed the same as Emi's.

"Really, though, thank you so much for everything. I'll be in the bathroom."

Lukewarm shower water bounced off her body, instantly sweeping away the assorted events of the day and filling her with a comfortable sense of satisfaction.

"I put a towel on top of the washer in the changing room, okay?

Oh, and here's a washcloth if you need it. The body soap's on the far
left-hand side."

A washcloth was offered through a crack in the bathroom door,
Rika's index finger pointing out the soap container.

"Did you eat dinner, by the way?"

"Ooh, to be honest, I'm about ready to die of starvation more than
anything else."

Rika broke into a broad, comforting smile at Emi's honest reply.

"Well, I'll whip up something quick for you, so enjoy the shower,
okay? You're good for anything, right?"

Rika left the changing room, allowing Emi a few moments to fully
enjoy the shower in silence.

"...Weird."

It was oddly difficult to calm down. She was overly aware of her
heartbeat, yes, but there was something about even that which com-
forted her.

Whenever she was struck down by foes in her quest against the
Devil King, there was always someone nearby to help her. Many of
them happily offered her food and board as well.

But she had never had a feeling quite like this one before.

It made her wish she could stay this way forever, as intensely pleasant and comfortable as the temperature of the water that coursed
down her skin.

It was as if a soft light kindled itself within her mind, like she was
being gently wrapped in an angel's wings.

"Well, here's to your good health. Cheers!"

The two glasses of cold mineral water clinked together.

Rika apologized for having nothing but leftovers to offer, but
the simmered meat and potatoes she warmed up were a feast for
Emi's empty stomach. She eagerly worked on the dish with her
chopsticks.

"If you've got that kind of appetite, I guess there really *is* nothing
to worry about, huh?"

Rika smiled, relieved from the inside out.

"But, still, be careful, all right? Sometimes injuries like that can relapse and get you in trouble later on."

"I'll keep that in mind. Thanks for everything, Rika. Really. I promise I'll pay you back later."

"Well, it's the least I could do! I mean, you lost your purse *and* your bank book! That'd be a disaster for anyone."

After some more chitchat, Rika casually turned on the TV.

It was nothing but news reports about the corridor collapse Emi was involved in. Rika flipped through the channels at light speed, until she stopped at a music program.

For Emi's sake, no doubt. Emi looked toward the TV stand, noticing a photograph propped on top of it. Her attention did not go unnoticed.

"Oh, that's my family."

The photo was shot in front of a factorylike building, with Rika, a couple that were presumably her parents, and another girl, essentially a younger version of Rika.

"Is that your sister down there? You sure look alike."

"You know, that's what everyone says! If you ask me, though, I've never seen the resemblance."

Rika smiled. Just then:

"Oh, mind if I get that?"

The phone was ringing inside Rika's bag. Once Emi nodded, Rika picked up.

"Hello?…Pfft. Wella *course* it's me. Who else're ya expectin', calling up this number?"

Emi looked toward Rika, surprised. This tone of voice she had never heard before.

"Oh, y'all got that? Cool. Nah, it ain't nothin' that expensive. I drink it all the time. Plus which, 'ell, Gramps'll drink anythin' if it says '*shochu* liquor' on the label, am I right?"

Rika had mentioned that she was born in the Kansai region of Japan. But the accent seemed a bit off intonation-wise from what Emi knew about the Kansai dialect.

"So I'm a-comin' back in August, okay?…Huh? Accident? Oh,

yeah, that was right close to my job, but I'm okay, so... You tell that to everyone else too, all right? Yeah. Byeeeee."

The short conversation ended. Rika was about to toss the phone on the table, but thought better of it and pulled up the charger cord plugged into the wall, inserting it into the phone jack.

"That was Ma. She was all worked up about the stuff on TV, but I didn't feel like goin' all at it talkin' about you all night."

"I don't think I've heard your original accent before, Rika."

"Oh, no? I didn't realize. I always fall into that whenever I'm talking to folks back home. We all live in Kobe."

Come to think of it, Rika did sound a bit different from usual ever since they'd met at the collapse site. Revealing more of herself, maybe. The thought made Emi smile.

"Wow. It sounds kind of fresh and new to me. I've never really left Tokyo at all, but I'd love to go out west sometime."

The work paid well by the hour, but she was hardly a wealthy woman, and she had never enjoyed anything close to resembling a "vacation" in her life. If it weren't for the Devil King...though she had entertained the thought of traveling around Japan for a while if she ever did slay him. But that was far in the future, if ever.

Emi focused back on her dinner. By the time the music program was over, she had polished off everything Rika put out for her.

"Wow. Nice job. Guess you're just fine now, huh?"

"Thanks to you. Should I go rinse off the dishes?"

Emi quickly stacked up the dishes and bowls, dividing them into "oil" and "non-oil" stacks as she placed them in the water.

"Thanks! Just leave them there, okay? I'll wash them later."

"Sure thing. Oh, uh, you mind if I watch the news?"

"Mmm? Not really, but are you sure?"

It was obvious what they'd be covering, no matter how long they waited. Rika's face darkened for a moment, but Emi nodded back at her.

"I want to check the weather and stuff. Besides, I'm sure they'll have other things on, too."

"Well, okay. I think *Press Terminal* oughtta be on right now."

Rika picked up the remote and navigated the channels. Emi returned from the dining table and sat where she was before, facing the TV screen. The top news was the collapse in Shinjuku, of course, but they dwelled upon it for a surprisingly small amount of time before moving on to the recent rash of street robberies across Tokyo.

"Man, that sucks. My luck's been so bad lately, I'm probably gonna run into *that* next."

The observation from Emi made Rika look at her from the side. Then: "Dahh! Aw, Emi, you're the best!"

"Huh? Wh-what do you mean, Rika?"

Suddenly, Rika gave Emi a hug from behind.

"Whoa! What's gotten into *you*?"

"Aw, you're just so *nice*, Emi. You're so *soothing*."

"Huh?"

For a moment or two, Rika swayed back and forth, rocking Emi like a cradle. Emi let it pass, not quite understanding her behavior. Soon, Rika finally spoke, still holding her.

"You know, ever since I went off to Tokyo, I've always tried to speak in standard Japanese. It was just so annoying otherwise."

"Annoying?"

Emi turned toward her quizzically. Thousands of people flocked to Tokyo from elsewhere in Japan all the time. Several people at the call center still sported obvious accents as they worked.

"Well, like, if you use standard Japanese, then you don't have to worry about people asking where you came from, right?"

Come to think of it…Emi knew Rika was from the Kansai area, but her friend never told her anything else about home.

It was, truthfully, something Emi never actively explored with her, lest she be tasked with completely fabricating her own childhood in response.

"If you're from Hyogo prefecture, then all people in Tokyo ever want to talk to you about is The Earthquake."

"Oh…"

Emi suddenly realized her motivation. She turned around within Rika's arms.

"And that's, like, *all*, too. Never anything else. So I stopped talking about my home, since it was just getting annoying."

Rika's eyes turned toward the family photograph.

"I was still just a kid during the 1995 Earthquake, but I'll still never forget that day. It was really scary. There were a lot of small workshops and stuff near our house, and we had a lot of damage in our neighborhood."

Emi was certainly aware of the history-making earthquake centered on Kobe and its environs. It was an era-defining event, a couple of decades ago.

"It was practically a miracle everyone in my family was okay. A lot of my friends… There were a ton of kids who lost family members. I was in grade school, but when class started up again, two of my classmates were gone. I tried to kid myself into thinking they moved away."

"…Wow. I hear you."

"So it really makes me mad, how insensitive some people are. They're just like 'Oh, how was the earthquake?' It pretty much flattened my granddad's workshop, and there were aftershocks the whole time we were at the rescue center. I was scared for days!"

Rika's voice was detached and calm as she spoke. She had clearly come to terms with it in her mind by this point.

"But the moment I take a step away from where I grew up, people treat it like some long-forgotten event. No matter where I go, no matter how much time has passed, when I mention that my family's from Kobe, they ask about The Earthquake first. It's like, can't they picture anything else about the place? Those sort of people, I really didn't want to be friends with them."

As Rika explained, she had to give up her hardline stance over time.

"That was, like, pretty much everyone I met, so I thought I'd never let myself talk to anybody if I kept dwelling on it. So I changed my accent so I could hide where I came from. Sorry I tricked you like that!"

"Oh, you didn't trick me..."

"But you're the first one, Emi. The first one who heard the word *Kobe* and didn't ask about the quake."

Rika finally separated from Emi, taking the glasses back to the kitchen for another round of mineral water from the fridge.

"Whenever you find that your life's gone completely upside down like that... There's just no telling how people will react afterward, you know?"

Emi could feel her heart pound for an instant at the nuance behind the observation.

"Some people out there, they try to take advantage of the chaos to do real bad stuff. Then there are people who really work hard to help out others, even though they have no idea what's gonna happen tomorrow. And it makes you think, you know? It's kind of like those old cartoons, where whenever you're pondering something, this little angel and devil appear on your shoulders."

Rika crossed her index fingers in swordlike fashion to illustrate her point.

"It made me think that, like, people really *can* be angels; they really *can* be devils. It all depends on what they choose to do."

"Angel, or devil...?"

Rika's offhand remarks triggered something. Emi pondered it for a moment.

"So anyway, that photo shows what my pop and granddad devoted themselves to for the next ten years after. They rebuilt their workshop from scratch, just a constant, never-ending effort. And even now, with the recession and so on, they still have enough old business connections to keep chugging along."

She put the glass down in front of her.

"But I'm telling you, today *spooked* me. I come all the way to Tokyo, only to see an accident like that...and another friend was *there*, too! I never even wanted to think about it."

*Another friend.* The words snapped Emi back to attention. Rika must have been close to the classmates she lost.

If things had worked out otherwise, it might have been Rika

herself. She was a mature adult because she had learned, at a deeply personal level, the terrors that disaster could bring. And now she was coming to Emi's rescue as well, doing her level best to help her out.

"Emi?"

"…Huh?"

"You okay? Sorry if I'm making you think about kind of weird stuff."

Rika chuckled to herself, then emptied the remaining mineral water into her mouth, as if drinking up the dark emotions locked in her memories.

"But, hey, we're all okay now, right? And you've really been a huge help to me, Rika. I appreciate it so much."

"Oh, stop. What kind of friends would we be if we didn't help each other out? No need to feel all weird about it."

At that instant, that feeling struck Emi again. That soft light in her heart. The warm…feeling. The comfort of knowing she was protected, head to toe.

"So, you know, that's why I don't really want to ask about you or anything."

"Oh?"

"I mean, where you lived, where you come from… I don't really care about that, Emi. To me, as long as you're a friend I can talk a bunch of BS with, and have lunch with, and go out on the town with sometimes, that's all I need."

"Rika…"

"Oh, and speaking of…"

Suddenly, Rika brought his face closer to Emi's, a sneering smile on her face.

"Who was that *guy*?"

"Eh?"

"The guy you were talking to out by the accident site."

"Huh? Uh… Oh. *That* guy."

She meant Maou. Of course she did.

"You know him? You sure acted like you did. He looked like a pretty decent fellow, so I couldn't help but wonder…"

"Hey! You just said you wouldn't ask me anything, Rika! That, and he's really not anyone like—"

"Romance is different, Emi! I won't let any of those wolves get near *you*, my little angel!"

"Oh, stop sounding like some weird, overprotective dad! He's just an acquaintance of mine…actually, less than that, even. He's a demon, not a wolf. Total demon."

It was no lie. He was certainly nothing *more* than an acquaintance. And he *was* a demon.

"A demon…"

"Emi?"

"An angel…and a demon."

At the site of that frightful accident, Maou had regained his demon form.

"What's up, Emi?"

She looked at Rika's face, the face of a woman who called her a friend.

She had felt a sense of warmth in the shower, and then at the dining table, when her friend hugged her; like her heart was within an angel's wings.

And the cause of it:

"The heart…of a human being?"

THE DEVIL
AND THE HERO
STAND STRONG
IN SASAZUKA

"Not *you* again. This early in the morning? Look, I have work today, so could you let me sleep some more?"

It was hardly that early. Emi, after all, had left the same time Rika went off to work.

Rika tried to stop her, suggesting she take another day to rest. But she didn't want to cause too much trouble for her friend, and the thoughts she dwelled upon over the previous night had driven her to room 201 of the Villa Rosa Sasazuka apartments as quickly as she could manage.

Since her own clothes were bloodied, she borrowed a blouse from Rika. She wore the same suit and shoes from the night of the accident as she clambered the Villa Rosa staircase and mashed a finger on the doorbell.

She expected that Maou might not exactly heave the door wide open for her, so she had an excuse in hand—a brown paper envelope she purchased from the convenience store. It was enough to capture Maou's notice as he cracked the door open, still not ready to remove the chain.

"Don't worry. There isn't poison or a razor blade inside or anything."

"I don't think I've received anything from you I *didn't* regret."

"Oh, well, in that case, I think I'll just keep this thousand yen—"

Maou snatched the envelope away.

"Okay, we're even now."

"Hey! I thought we promised you'd stop interfering with us for a while."

"I think me rescuing you from the cops more than makes up for that."

"Ugh, you stupid little—"

Emi interjected before Maou could finish his evaluation.

"Yesterday!"

"Uh?"

"Was Ashiya...I mean Alciel all right?"

A look of clear suspicion crossed Maou's face.

"Did you get clocked in the head or something last night?"

"We're talking about him, not me. He wasn't hurt or anything?"

She knew this was an inelegant way of picking his mind. But there was no other way to broach the topic.

"No, no injuries. Major blow to his ego, though."

The look of suspicion remained on his face.

"And he didn't turn back into his demon form or anything, either."

"Ah...!"

"What? Isn't that what you were asking about?" Maou snorted at Emi, who was unable to hide the shock. The confrontational tone drained from her voice.

"How do I know you're telling the truth?"

"Well, what if I said he *was* a demon? Would you bust in here and kill us?"

"I..."

Maou continued, not expecting a useful response.

"He could tell I reverted back, too, for a little while. He spent all night crying about 'Ooooh, I failed to serve my liege at his hour of need,' et cetera, et cetera, and now he's sleeping in this morning. What the hell am I gonna do for breakfast now?"

Ashiya had remained staunchly human. Internally, this disturbed Emi.

Rika's monologue suggested to her that Maou regained his

demon form temporarily because his body had consumed the terror and anguish from the nearby survivors, converting it into magical force.

If that theory proved true, Maou could have used the power he had before yesterday to summon any manner of disaster. Say, an earthquake strong enough to make an underground corridor collapse. And he could repeat the process, continually feeding off the negative emotions of his victims, until the Devil King Satan finally resurrected himself. And if this *was* Maou's plan, there was no reason for him to hesitate any longer.

Satan, in his conquest of Ente Isla, was a cruel, merciless tyrant, one who thought of a human being's life as no more consequential as that of a blade of grass. It was easy to picture him immediately moving to take action.

So she flew to his squalid apartment in a state of half panic...and found the same dopey-looking face peeking out behind the crack in the door, whining about how he needed to be on time for his shift. What was this Devil King thinking, going on with his human life? It was beyond Emi's comprehension.

His next question brought Emi into an even higher plane of bewilderment.

"But, hey, were *you* all right? I saw your forehead. And you used some of your power when you put Chi to sleep, didn't you?"

"...What?"

Emi froze on the spot.

"What are you...saying?"

"What do you mean, what am I saying? I'm just asking if you're okay. Your power isn't back, right?"

The easy explanation would be that she had suddenly, inexplicably, failed to comprehend the Japanese language. If only it were that easy.

"Are you being...serious?"

"What? Am I not allowed to be concerned about people?"

Maou acted honestly peeved as he fired back.

Emi could feel the blood drain from her face. She felt sick. What could this man possibly be saying to her?

She was gripped by an intense loathing, one far stronger than what rose up upon her first encounter with Maou and Ashiya in Japan. It was almost the same hatred as she felt the day she learned of her father's death.

"I am not so weak…that my enemy should be *concerned* for me."

That was all she could say, at the end of it.

"Oh?…Yeah, I guess so, huh?"

That was all the response Maou had to offer.

"Anyway. If that's all you needed, you mind leaving me alone?"

"With pleasure."

Emi quickly turned to make her exit. She wanted to feel out Maou a bit more, in hopes he'd drop a clue to the riddle behind his transformation. But if she stayed here any longer, she honestly wasn't sure what the disgust bubbling within her chest would make her do.

Maou looked on, concerned, as she left. Whether he understood her feelings or not, he plainly found her behavior puzzling. Suddenly, something sprang to his mind.

"H-hey! Emi!"

But Emi showed no sign of stopping, in a hurry to leave as quickly as possible.

"You're gonna slip if you—"

He wasn't quite able to relay the intended message before the moment came. The sound of corrugated iron panels loudly scraping against each other greeted his ears.

"Ah!"

That was all the reaction Maou heard from Emi.

The corrugated-iron stairway structure, replete with peeling paint and visible rust, had long been tilting to the side, the result of long years of supporting itself against the wind, rain, and weight of time. It had achieved an odd concave shape, just barely skirting legal regulations.

A soundless scream was heard as the weight so cruelly placed upon these stairs consumed its potential energy and tumbled to the ground.

"—if you go downstairs in those heels."

Maou finally completed the sentence once the noise died down.

* * *

A sulky-looking Ashiya, wearing a jersey he had lying around on the floor, opened the cabinet that held their first-aid kit.

Atop a stack of job-search magazines bound with twine in the corner, Emi sat staring into space, unable to figure out where to direct her emotions any longer.

Considering she had slipped the moment she set foot on the first step, her injuries were miraculously light. Unfortunately, her suit, which had survived intact up to this point, was now a ragged mess of dirt and tearing. One of the pumps that flew off her feet landed right on a concrete-block flagstone, adding a patchwork of scratches to the external leather.

As for Emi herself: One sprained finger, caused by reaching out and jamming it against the handrail. Bruising on her buttocks, which was the first to hit the stairs. A scrape to the bridge of her nose, as she landed facedown below.

Overall, far more serious than the damage she took from an entire underground corridor collapsing upon her.

"My... The Hero Emilia had the Devil King—in a different form, yes, but still the Devil King!—cornered in his lair once, and now she's been roughed up by falling down the stairs of our apartment? A black mark on His Demonic Highness more than anyone, perhaps, but..."

The impact on her forehead also reopened the wound from the previous night. Blood was beginning to show on the bandage, making its way past the gauze below. The dressing itself had turned brown from the dirt and would need a change shortly. Ashiya, however, looked dejected as he showed the emergency kit to the Devil King.

"Nothing in here but adhesive tape. We did buy gauze and so forth somewhere else, no?"

"Maybe. We weren't planning on anything as rough as this. We'll probably have to go buy some stuff. Hey, Ashiya, you mind going out to the pharmacy by the rail station and buying bandages and gauze? They oughtta be open by now. I don't want this girl yelling at me even more."

"Yes, my liege. May I be permitted to borrow Dullahan from you? I have other shopping to take care of as well."

"Permission granted. Hey, if you got *that* much money on you, why don't you cook something better for me?"

"I am afraid, Your Demonic Highness, that your spending habits are such that I have to build my own stash and save my money carefully. I will return soon."

Maou snorted derisively as he heard Ashiya, still wearing the morning's jersey, pedal off.

"You better get that disinfected for now, at least. I have some stuff over here, so let's get that washed and…"

Maou sat down in front of Emi, wet towel in hand. Emi, snapping out of her torpor, snatched it from his hand.

"D-don't touch me! I'm not a child! I can do it myself!"

"Sure, sure, sorry. Tissues are over there."

The box of tissues that Emi had flung at Maou still laid where it fell. She wiped the dirt from her nose and forehead, then used another tissue to apply the disinfectant. Then, she was struck by a crushing wave of sadness.

"What, does it sting?"

"No!"

Emi answered Maou's simple question by throwing the bottle of disinfectant, lid still open, full bore at him.

"Whoa! What was that for?"

"Shut up! What is *with* you, anyway?! You're the Devil King, you idiot! Why don't you *act* like one and start wrecking this world already?!"

"Huh? Where'd all *that* come from?"

Maou was honestly surprised, unsure what Emi was trying to say. Emi continued shouting.

"What?! Who the hell ever heard of a dirt-poor, junk-food-eating, rising-star-in-the-workplace, loved-by-teenage-girls Devil King?!"

"Ngh…"

Maou was taken off guard by this astute observation, but quickly rallied. "Well, *I've* never heard of a Hero who started crying after falling down the stairs and had a demon fix her up!"

"And what kind of Devil King sends his minion off to the pharmacy for the Hero's sake?! And what kind of Great Demon General actually says *yes* to that?!"

"Ergh..."

Emi began shouting like a toddler, unable to process her raging emotions.

"Why are you so damn *kind* to me?!"

The screamed question hit Maou where it hurt.

"Why are you kind to me, to other people, to the whole *world*?! How can... How can you be so *nice* all the time?!"

Maou was at a loss to answer. The unexpected sharpness of the query stabbed directly into his heart.

"And if you *can* be so nice...then why... Why..."

Emi shouted through the tears.

*"Why did you kill my father?!"*

The scream made the apartment's wooden frame shudder. The moment of silence afterward seemed even more deafening.

Emi sobbed, out of breath. Maou stood there, unable to give any response.

"The...the Devil King I pursued was a malicious monster! He treated people like they were nothing more than insects! He loved nothing more than the despair, the blood that ran across the world!"

"I—"

"You turned our fields into gigantic firestorms! You crushed our castles with your lightning! You washed away entire towns with your floods! You allowed your horde of demons to perform any kind of savage brutality they wanted! Devil King Satan! Even when you die, I will *never* forgive you! You took my home, my father's fields, my father's *life*, my peaceful, quiet childhood...! Everything! And I'll never forgive you!"

"Emi, I—"

"But why... Why are you...being so nice to me...?"

It was clear that Maou's mental makeup had veered considerably away from his time on Ente Isla.

He was a tyrant back then. Even now, he remembered how he treated the world as his personal plaything and resolved to eradicate the human race from all the land. That desire, at least, was still there. So why was he presenting no resistance to the idea of living a comfortable life in a human-dominated world?

"I...I haven't really thought deeply about it."

Maou, unable to formulate a clear answer in his mind, forced the words out anyway.

"But...well, sorry, I guess."

"......"

Emi did not reply. Instead she looked up with her red, tear-moistened face at the man in front of her, mouth open as she stared.

His approach was casual, but Maou was apologizing from the heart.

"I mean, I didn't know anything about any Hero at first. I was busy taking over the Central Continent and controlling my demon forces, so I guess I didn't really pay full attention to what was going on, over on the surrounding islands... Well, I don't mean to shift the blame to Lucifer, either, though. But what could I have done? Demons and humans... Well, we're *always* in conflict with each other."

He was clearly frustrated with himself. His eyes swiveled from one point in the air to the next, gesturing as he tried his hardest to formulate a decent excuse.

"Plus, you know, at the time, I guess I didn't really understand humans all that well, so..."

Emi was not expecting Maou to come up with much, but *this* reaction was wholly unexpected. She turned her reddened face to the side, the realization that she had exploded in front of Maou filling her with shame.

"Hello, I was—"

That was the scene so suddenly interrupted by a familiar voice. Emi and Maou quickly turned toward the door. Ashiya walked in, as if guided inside, and behind him was Chiho, frozen as she noticed the state Emi and Maou were in.

Ashiya was just as lost himself, forgetting to close the door as he witnessed the scene.

Chiho, in her scarlet-tinged school outfit, was holding a paper bag printed with the logo of a Japan-style sweet shop located inside a Shinjuku department store.

"Uh, I…I ran into Miss Sasaki there, and she stated she wanted to meet with you, and so…"

Ashiya stammered out his explanation, pharmacy bag still in hand. After a moment standing there in shock, Chiho dropped the bag she was holding. Judging by the heavy clank, one could figure the bag contained a can of *senbei* rice crackers, not that it mattered right now.

Maou could guess what was running through Chiho's mind.

Probably, she still felt bad about last night. Not only did she get Maou caught up in a disaster, but her selfish request had also led to repercussions in his personal life.

So to make up for it, she dressed up in her finest outfit and decided to stop by with something to snack on as a gift. By modern teenager standards, it was a tremendously polite gesture.

And then she ran into Ashiya, his roommate, near his apartment. Chiho hadn't exactly had a deep conversation with Ashiya yesterday, but he knew who she was, and she knew he was at the disaster site. And Ashiya, ever the gentleman, must have kindly escorted her up the stairs.

As attentive to detail as Ashiya always was, he had doubtlessly told her of Emi's morning visit. Chiho must have accepted the news well enough, given that she was here now.

So he came in expecting an injured Emi. Not a sobbing, red-faced Emi, along with a panicked-looking Maou trying his hardest to make excuses. It was simple to picture how she would gauge *that* situation. What's more, thanks to her trip down the stairs, Emi's suit was more than a little ripped and damaged. All of this raced across Maou's mind in the course of a single second.

The nervous step backward Chiho gingerly took turned all of this guesswork into confirmed belief.

"Uh… Ha-ha! M-maybe, uh, this isn't the best time…" she stammered.

"Ch-Chiho…"

Emi, no doubt reaching the same conclusion as Maou, rose up in a panic, realizing that Chiho was misunderstanding the scene in dramatic fashion.

"I guess it's true…that…Maou and…Yusa… They really are…."

Chiho's knees were shaking. Her eyes were emotionless, but the smile on her face was taut and fraying at the edges.

This was turning into a serious misunderstanding.

"N-no, Chiho, that's not it at all! This is…"

"Chi, listen, just calm down for a…"

"I-I'm sorry!"

Not willing to lend an ear to Emi's and Maou's wholly ungrounded excuses, Chiho spun herself around and galloped out. Her school-uniform loafers kept her safe as her footsteps clanged their way downstairs. The three of them listened on, still frozen.

"That was…bad, wasn't it?"

Emi muttered the words flatly, the soul removed from her body. Maou turned his face upward, a hand covering his eyes.

"P-perhaps we should pursue her and get this straightened out?"

Ashiya took a look around the area beneath the stairwell. There was already no sign of Chiho.

Snatching the pharmacy bag from the nervous, twitching Ashiya, Maou threw it at Emi. She caught it instinctively.

"Look, just go home, okay? Nothing good ever happens when you're near me!"

There was no responding to his verbal and physical abuse.

The unexpected Chiho factor had drained all the tenseness from the apartment.

"Oh, dear, Mr. Maou, that wasn't very mature."

That was why even Ashiya, still frozen near the open door, didn't notice at first.

"Picking on a woman like that! This isn't grade-school recess, you know."

"Aaaghh!!"

He had failed to realize until that instant that a pillar of gold was standing behind him.

"M-Ms. Shiba!"

Her long, medieval-styled, marigold-print dress shone in the morning light. A peacock feather, painted a bright golden color, stuck out of her wide-brimmed hat, the same color as the dress. Her golden hair, reminiscent of French nobility, reflected the sun's rays atop her body. She carried a bright yellow handbag with elegant handles that resembled strings of pearls, and she completed the package with a shawl replete with lime-green lamé strands, white enamel heels, and false eyelashes that resembled a field of grass growing on the seabed, so long that even the most egregious shojo manga artist would run for the hills if asked to draw them that length. She was Miki Shiba, the owner of the apartment, and she had appeared without a sound.

It was Ashiya's outcry that finally made Maou and Emi notice the corn-on-the-cob-shaped landlord behind him. The golden light around her seemed to form an enormous yellow halo as they basked in her presence.

"This your girlfriend I assume, Mr. Maou?"

The gravelly voice seemed to belong to a woman fairly on in years, but Shiba's wine-barrel-sized frame readily foiled any attempts to guess her true age.

"My name is Miki Shiba, and I'm the landlord here at Villa Rosa Sasazuka. It's good to meet you!"

Emi squinted, as if trying to see through the glorious sunlight in front of her. Nodding back was the best she could manage.

"Feel free to call me Mikitty, by the way."

"Uh, sure…"

There was no other response to give.

"I had come to visit, Mr. Maou, Mr. Ashiya, in order to inform my tenants of certain upcoming matters…but I see you are both rather occupied at the moment?"

With these overly prying words, she handed a piece of paper

over to Ashiya, offering a whiff of her elegant perfume as her arm extended forward.

"But regardless. We have had quite a spate of earthquakes as of late, no? I've felt it necessary to perform seismic reinforcement on this residence, so I came to inform you of some construction work in the future."

While this had been the case since they first met, for some reason, Maou had trouble dealing with his landlord. He didn't mind the sassy, cheesy extravagance at all, but for some reason, his internal demonic sixth sense always told him that Shiba was a lady not to be defied at any cost.

The piece of paper contained a schedule for the reinforcement work, a notice that residents would need to vacate the property for a one-day period, and another notice that this would not change their monthly rent. The landlord's seal was on the bottom, alongside a glossy, golden kiss mark. Maou made a conscious effort not to let his reaction to this show.

"But, there has certainly been quite a few earthquakes, hmm? Especially *lately*."

Shiba made the casual observation as she sidled up to Maou.

"Y-yeah…"

"In fact, I wonder if we'll have another one today, even."

"I…I couldn't say."

"And speaking of that, on my way here, I happened across a charming young woman running down the road. Crying the whole way, I may add!"

She smiled as she leered at all three of the apartment's residents simultaneously. It was a fairly impressive physical feat. "I believe she was heading for Sasazuka station as well…"

It was that instant.

"Did it…shake just now?"

Only the ever-elegant Miki Shiba chose not to nod her head in response.

"Mr. Maou?"

"Uh."

"If you've involved her in this, I would *hope* a young man would see matters through to the end, hmm?"

"Wh-what do you…"

Maou was thrown into confusion, unable to comprehend his landlord. But as he stood there, the shaking grew stronger and stronger.

"Y-Your Demonic Highness! Th-this shaking!"

Ashiya was shouting.

"Chiho!"

"Did you honestly think that charming young woman receiving an idea link and being subject to that sonar strike was a complete coincidence, then?"

A single sentence was all it took from the landlord to turn the others into stone.

"I would think that *you*, of all people, would understand the power behind people's thoughts and wills. Perhaps you had best hurry, before it is too late?"

There was something lurking underneath that thick makeup. But what?

"See? You can hear it, no?"

A loud rumble coursed across town.

✳

"Argh, I feel *horrible*! I think I'm gonna get Gate-sick!"

"Please try not to vomit if you caaaaan…"

"No guarantees, man! Erp…"

"Hang in there, pleeease! I doubt we'll have time to relax once we reach the other side."

"Uh? You catchin' something over there? Grhh…"

"A man-made magical reaction, picked up by our sonar readings. It's far too large to be purely the latent magic of 'Japan.'"

"So Emilia's in trouble?"

"Possss-ible! We may need to prepare for battle!"

"Right! Let's hurry! I can take this!"

"Yes, sir! On our waaaaaay!"

"Oooogh! Stop making it shake so much!"

❋

Chiho sprinted at full speed, crying. Whatever Maou and Emi had to say, that was *not* the kind of situation she had the wherewithal to calmly pick her way through.

*I really do like Maou.*

*But I'm just a new girl on the job, someone he's only just met. I can't do anything about the history Maou and Emi Yusa have between them.*

*It had to have been my first love. With Maou, I was full of spirit; I had a drive, a goal I could push to achieve with him. The high school boys, all mooching off their parents and partying all night; they're nothing compared to him.*

He wasn't particularly tall or handsome, but Chiho had still fallen in love with him.

Now that was gone, her heart ripped into a million pieces, and she had no idea what to do. So she ran as hard as she could, plunging into the crowd around Sasazuka station, running into an electric pole, tripping over a parked bicycle, colliding head-on with a pedestrian.

"S-sorry!"

She apologized, too ashamed to bring her head upward.

"Oooh, *this* looks like a good one."

The voice, coming from a head or so taller than Chiho, was ringed with a bitter coldness wholly unfamiliar to Chiho's ears.

"I had been following you since that last mistake, but I didn't think you would be caught up in despair for them so easily."

It was a young man, on the small side. He looked normal enough— long, flowing hair, T-shirt, and jeans. He couldn't have been much older than Chiho, either.

But what about those eyes? Those purple eyes, with pupils that seemed to shine a rainbow of ominous colors that Chiho had never seen before?

"Chiho Sasaki. Allow me to take that hatred and despair the Devil King and the Hero brought to you, and make it a reality!"

They were in the middle of the midmorning Sasazuka bustle. Two people stopped in the middle of it caused a traffic situation in and of itself.

"Hey, get outta the way!"

A young, fashionably dressed man drowsily warned the stranger, placing a hand on his shoulder.

"…!"

Suddenly, the T-shirt ripped itself apart in the area the hand touched him. The young man was blown away by the thing that popped out of his shoulder, plowing into a line of parked bikes.

"Ahh…!"

Chiho let out a scream, deep within her throat. Other passersby stared at the man, unable to fathom what had just happened.

It was a wing. A set of large, jet-black wings, jutting out from this person's back.

"The hunt has begun. Today, I will surpass the Devil King for good."

At that moment, an elevated Keio rail line collapsed, the victim of a mysterious explosion.

Maou and Emi ran, Ashiya a small distance behind them.

The rumbling they heard right after the explosion couldn't have been caused by anything other than the influence of something magical.

Judging by the landlord's warning, it was clear she was, to say the least, no ordinary person. But there was no time to get to the bottom of that.

"Hang in there, Chi!"

Maou kept running.

"Look!" Emi pointed ahead.

"…What in the world?!" Ashiya groaned to himself.

The rail line had fallen. The elevation bridge had collapsed to the ground, crushing the shopping mall adjacent to Sasazuka station. They could detect residual magic in the area, but this was nothing like the barriers Maou had impulsively built to rescue people.

Beyond the mess, on the Koshu-Kaido road, Maou could see two figures in the air, the Shuto Expressway spanning across the sky above.

The enemy no longer had any reason to hide themselves. The bystanders that had escaped harm stood off in the distance, staring at the rubble and the figures in the air.

"Them…!"

"Who…are they? How could they have…"

"How do you *think*?!"

Maou began to climb up the rubble, dodging the broken power lines and making his way past a mountain of detritus that was liable to collapse again at any moment. Emi and Ashiya followed behind.

There were two of them: a man flapping his giant wings as he carried something at his side; and another, this one floating in the air, the hood on his ghostlike robe covering his face.

As they surmounted the rubble, Maou detected something. Something returning to him once again. Why? He should have been overjoyed, but instead he found it disturbing. It wasn't something he planned to regain *this* way.

A nagging thought like that never would have occurred to him during his demon-realm days. But now—

"Good to see you, Lucifer! Brought a new playmate with you?"

The winged figure in the air replied with a spate of dark laughter. "Well, well! The Devil King Satan! Or should I be referring to you as Sadao Maou instead? And how nice to see Alciel safe and sound!"

"Lucifer…? It couldn't be…"

"N-no… Why are you here *now*…?"

Emi was at a total loss for words. Ashiya shook his head, unable to believe the sight before him.

Only Maou remained strong, his stern expression unchanged as he glared at the two floating figures.

Lucifer was the Great Demon General whom Emilia the Hero had slain first. The fallen angel who arose a demon. The general who governed the invasion and capture of Ente Isla's Western Continent.

"How long has it been, Emilia the Hero...that is, Emi Yusa!"

"No... No way..."

"Oh, yes! Your sword may have pierced through my body, and yet I am here now, before you!"

The Great Demon General Lucifer sneered, the ominous black wings befitting his fallen-angel title. At his side, like a mother carrying around its kitten, he held an unconscious Chiho.

She did not appear to be injured. But why did he decide to capture *her*?

"All thanks to your new friend, isn't it?" Maou nodded toward the hooded figure as he spoke. "When I retreated and sent a squadron over to the Western Continent to investigate, I still had no faith that you were dead. I never imagined in a thousand years the humans could defeat a Great Demon General, so the investigation was likely less thorough than it should have been..."

"And thanks to that, I survived."

"Yeah. You weren't a *pure* demon. Not like Alciel, Malacoda, and Adramelech. But with your heaven-born blood, I figured that capturing the Western Continent would have been a cinch, even if it *was* a Church stronghold. Too bad I was wrong."

"Too bad indeed! I devoted my all to eradicating the humans on the island, to fulfill the mission granted to me. But..."

Lucifer turned his glare toward Emi. "But the Hero's armies overwhelmed me. That much, you already know."

"Would your friend mind telling me the rest?" Maou asked.

"Well?" Lucifer turned toward the floating robed figure next to him.

He laughed, as he seemed to give his partner a nod. "Certainly. I am—"

"—Olba Meiyer, one of the six archbishops of the Church?"

The man stopped cold at Maou's prompt guess.

"…!" Emi's mind was in utter disarray. The name was too familiar to her. "Olba? That's a lie! Olba is my—"

"—your companion, who sent you to this world, then tried to eradicate both you and me. Right?"

"…You knew of that?"

The figure interjected, a tad crestfallen that the thunder was stolen from him as he raised his hood. It revealed a calm, benign-looking man, aged fifty or so. His tonsured head, the symbol of a high-level Church bishop, shone in the morning sun.

His pure white archbishop's robe, embroidered with blue and silver thread, flapped in the strong wind blowing between the nearby buildings.

"Us demons, we practically invented evil, you know. I can always tell what a villain is thinking, start to finish. You're the guy who was behind Emi when she entered the Gate, right? Once I heard that, I pretty much guessed the rest. No one else had the chance to take a shot at me and Emi."

"No… No! Olba, why are you with Lucifer? You didn't—"

"Everything began after Lucifer lost to you, Emilia."

The archbishop Olba cracked a thin smile, his voice rising to crescendo as he prepared the epic tale he was about to spin.

"After you destroyed the demon forces, you didn't want the Hero lording it over you, so you tossed her into another world and consulted with Lucifer while she was still powerless to do anything about it. Then you secretly wiped out the rest of the Hero's crew in order to protect the vested interests of the Church. The end. Any corrections I need to make?"

Once again, Maou stole the limelight.

What's more, judging by the way Olba's mouth opened and closed in stunned silence, he had it right. Maou laughed a hideously mocking laugh.

"That scenario's been done a thousand times before, baldy! You think this girl was gonna try becoming goddess of the universe or something? Even a low-budget B movie would come up with a better script than that."

Maou nudged Emi as he spoke.

"Hey, stop that!"

Emi was still in a state of shock, but the nudge was all it took to bring her back to reality.

"...Baldy? B movie?"

Olba was shocked for different reasons.

"Um... Your Demonic Highness? I would hardly call him naturally bald."

For some reason, Ashiya found it apt to defend him. Ignoring it, Maou defiantly stood before his two enemies.

"See, this is why I hate heaven. You people all say one thing and think the exact opposite. It'd be much more humane for everyone if we demons ruled the roost instead. I can probably guess how you got Lucifer on your side, too. Did you bait him with the chance to return to heaven?"

"H-how did you—!"

"Don't 'How did you' me. Could you at least *try* to be a little original? I guess you were just B-movie caliber, too, Lucifer. Seeing you fall for this idiot makes me want to cry."

"Y-you accursed devil!!" Olba's voice cracked as he flew into a rage.

"If you're gonna float up there, baldy, and start crying just 'cause I'm telling the truth, you *really* should have come up with a better script!"

The sheer abusiveness behind Maou's seemingly never-ending invective left not just Olba and Lucifer open-mouthed, but Emi as well.

"And now you're gonna be all like 'Oh, *nooooo*, you have angered Lucifer! And you will not be able to flee like last time! Die where you stand alongside the Hero!' That is *so* lame, man! Even the villain from some kid's *sentai* show would come up with better lines than that!"

"What is a '*sentai* show'?! What are you going *on* about, you stupid idiot?! Plus, they kind of took Chiho hostage, remember?!"

Unable to take any more, Emi slapped Maou in the back of the head.

"You could at least know your place right now! They were both ready to confess all their evil deeds! So stop heckling them already!"

"Your Demonic Highness! When on earth did you have the chance to watch any movies?! Such a waste of money..."

Emi and Ashiya laid out upon Maou in tandem, albeit for somewhat unfocused reasons. Tears of frustration came to Maou's eyes.

"Man, that *hurt*, you bastard! If I let them go first, you probably would've fainted from the shock, all right?! So I made a little effort to cushion the bad news for you instead! That, and come *on*, what's a movie now and then gonna hurt?! *I'm* the one bringing home the bacon!"

Neither Emi nor Ashiya were willing to give in.

"I don't need you fawning all over me like that!"

"*I've* wanted to stop playing househusband all day and enjoy a little entertainment too, you! But I held myself back!"

"Stop this! All of you!"

It took Olba shouting at the top of his lungs to halt the argument.

"I deigned to listen to you, and my reward is all this nonsensical blubbering? You will pay for this, Devil King Satan!!"

"That is *so* amateur hour, man. Couldn't be more unoriginal if you tried."

"Grrrnnnnhhhh..."

Olba's face had reddened to the point where one could fry an egg on it.

"Hey, mind if I ask you a question, Archbishop Cueball?"

Maou picked at an ear as he spoke, flicking the results out to his side. "How many people did you attack in order to prop Lucifer's magic levels up?"

"...!"

"Huh?!"

"Whaa?!"

"...You are perceptive indeed, Your Demonic Highness!"

Maou lowered his tone as he continued over the startled reactions of the other four.

"Lemme ask you, Emi... Where do all the gods and devils live in this land? In Japan?"

"What? I don't know..."

"They're inside the hearts of the people. Tell me you at least *thought* about that by now."

"The hearts of...the people?"

"Yeah. The people of this nation aren't ruled by their gods. They roll over to the evil side, or the holy side, with a snap of the fingers. Look at the divinity, and the evilness, you see in a person whenever they're forced into extreme circumstances. *That's* our source of power! The way we can gain power in this world!"

"It...is? Then..."

Maou nodded back, then turned his gaze back toward Lucifer.

"Seeing a demon in all his glory like that would make most people wet their pants. They'd be too scared to do anything. These are probably the guys behind that string of robberies."

Emi turned to Olba, all but asking him to deny it. But Olba said nothing. How long had they been here? They couldn't have gone without food or drink that entire time. How did they stay fed?

"*That* was why I reverted back to my old form a little bit yesterday. People were despairing their impending death all around me, and that forced its way into my body."

There was still a part of Emi that begged for Olba to say it was all untrue. But, even so, she still couldn't understand why Lucifer and Olba were working together.

"They sucked in all the negative energy, all the fear and sadness. All that power that drove the first magic sniper attack, and yesterday's earthquake... How did they get all of that, hmm?"

Just then, Emi recalled the morning after the magic-blast attack, as well as the news she saw in Rika's room. Her face wrinkled.

"So if you want to gain enough magical force to return to Ente Isla..."

"You have to cause a huge disaster! Sucking power out of one or two people isn't gonna cut it."

"No..."

"I kind of like this world, you know? It's been a real fresh experience for me, being human. It's been a good world to me, and I don't want to screw it up like that. I want to take a different approach. So…"

With a grin on his face, Maou looked up at the two figures above him. "What next? Wanna do it here?"

He could tell that even this was enough to faze them.

"B-but, Devil King! Don't you care about this girl at all? We're fully aware of your relationship! We know you've been intimate!"

Maou had to laugh, resigned, at how plainly villainous Olba was acting. "Hey. Emilia the Hero. I really hate bishops, but I'll tell you what I hate more, and that's traitors."

Emi's gaze shot between Maou and Olba for a moment, but soon it was fixed entirely upon the archbishop.

"Yeah… I hate demons and traitors, too."

"You sure about this? You've been saving that power for a while. If we fight here, you might never be able to get back."

"Good things come to those who work earnestly."

"*That's* what I like to hear."

Emi flashed a bitter smile.

Maou smiled as well, as he gestured upward. "C'mon, let's do this! I'll pulverize both of you! And I'm gettin' Chi back, too!"

The majestic, larger-than-life air he presented reminded his observers of a Devil King from another time.

"B-but, Your Demonic Highness!"

Ashiya, naturally, stepped in from behind to ruin the moment.

"We need to fully gauge our opponents. Unless we thoroughly understand why they chose this moment to suddenly unfurl this trap for us, it'll be too dangerous to move things forward recklessly…"

"Sound advice, Alciel. Let me show you," Lucifer said, his wings seeming to glow for an instant as he spoke.

There was a whoosh, followed by a short, cut-off groan. Maou and Emi turned around.

Ashiya was on the ground, blood spurting out of a wound on his left breast, as if he had been shot.

"A-Ashiya!" Maou screamed.

"My! Look at the force she belted out for his roommate Alciel as well! You must have plunged this girl into the depths of despair for me!" Lucifer's smile was a sneer, his words pitying.

Seeing Ashiya bleeding on the ground caused panic to spread across the area in an instant. Even with the previous bridge collapse, a large audience was still looking up at Lucifer, demonstrating the uniquely Japanese lack of ability to sense danger. Lucifer muttered downward, not paying a moment's notice to the fleeing throngs.

"Your immaturity will be your downfall. Imagine, such a small thing causing such vast, ballooning clouds of despair and sadness!"

"You...you're going into Chi's heart..."

Maou blinked helplessly.

"Negative feelings are so easy to control when they're directed toward a unique target. I've grown able to fire bolts of magical power that will have a more punishing effect on the both of you, and *only* the both of you, than ever before. Watch!"

Lucifer's wings glowed darkly for another moment. Countless streaks of light coursed toward the ground.

"Dammit..."

The sheer number, and their speed, was too much for a human's weak legs to completely avoid. Clicking his tongue in frustration, Maou raised his arms, then brought them apart from each other. The streaks of light followed his hands' direction, redirecting themselves toward a nearby building.

With an explosive rumble, every window in the multifloor edifice shattered, the people inside flying out like wasps from a fumigated nest.

"Devil King! Alciel's...!"

Emi picked up the head of the completely immobile Ashiya. The blood showed no sign of stopping, and his skin was rapidly turning the shade of a sheet of paper. Bringing her hands to his neck and wrist, she found only a weak, rapid pulse.

"...Careless!"

"That's the pot calling the kettle black, don't you think?"

"Ngh!"

The second volley launched outward. Maou brought his hands upward in the same motion, but:

"Crap, I don't have enough!"

"Whaaa?!"

There was still a small amount of magical power, borne from the nearby fear they encountered as they crossed the bridge rubble. But Maou had not actively tried to absorb it within himself. Diverting a single round of Lucifer's mind-controlled magical bullets had made him run out of gas already.

Emi instinctively covered her head, unable to launch an antimagic protective wall with her holy force while covering for Ashiya at the same time.

The blasts Maou failed to divert thudded against the concrete.

"Whooaahhh!"

Maou's scream was swallowed up by the asphalt dust thrown into the air by the explosion. The shock wave from the magical blast coursed across electric lines, poles, and buildings, and in an instant, Sasazuka station had transformed into something resembling a battlefield.

"Ha-ha-ha! I had no idea my first taste of destruction after my defeat at Emilia the Hero's hands would feel so wonderful!" Lucifer's howling laughter echoed across the area. Sasazuka station, its air choked with toxic dust, seemed like hell on earth.

The neighborhood had ceased to function as it once did, what with all the fleeing people, the people who had failed to flee in time, the impossible-to-imagine explosions, and the sheer, otherworldly bizarreness of the scene.

"Don't get distracted, Lucifer! Our mission is to destroy Emilia and the Devil King!"

Lucifer sneered to his side at Olba, who was bellowing at him as he gauged the fight.

"You dare to butt in on *my* business?"

Olba flinched for a moment at the impact of Lucifer's threat, but he kept his emphatic tone as he continued, sweat beading on his brow.

"Y-you haven't forgotten that *I* am the one who controls the Gate which shall serve as your bridge to heaven?"

"...Damn you."

Lucifer rolled his eyes in frustration, then turned them upon Chiho, still under one arm.

"You have nothing to worry about. As long as I have this girl, the Devil King and Emilia the Hero will never flee from us."

Once the dust settled, the only thing left on the ground was Ashiya's blood. Maou, Emi, and Ashiya were gone.

"Lucifer!"

"Calm yourself. They can store up as much power as they want, but they will never have enough to resist us. After them!"

The pair glided across the Sasazuka sky.

"What? That was all a bluff?!"

Maou and Emi were using the cover offered by an alley to escape from their airborne pursuers. But Ashiya was leaving a trail of blood dots as they carried him on their shoulders. It would be followed, no doubt.

"Well, what do you *want* from me? I used up pretty much all of *my* magic force, too."

The potted plant in the garden they faced suddenly shattered with an enormous cracking sound.

"Did they shoot that?!"

"What do *you* think?!"

Unable to even turn around to see behind them, Emi dove behind an electric pole, while Maou hid in the eaves around a private residence. But, since they were carrying along the larger Ashiya behind them, it was akin to a bear hiding behind a laundry basket.

"Come on! Where's all the bravado from before?!"

An enormous ball of magic crashed into the home Maou hid near, accompanied by Lucifer's thundering voice.

"Uwaahh!" Maou and Ashiya were easily blown aside by the blast, not even able to attempt a clean landing.

"H-how could this be...?"

Emi was appalled at the sight of Lucifer, a demon with no qualms at all about collateral damage. If there was anyone inside the home that blast just leveled, there was no time to check.

"Let's go!"

Maou still tried his hardest to flee, picking up Ashiya by himself, no longer even pretending to fight.

"Oh no you don't!"

Lucifer made a gun with his hand, aiming it straight for Maou's back.

"Look out!"

Emi's shout came too late. The shot struck Maou at the edge of his shoulder, sending him to the ground with Ashiya.

"Ow, ow, ow, ow, owwww," Maou hissed in pain. "This body's so damn fragile! I always knew it was, but *ugghhh*, it totally is! Dammit! I don't want to die!"

"What are you wailing about? You call yourself Satan, the Devil King?!"

Emi jumped out of her hiding place, putting Maou and Ashiya behind her as she glared at Lucifer.

"...Hmmm? Emilia? Are you trying to protect the lord of all demons?"

Lucifer laughed a chiding laugh. Emi ignored the bait.

"This isn't what you're fully capable of, is it, Lucifer?"

She had to buy time. They needed a grip on the battle situation. Ashiya was near death, and it was doubtful Maou could help the cause any longer.

More than anything, as long as Chiho remained ensconced under Lucifer's arm, she couldn't just strike wildly at him.

"...So?"

Lucifer didn't deny Emi's words.

"Those finger blasts, and these balls of magic... This isn't the Lucifer *I* remember fighting."

"...It is more than enough to bury the three of you now."

Lucifer had opened the window a crack. Emi lunged at it.

"Any demon who acts like he has it in the bag always loses, in the end."

"Yeah!" Maou interjected. "That's the biggest lame trope in the—*arrghh*!"

Emi, not looking back at the wailing Maou, gave him a swift kick. He groaned in response.

"So, basically, you're the same as I am. Neither of us can unleash their true force right now. And…"

Olba, for reasons known only to him, slowly followed behind Lucifer.

"…*you* can't afford to waste energy, either, am I right? You *are* still a bishop, after all. Unlike Lucifer, you can't just do something evil to restore your powers. You *wish* you had it so easy."

Olba certainly could have heard her, but refused to respond.

"But even I lose my patience sooner or later. Emilia the Hero didn't build that name getting beaten up over and over."

"Wait! Don't do it now—*ooof*!"

Emi's back heel stopped Maou midsentence once again.

"You *touched* my foot, you perv!!"

"Is grabbing your foot because I wanted you to notice my bloodied husk on the street a crime punishable by a boot to the stomach?"

Maou staggered to his feet, but he was plainly not well. Ashiya, still balanced on his shoulders, was liable to make him collapse at any moment.

"…If you die, I'm leaving you here."

"Don't worry about that. If I let one of my own minions kill me, it'd be an embarrassment to my entire bloodline."

With that, Maou suddenly grabbed Emi's hand, pulled at it, and began staggering his way away.

"Wh-whoa! What're you doing?!"

Maou's arm was unexpectedly strong as it pulled Emi along. But this was no opponent he could flee from by tottering around with uneasy steps.

"What are you trying to do now? You cannot escape me."

With an easy smile on his face, Lucifer shot Maou again. He fell as the blast tore through his leg.

There were screams around them as the bloodied trio vaulted into a wide-open intersection.

"Oww…"

"What are you *doing*?! Are you trying to die?!"

"Heh-heh… Does it look like I'm about to…?"

Emi tried to support the collapsed Maou, but Lucifer and Olba followed along, like a pair of vultures looming over their weakened prey.

"Heh-heh…"

"Stop laughing! Ugh, you make me sick! This isn't a joke! If anyone's killing the Devil King, it's *me*! Why do I have to sit here and get killed right next to you?!"

Maou and Ashiya were sprawled out in a car lane on the street, neither moving a muscle.

By sheer luck, it was the exact intersection, restaurant and all, where Maou and Emi first encountered each other in Japan.

A finger blast from Lucifer scraped past Emi's nose before smashing through Maou's shoulder. The force of the shot sent both of them to the ground.

"Pathetic! *This* is the Devil King that stood tall above me? That had Ente Isla in the palm of his hand?!"

The pity in Lucifer's smug laugh was almost palpable.

"…Hurry up! We can kill the both of them at once! I have to retain my powers for the Gate!"

Once Olba stopped speaking, he reached into his robe and pulled out…a pistol. Emi's eyes opened wide at the sight.

Firearms, of course, were unheard of on Ente Isla. Either Olba or Lucifer must have come across one in this world.

Olba must have been an active participant in the string of street robberies, not to mention the first sniper attacks upon Maou and Emi.

During her journeys across Ente Isla, he was a humble servant of the Church, one who held the title of archbishop in high esteem and easily won the respect of his peers. With his heavenly powers and fatherly smile, he had provided Emilia and her friends with solace and comfort across their voyage. Now there was some other force behind that façade, one brandishing a deadly weapon at her. Emi—Emilia—gnashed her teeth in sadness and frustration.

What could have changed Olba so much?

The corrupted clergyman, paying no heed to Emi's emotions, pointed the gun barrel toward the fallen pair.

Just then, Emi heard several sirens approaching from afar. The police and fire department must have started casing the area. Thousands of people must have witnessed Maou and Lucifer by the time they reached this intersection. Of *course* the authorities were called. But trying to take on Lucifer right now would only add to the victim count.

Maou took in the scene, as much as his rapidly fading mind could amid the blood loss and fatigue.

"...Good. Good. Now they're probably gonna..."

His voice was too soft to be heard by anyone. Then:

"Emi, hold on." He took the hand of the girl who had fallen, defeated, next to him.

"Mmm?"

A soft, white light enveloped Maou and Emi. By the time Lucifer's magical blast and Olba's bullet reached them:

"...He had enough power left to teleport them all?"

All that remained was the blood Maou and Ashiya shed. The three of them were gone.

"Lucifer!"

"...He waited for just this situation. He couldn't have enough power left to go far. It'll be easy to track him."

"...Gah! You scared me!"

Emi was shocked that Maou used his teleportation magic without warning, but now was no time to chide him. They needed a grip on their situation.

They hadn't gone far. In fact, they had simply returned to the area they first saw Lucifer, so his magical trail would no doubt be followed shortly.

·What differed from before was the masses of typical Japanese onlookers (*still* no sense of danger at all!) and the police and fire vehicles tending to the victims caught up in Lucifer's magical blasts.

"But...but what're you trying to do, taking us here?"

This time, they truly had nowhere to go. They lacked the strength for it. Judging how their foes made quick work of that residence earlier, Maou and Emi knew they hadn't hesitated for a moment to consider the innocent victims.

"...Hey! Don't die on me! You okay?"

"......"

Maou was breathing, but his face was completely white, likely due to the bleeding. Ashiya, meanwhile, was beyond white and into the realm of light blue, teetering on the brink of death.

"You didn't come here for the ambulances, did you?"

"You...kidding me...?"

"Well, what, then?! If you just stay here, you're both gonna die!"

"I...know."

Borrowing Emi's hand, Maou somehow forced himself to sit up.

"Just a little...more, I think."

"Oh, you still have some kind of trick up your sleeve, now?"

A forlorn voice loomed over them. Looking up, they were greeted by the same sight as before: Lucifer and Olba floating below the towering Shuto Expressway. Teleporting this short distance away was nowhere near enough to lose them. They were at the end of their rope.

"Lucifer! We're only attracting more witnesses with these delays!"

"Ah, you're always so flinchy, Olba. If there are too many, I can always cull them down a bit."

Emi shuddered. Lucifer's magical power skyrocketed as he spoke those disquieting words.

"Wh-what're you gonna do?!"

"Who can say? A terror bombing? Destroying the Shuto Expressway? Countless victims? I think it a good fit for this nation."

Lucifer flashed an evil grin.

"But I don't need the Devil King returning to life...the way he did underneath Shinjuku."

A light zoomed past Emi.

"Ngh! Ah…"

The groan came from within Emi's arms.

"Satan!!"

Lucifer's blast of light had shot through Maou's chest. A black hole opened up in his midsection, and the light flickered out of his pupils in an instant. The strength drained from the hand supporting Ashiya, collapsing his body to the ground.

"No! You're the Devil King! Stay here for me!"

Maou leaned heavily upon Emi's arms. She slapped his cheek several times, with no response.

"No! You're kidding me! Come *on*, Satan!"

She tried to lay him down to perform CPR, but seeing the hole in his chest made her gasp and freeze on the spot. The area of the body where his heart was located had been cleanly pierced through. There was no way to revive him.

Lucifer watched the pair, a satisfied smile on her face.

"My work is done. You can have the girl back."

He flung Chiho away from his arm like a wadded-up piece of paper.

"Chiho!"

Emi raised her tear-stained face, lunging toward her landing point, but:

"Ngh…"

Her fragile human body was capable of being crushed simply by having a girl land on it from several meters above. Emi's leg, which was poised beneath the falling Chiho, was now twisted in assorted unlikely directions.

Lucifer, watching this unfold from up high, let a sadistic smile unfold over his face.

"It is time to complete my contract with you, Olba. I hope you will hold your end of the bargain."

He opened his arms wide, to both sides of his body. Massive amounts of magical power, far more than the force that pulverized the house from before, flowed into his palms in a torrent.

"Wh-what're…?!"

Emi, holding back the pain, looked up at Lucifer. But Lucifer wasn't looking back. His eyes were on the Shuto Expressway above.

"Lucifer! Lucifer, stop!"

She shouted it from beneath Chiho, fully understanding his intentions. But it was nothing that could stop a Great Demon General.

"...Such a beautiful voice. Go ahead. Sing a beautiful chorus for me, alongside the roar of destruction and the screams of despair, until the end finally arrives!"

He unleashed his balls of magic toward an expressway bridge support.

"Farewell, Emilia the Hero! You will follow in the path of Alciel and the Devil King!"

A pair of explosions completely vaporized the support.

Every man and woman in the area looked toward the sky. The black concrete roadway above them rumbled its way downward, like some otherworldly being emitting an alien roar as its jaw descended upon them.

There was no way anyone could stop the tilting expressway from collapsing any longer.

The road panels began to come apart, cars plunging downward amid the chaos.

Emi hugged Chiho's head tightly as the expressway fell, snuffing out even the crowd's crazed screaming.

Their faces and bodies were covered in darkness, their souls filled with despair and helplessness, as their consciousness and vision were cut off.

"Total B movie. Just like...I thought."

No one noticed the smile that had come across Maou's face.

✳

Emi opened her eyes.

She remembered resigning herself to her fate, but if she was awake, she must have avoided death.

But she couldn't have emerged safe from having the Shuto Expressway fall on her. What happened to…?

"…Ngh!"

She moved her body. Something was draped on top of her. She remembered it was Chiho, thrown down upon her by Lucifer.

"Chiho!… Oof!"

Trying to get up, Emi noticed the state of her leg for the first time. As she did, a swell of pain rushed across her body, like her blood was boiling. But she didn't mind. It was all the more proof she was alive.

"Ngh…ergh…"

Chiho groaned. Slowly, Emi extracted her body from below, keeping a close eye on her leg as she placed the other girl on the ground.

"Chiho! Chiho!"

"…Ah."

Slapping her cheek, she found Chiho waking up far more readily than she guessed. She was less knocked unconscious, it seemed, and more put to sleep by Lucifer's force.

"Yusa… Nnh…!"

She had recognized Emi, but Chiho still grimaced, apparently in pain.

"Those wings… That scary guy…"

Emi looked upward, her memory jogged by Chiho's rambling. Yes. If they were safe right now, then Lucifer was the one menace they had to watch out for. But the sky above them was cut off by a vast, uniformly black presence. What was blocking it out?

The Shuto Expressway had collapsed, making a hideous groan that portended doom as it did. *I was almost directly below it. So why am I still here?*

"Heh-heh-heh…"

Emi shuddered as he heard the low, guttural laugh.

He was darker than the most profound of darkness, his body emitting a light blacker than ink. The horn that Emi had smashed to pieces once upon a time was still missing, but there was no way to wipe away the magic force, the foreboding strength, the sheer presence looming over her.

His eyes were as red as a river of blood, but his skin was white, cold, as if not a drop of blood flowed through it. He was over two meters in height, his wings emitting an aura of sheer murky blackness.

What stood before here was not Sadao Maou, shift supervisor at the Hatagaya MgRonald branch, the man Lucifer had just murdered with a shot through the heart.

"You have my gratitude, Lucifer… Thanks to your hard work, I have finally regained this form."

His form was as magic itself—enough magic to support the entirety of the expressway.

"Satan… The Devil King…"

Before her eyes was the Devil King himself, the demon lord who had plunged Ente Isla into a hellhole of misery and gloom.

The long, slitted eyes of the terrifying demon tyrant were now fixated squarely upon Emi—Emilia the Hero.

At that moment, Emi was stuck with an indescribable wave of despair.

"Wh-why…?"

Lucifer stood there, panic-stricken, hand covering his face in disbelief. He knew he had just struck Sadao Maou dead. Even if he *was* the Devil King, no mere corpse could have drawn in magical force from the desperation that reigned around it.

But here he was now, the Devil King Satan, standing before his eyes.

The jaw-droppingly massive power he wielded, enough to keep the Shuto Expressway up with a single hand, was on a completely different level from what he wielded in the corridor in Shinjuku. This was the Devil King himself; that much was irrefutable. How much power did he take in? How many human beings were within his range for that?

To Lucifer's credit, he felt no sense of fear or despair at the sight. The despair had all been sucked out of him by Satan. As Devil King,

Satan was on a plane of existence he could never surmount. The difference between a Great Demon General and his master was like a sheer wall of strength, insurmountable by any force.

Then, things began to move.

"Emilia the Hero..."

The Devil King opened his mouth.

The mere timbre of his voice was enough to make the crowd of uninjured onlookers still nearby quiver in fear.

"Ah...ah..."

Chiho spoke for all of the human beings watching the Devil King. His existence itself was pure fear, the mere sight one of anguished pain.

Olba, for his part, was scared stiff at this unexpected turn of events. He did, however, still remain in the air, which must have required quite a bit of dexterity.

That was the amount of power, of will, of sheer magic instilled within the Devil King's voice. There was no longer any trace of the bloody pulp that Lucifer had toyed with so malevolently just a moment ago.

"......"

Emi could not respond.

Satan, the Devil King, had regained his original powers. In which case, no matter how one interpreted this, *he* was now the enemy. Lucifer and Olba were formidable enough as foes, but with the Devil King joining the fray, Emi alone had no way to compete.

There was no question what would come next. The Devil King would use his regained magic to throw this world into utter chaos, just as he had cruelly done to Ente Isla.

The mental image flashed across her mind in an instant.

The fear of death was quickly followed by a sense of utter despair, the despair of a world about to breathe its last.

Or it was supposed to, until the next moment.

"...Jeez, Emi, you don't have to *ignore* me!"

"Uh. Huh?"

Even Lucifer, to say nothing of Emi, required several moments to realize it had come from the king of demons, the embodiment of evil that stood before them. Chiho, who was visibly shaking in fear, stopped cold.

"Um…me?"

"Who the hell do you *think* I mean?! Snap out of it! You gotta do something about *him*!"

Satan used his free hand to point out Lucifer.

"Uh…guh?"

Emi was flabbergasted, her brain having difficulty parsing his words.

"Hurry *up*! This is *heavy*, man!"

Looking up, she saw the battered remains of the expressway, held in the air by the Devil King's magic power, begin to ever-so-softly float downward.

"I'm out of practice with this magic… Like, seriously, this really sucks."

All Lucifer, Emi, even Olba could do was gape silently at the Devil King, who was whining like a sullen teen as something resembling a bead of sweat began to flow down his head.

Only Chiho was able to speak, her voice soft and detached at this strange creature before her.

"Is…that *you*, Maou?"

"How do you get…*out of practice* with magic?" Emi finally came to. This was *not* how the Devil King spoke back in her homeland.

"I just…am, okay? Please…hurry…"

Apparently his one-handed magic performance was meant entirely just to show off. Once his strength reached its limits, the Devil King began to crouch down heavily, as if bearing a great weight with both arms. His magic was keeping up not only the heavy panels that comprised the Shuto Expressway, but the other cars and people caught up in the collapse, all of them stopped cold in the air.

"Ngh… Oof!"

Satan repositioned himself, standing squarely on the ground to spread the weight evenly. Emi realized that the effort had actually boosted his magic power for a few moments.

"This is *so* stupid."

Emi smiled as she chided him, then scrunched her face as the pain from her broken leg came back to the forefront.

"You have to be the dumbest Devil King in the universe. I thought you were dead! Why are you standing there?"

The pain wasn't enough to stop her.

"How should I know? They said on TV that you don't die right when your heart stops. Like, your brain's supposedly still alive for a few minutes after, you know?"

Satan smirked at Emi as he spoke. Emi was dumbfounded.

"So…that's what you did? Because we were in so much trouble?"

"Pretty much. I mean, if Lucifer started just fighting you normally, you would've been dead in two seconds. But the weird thing about bad guys… We're lazy, so we try to finish people off with one shot. That's what I was betting on. Kinda cut it close there, though, huh? Good thing they were working off a B-movie script."

The Devil King acted like he couldn't care less as he continued, but his tactics seemed impossibly reckless to Emi. If Lucifer hadn't triggered a disaster of epic proportions for him, Sadao Maou would have been dead by now.

"But quit derailing. Can you help me out? This stuff's heavy! Like, seriously, I'm begging you here!"

He had put Emi through an emotional roller coaster, and *this* was the thanks she earned. She was beyond relief, beyond exasperation, and comfortably settling into a quiet, intense state of anger.

"Not gonna happen. I'm the Hero! Heroes don't lend a hand to the Devil King!"

"Mmh…!"

Lucifer grunted as he saw Emi stand up, gingerly handling her injured leg.

The Devil King's words were completely beyond his understanding. But he could still see what was unfolding. Even after regaining all of his demonic powers, he still wanted to join arms with the Hero to save the people of Earth.

"So stay where you are for just a few more moments."

Emi brought her right hand up to her forehead.

"That's all I need to finally end this!"

"Y-Yusa…?"

Emi smiled at the completely awestruck Chiho.

"Just sit back and watch, okay?"

Emi raised her hand over Chiho's head. In an instant, Chiho's body was covered in a transparent sphere, shining its golden light against the ground, an antimagic barrier powered by her holy force.

"Yusa! What's going on?"

Emi flashed Chiho a brighter smile than before.

"I don't know, Chiho… I think I just want you to know."

With that, Emi quickly brought her hand downward.

The transformation happened in milliseconds.

Emi's jet-black hair flowed in the wind as it emitted a pure, healing light. A blinding shine, like a bolt of pure sunlight, imbued itself within her right palm.

"O great power, I summon thee, to smite the forces of evil!"

"Wh… Whoa…!"

Lucifer edged backward. A gale began to blow, Emi at its center. No simple wind would be strong enough to physically affect Lucifer. The power Emi summoned was something quite different.

"Holy…magic…"

"I am the Hero. Worlds may change, but the truth will never waver!"

A pillar of sunlight shot upward from the ground, out from the darkness beneath the cloud of twisted rubble above them.

Her hair now shone like silvery strands of silk, and her scarlet eyes were fiery enough to crush any evil they perceived.

A flash of light ran across Emi's right hand, forming the shape of a sword. Her body was infused with Holy Silver, the heavenly metal guarded by the Church of Ente Isla since ancient times, and now it resonated at the call of her holy force.

The name of the sword that Emilia Justina forged with this Holy Silver was the Better Half, an evolved blade whose scintillating powers were charged by the holy force of its owner.

The golden light that protected her body was the Cloth of the Dispeller, woven with the wings of the mighty Seraphs, a garment worn only by the Hero. Its power depended greatly upon the holy force of the one who bore it.

Now this holy force filled her body, healing all of the wounds "Emi" had sustained. Her broken leg, and the scar on her forehead, all disappeared without a trace, as if they had never existed.

"Hmm... I can't manifest my sword past the first level. This might get a bit hairy."

The pillar of sunlight mumbled to itself, frustrated.

The thin-bladed sword, really more of a rapier, and the Cloth of the Dispeller that only covered her forehead, chest, and legs, were both a disappointment. The fact this had all manifested itself over her business attire also made for a less than flattering patchwork look.

"Well, so be it. They're on just as unfamiliar ground as I am. No point worrying about my appearance right now."

The blaze of sunlight that Emi's form had become drew its sword, and leveled the coil of light straight toward its foes.

"Lucifer, the Great Demon General! Olba, the fallen archbishop! I hereby condemn you for the sins you have committed against this world!"

She was now Emilia Justina in body and soul, the Hero who had driven the evil from Ente Isla.

"Oooh, nice one!"

The Devil King marveled appreciatively at the celestial figure she cut.

"Shut *up*! You're up next once I beat these guys, so hurry up and say your prayers!"

"Yeah, yeah. Try to be quick, could you?... Oh, but before that."

Suddenly recalling something, the Devil King raised his right hand upward once more.

"Take a nap for me, people!"

He snapped his fingers as he spoke the very unmystical incantation. With that, all the onlookers staring from afar at the otherworldly demons beneath the expressway froze, covered in a dull green light. And that wasn't all. Suddenly, silence reigned. Everything seemed to stop—not just the people, but time itself across the area.

"Hey! What'd you just do?!"

Emilia glared at the Devil King, who shook his head as he lowered his hand.

"Magic barrier. I don't want people seeing *too* much of this, and besides, I don't want to get too many more of them involved in the fight. That, and the media, too; forget *those* guys. So I shut away the local area."

He acted like there was nothing to it, but it was impossible to guess how much magic force such a feat required. It was also impossible to imagine a Devil King who even cared about trivialities like being watched.

"So try not to let those guys escape the barrier, all right? 'Cause if they do, that's gonna be a pain for both of us... Oof!"

Apparently the Shuto Expressway was a heavy burden, even for a Devil King with seemingly limitless power in his hands. Smirking a bit at the plainly encumbered demon master, Emilia readied her holy sword as she faced Lucifer.

"So! It seems I had best leave nothing on the table myself, then!"

Lucifer had all but resigned himself to his fate. As unbelievable as it seemed, the Devil King and the Hero had forged a pact in this world. And now they both had their sights upon him, the full brunt of their demonic—and holy—magic backing them up. Magic they had no simple way to replenish.

Were they even *thinking* of returning home?

"...Hah!"

Lucifer flew high into the air, then unleashed a countless barrage of magic bolts, a seemingly endless river of light from his jet-black wings.

Emilia brushed away the barrage with a single swipe, but the bolts of magic changed trajectory. Every one of them struck the Devil King in the back.

"Owwwwwwww! What the *hell*, man?!"

"Sorry! Just an accident!"

Emilia shrugged off his protests as she drove her foot to the ground. It did not seem that powerful of a stomp, but it was all she needed to propel herself toward Lucifer, like a great arrow of gold.

"Haaaaaahh!"

Lucifer only barely dodged the divine streak of light.

With a flap of his dark wings, the demon began to dart across the air, faster than even Emilia's sudden burst of speed.

"Think you can catch me?!"

The side of Lucifer's hands glowed black, unleashing a barrage of dark blades as he himself struck at close range. It was an expertly timed wave attack.

Emilia did not even attempt to dodge. Her Cloth of the Dispeller shone even more brightly as she balled herself up in the air.

The dark blades, and Lucifer's fist, all bounced harmlessly off of the bright light.

"Nice try. But not good enough."

Lucifer snorted.

"Hah! Talk all you want! Your defense is far from impervious. And you failed to dodge my attack at all! In your state, your blade would never reach me!"

As if to confirm Lucifer's assertion, a drop of blood began to fall from Emilia's forehead. It trickled from the exact same location where "Emi" sustained her injury in the food court.

"Your agility in the air was never a match for mine, even in times past. I can still gain magic force in this world! Time is on my side!"

He had a point. If Emilia, who had no way to replenish her holy force, was caught in a marathon struggle, she would inevitably peter out sooner or later.

"Sorry, but I will *not* allow that to happen."

An unfamiliar voice came from above the two of them.

A large mass of rock flew downward, zooming between Lucifer and Emilia.

"You!"

"*Him?*"

It was a gigantic body, one with bloodless white skin and a demonic, gnarled, locustlike tail. At its tip was a forked, clawlike spike.

"Far be it from me to fight in tandem with the Hero...but I have sworn my loyalty to Satan, the Devil King!"

It was Alciel, the Great Demon General, and a demon who once plunged the Eastern Continent of Ente Isla into a tornado of despair.

"And thus, my current foe...is you, Lucifer!"

The jarring voice, like running one's fingernails across a chalkboard, was clearly reminiscent of the human Ashiya's sarcastic tone.

"Oh, yeah. Guess you weren't around, huh? But how'd you come back to life from *that*?"

Whether here or at the Shinjuku food court, Alciel was apparently doomed to be forgotten about quickly, whenever crisis struck. It was difficult to tell if this bothered Alciel, given that his animal-like demon face betrayed no emotions that a human could pick up.

"I was near death, Your Demonic Highness, and you granted me enough magic force to revive myself. No more, and no less."

"Huh. Neat. But what've you been doing since then? You weren't *here.*"

"I had...ripped through my pants, so I went back to the apartment to fetch my general's cloak from the closet."

He *was*, come to think of it, wearing a gigantic robe. It was made of a thick, heavy cloth emblazoned with the seal of the demon realm, a garment designed to symbolize the dignity of his role as Great Demon General. On one side was the bright, glittery general's emblem, a mark that only the Devil King's four closest officers were allowed the right to bear.

It allowed him to strike a bold presence, one truly worthy of the name Alciel, Great Demon General and commander of the successful invasion of Ente Isla's Eastern Continent.

For the first time, Emilia discovered that a demon's garb was for more than mere flash or intimidation. Though, for a human going face-to-face with a demon, whether said horrid monster was flashing his privates or not would never be the first priority.

"...Well, great. Don't expect me to get all friendly with you, though."

"Nor will I, Hero. Once this battle is over, we will be enemies once more."

"Perfect."

As she spoke, Emilia looked Lucifer squarely in the eye and slashed her hand to the side.

The beam of light this emitted instantly melted away the gun in Olba's hand as the archbishop attempted to shoot Alciel in the back.

"Gah!"

Alciel did not so much as toss a glance behind him. "Do not expect my thanks for that. That bullet would hardly even faze me."

"Oh? Lofty words, there. That wasn't exactly the case a few minutes ago, if I recall."

"...You worthless fool!"

Lucifer interjected, showering Olba with abuse. "You had almost brought the Devil King to his knees! You could at least fight like you mean it!"

"But...but we'll be unable to return."

"Perhaps not! But we *certainly* won't if we lose here!"

"...Damn you all..."

Olba finally recollected himself, his face belying his resignation. He seemed to be wholly unarmed, but the holy power within him was palpably welling up.

A clash between holy and demonic, between heaven and hell, was about to begin.

"Jeez, Alciel. Thanks for running off like that."

Meanwhile, the Devil King was muttering to himself.

"Ugh... I've got nothing to do. And I probably look terrible."

UniClo's line of sweat-wicking T-shirts and stretch pants, utilizing the latest advances in sewing technology, was proving remarkably resilient. Unlike the fashionable denim he had ripped through in the Shinjuku underground corridor, they were still managing to cover up the important bits without tearing, even after the wearer ballooned in size. In terms of keeping the Devil King safe from indecent-exposure charges, no one had anything to complain about.

"This...this isn't a movie, is it?"

Chiho was still conscious, the sole witness to this clash of holy and demonic forces. Inside her holy antimagic barrier, she watched on, a stunned look on her face, as the unearthly battle unfolded. Her mouth was agape, and even the pain in her body seemed to fly away, no longer relevant.

Alciel used his force to throw countless enormous pieces of rubble into the air. As if on cue, they hurtled toward Lucifer and Olba at dizzying speed.

Emilia climbed aboard one of them, thrusting herself toward her foes. Although it pained him down to the bottom of his soul, Alciel took control of the rock Emilia clung to, the spike on his tail twitching.

"Heavenly Flame Slash!"

The holy sword fell, launching a horde of flaming blades that rocketed toward Lucifer's shoulder. Lucifer staggered back midair, but the wound was not serious.

"Emilia, have you lost your mind?! Teaming with the forces of evil... The Church will never forgive this!"

Olba's invective seemed hopelessly out of touch as he dodged the detritus Alciel flung at him. Emilia laughed, as did the Devil King, still engaged in his Atlasian labor on the far side of the battle.

"Silence, betrayer!"

"Don't give her that crap, baldy."

"That's hardly anything *you* have the right to say."

"...*You're* one to talk."

Even Lucifer and Alciel felt impelled to comment.

Olba, not expecting this unanimously scathing response, was

stunned for a moment—just long enough for one of the smaller pieces of debris to strike. It would have killed any regular man, but he was still an archbishop of the Church, fallen as he might be. He shook his head and grunted.

"...Yes. So I let my guard down for a moment."

Small shards of metal and concrete were scattered all around Olba. He must have guarded at the last moment. But he was still faintly bleeding from his head, where his protection failed to reach in time.

"......"

"You call *that* letting your guard down?"

As the Devil King commented from afar to no one in particular, Alciel went on the offensive, confronting Olba at close range.

"Away from me, foul demon!"

"......"

"Whoa, Olba's digging himself a major hole with his mouth."

Alciel was in the habit of never speaking unless necessary, leaving the Devil King to provide running commentary instead.

"But this is turning into a kind of weird battle. Are those guys really aware of who's on whose side any longer?"

Out of a corner of his eye, he spotted Chiho's eyes darting to and fro, her body still protected by Emilia's power. She made eye contact with the Devil King several times, a puzzled, indecisive look on her face whenever she did.

"Dahh... Guess there's no making excuses for *this*."

The Devil King bitterly resigned himself to a long explanation afterward.

"Heavenly Ice Dance!"

Emilia's sword clashed against Lucifer's magical barrier, the competing forces producing a frigid tempest.

"Nn...gh..."

Something resembling frost began to rain down upon Lucifer's wings.

"That ice has the power to freeze out magic, blocking its effects. Your speed has abandoned you!"

Emilia's sword boldly tore through Lucifer's barrier, leaving a slash wound that ran across his chest.

"Grraaaahhhh!!"

Lucifer attempted to keep away from his foe.

"Not so fast!"

Emilia closed the gap, using the debris kept in the air by the Devil King and Alciel as footholds.

"Ngh!"

Lucifer shot out bolts of black flame to keep her in check, but Emilia let them hit her, not attempting to dodge. They were all dashed to embers by her Cloth of the Dispeller before they could strike home.

Alciel, meanwhile, was closing in on Olba.

Olba's specialty in battle was maintaining the rear ranks, providing the support that saw the Hero Emilia's band of fighters to victory. He alone against a Great Demon General was nothing even resembling a fair match.

Forced to devote himself entirely to defense, he looked toward Lucifer for support. But Lucifer himself was facing long odds before the Hero's strength.

Just when Emilia and Alciel closed in on their opponents:

"...?!"

"...?"

A loud roar echoed across the ground. Everyone stopped. They had felt the sudden release of magical power that accompanied the rumble.

"Satan..."

"Your Demonic Highness..."

Emilia and Alciel focused their gazes upon the Devil King.

The lord of demons responded with a contrived laugh, looking every bit the human being he was before.

"Ugh. That was so, *so* heavy. But I got it all down gently! So we're all okay now! I rock!"

The rumble was the sound of the rubble from the collapsing Shuto Expressway landing on the ground, guided in slowly by the Devil King.

"So! I think now's a good time for me to get involved."

As he spoke, the cars, rubble, and people locked inside the magical barrier landed softly on the ground around him. For the Devil King, that much work required only a trivial effort now.

"Let's get this over with, okay? Besides..."

The Devil King's magical force shimmered like a dark haze, the force of an erupting volcano behind it. Alciel flashed a faint smile, and once again, Olba collapsed in fear while keeping himself aloft.

As for Lucifer, the look on his face was one of pure frustration.

Only Emilia understood what the Devil King was most concerned about at the moment.

The sun was at its highest point in the sky. It was almost lunchtime.

"I'm gonna be late for work at this rate. I promised Chi I'd teach her how to do maintenance on the ice cream machine."

"......"

A passing glance from the Devil King would be enough in itself to knock a normal human being unconscious. To Chiho inside the barrier, the look instead made her blush despite herself.

Alciel's eyes turned upward as he groaned to himself. Emilia noted how strangely charming the Devil King looked as he grinned, then slapped herself for entertaining the thought for even an instant.

"Right. Anyway. You guys. I had this wondrous plan for taking over the world, and you made me just stand by the side this whole battle like an idiot!"

*That* was what riled him the most. Apparently.

But before anyone had a chance to bash him for it, the Devil King brought the full brunt of his glare upon the still-collapsed Olba.

"Uhngh...hhh...!"

The sheer force behind the demon's sharpened stare was enough to send Olba flying, as if batted away with a giant hammer. His body slammed against one of the fallen expressway panels, knocking him out cold as he made a depression in the concrete.

"Pathetic! Pathetic, Olba!"

Howling with laughter, the Devil King spent not a single moment looking back at the archbishop. In the next instant, it was Lucifer he stood before.

Neither Lucifer, nor Emilia as she watched from afar, could follow his movements with the naked eye.

"You... Your Demonic..."

All Lucifer could do was nervously back away from his former commander.

"You think calling me *that* will please me at this point?"

In demonic society, defying those in the upper echelons was generally a serious taboo. And even half angel as he was, Lucifer had long since fallen to the darkness.

"Yo, Emi. What should we do with this guy?"

The Devil King turned toward his mortal enemy, face livid with sadistic glee.

The Hero seemed almost bored as she answered her own mortal enemy in return.

"Hmm, let me think... How about we make him take responsibility for messing up the city?"

"Good idea. Also, if I'm late for work, that's on you, Lucifer, you got that? If this screws up my perfect-attendance record, what're you gonna do about that? Huh? What the *hell* are you gonna do about that?!"

"Wh-*what?!* I don't understand!!"

As Lucifer screamed, bewildered, Alciel muttered to himself, "Something the likes of us will never be able to understand, I fear..."

"In any event, I'll be helping myself to your magic power." The grin on the king of all demons' face was gleeful.

"We'll take care of your punishment after that," the Hero whispered, her voice emotionless as she clanged her knuckles against the midpoint of her blade.

"Ahh...hhh..."

Lucifer, faced with the glorious light of heaven and the deepest pit of darkness, could do nothing but gurgle helplessly.

"If you call yourself a Great Demon General, at least *try* to take it with some dignity!!"

With the Devil King's shout, light and darkness thundered across Sasazuka.

"So, how do you plan to make up for all this?"

Lucifer, no longer in possession of his fallen-angel form, could do nothing but be silent at the Devil King's—or Maou's, to be exact—question.

He was on his knees. On his knees, as a fragile, weak human being, atop the asphalt road, rubble, and chunks of concrete scattered to and fro, the postbattle scene one of total ruination.

Lucifer, the Great Demon General who had turned the Western Continent of Ente Isla into an inferno of punishing hellfire, was now upon his knees in front of the Hero and the Devil King.

In Sasazuka. In Tokyo. In Japan.

"I can hear the news guy now: 'Due to a disaster of unprecedented proportions, the Shuto Expressway and Tokyo-Gaikan Expressway are impassible from Hatsudai to Chofu,' et cetera, et cetera. Oh, and the Koshu-Kaido road. *And* the Keio rail line; that's totally blocked just before Shinjuku. And, you know, I tried to be careful, but we might be dealing with some deaths here."

"It would be a bit of a miracle if there weren't any, Your Demonic Highness."

Ashiya, back to human form and completely unscathed, was doggedly attempting to keep his Great Demon General robes from falling off his body.

"But if it weren't for your great powers, anyone in the cars caught up in the Shuto Expressway collapse wouldn't have had a chance. The cars on the Koshu-Kaido road, too. And it's nothing short of a miracle that the nearby houses and such weren't more badly damaged."

"Yeah, well, people like us usually don't start goin' at it in this world. I bet at least a few people didn't evacuate in time. I tried to make the magic barrier as large as I could manage, but who knows if I got everything covered under it…"

Lucifer remained silent.

"I have an idea." Emi, dressed in a business suit that had all but fallen to tatters due to her falling down the stairs at Maou's apartment then joining a life-or-death clash of ponderously enormous magical forces, spoke up as she looked down upon Lucifer.

"Why don't we just hand this guy over to the cops? We could say he was some kind of terrorist bomber or something."

"I was thinking that too, but… Like, maybe that'd cause a big furor to start out, but there's no actual evidence at all, and plus, it'd be kinda pointless anyway. I bet the cops wouldn't mind closing the book on that string of robberies, though."

The pants and shirt on Maou, stretched to the very limit of their fibers following their owner's recent transformation, were now hanging loosely off his body, as if draped on a deck chair.

"Yeah, I'm sure, but…I mean, what're we gonna do about all *this*?"

"Beats me. Not like a Great Demon General drained of all his magic power is gonna help us much."

Said draining and absorption of Lucifer's magical force was the one and only reason why the suddenly-human demon officer was so meek and docile now.

Ashiya himself still retained some magic, obtained the same way Maou had obtained his just now, and Emi had yet to exhaust her supply of holy force either. For Lucifer, whose stores had been fully tapped, there was no chance of even scratching them.

"Um…"

Chiho was the one who sheepishly interjected. She had no obvious injuries, and except for a light case of exhaustion after having Lucifer suck all the negative emotion out of her, she was fine. Compared to Maou, she looked oddly refreshed and ready for the day.

"I-I guess this is kind of a silly thing to ask at this point…"

"What's up, Chi?"

The response, and the voice that delivered it, was unmistakably Sadao Maou. But Chiho still clearly recalled the enormous creature that had taken his form just minutes ago.

"Well, what…what *are* all of you?"

It was the obvious question of the hour. Maou, Ashiya, and Emi exchanged glances.

"Well…like, it's kind of embarrassing to just put it out like this, but I'm the Devil King over in another world."

Maou honestly did look embarrassed, distractedly scratching the side of his face with a finger, as if someone had just revealed one of his hidden nerd hobbies to his coworkers. It was enough to make Chiho burst into laughter even before she could process his words.

"Yeah, not that you believe it, huh?"

Chiho waved her hands in the air nervously. "Oh, no, no, no! I mean, I saw all of that…stuff you did, so. And that's how you did all *that*, too, right?"

Her finger was pointed at the crowds of onlookers, overturned cars, and other debris scattered around the area, still frozen in time underneath the magical barrier.

"Yeah, more or less. But, you know, that much is pretty easy, so…"

"Your Demonic Highness, I know humility is considered a virtue in Japanese society, but you really shouldn't be afraid to take more credit here."

Ashiya was already back to his usual griping-househusband tone of voice.

"These guys are all demons, keep in mind. Myself, I'm all human. Okay, half angel, but—"

The utter seriousness of Emi's interjection made Chiho spasm in laughter once more.

"Oh, come on, Chiho!"

"I-I'm sorry! It's just so…goofy!"

"Wait, you're half angel? 'Cause that's news to me."

"What? How could you *not* know? You're the Devil King! Who did you think I *was* this whole time?"

Emi snapping back at Maou's half-baked response was all it took for Chiho's laughing to grow louder.

"I just thought that… Ha-ha-ha-ha! That angels and demons and stuff… They were all just these big made-up things, but…seeing you all…right here…"

The effort to speak while laughing eventually caused Chiho to choke on her own words. Emi worriedly slapped her on the back a few times.

"Well, look, Emi, you weren't exactly sharing your personal info with me over there, right? I just thought you were, like, a really strong human, is all."

"Oh, so you thought a regular human could just walk around with enough Holy Silver in her body to summon her sword?"

"…Guess not, huh? Well, *that* sure explains a lot. I wondered how you could transform like that."

"If you think *that* was a shock, imagine finding you guys looking like *humans* for the first time!… Breathing okay now, Chiho?"

"Y-yeah. Sorry."

Emi brought her lips to Chiho's ears as she composed herself after her laughing fit.

"You see now? There's nothing special at all between me and Maou, so quit worrying, okay?"

"Y-Yusa…"

All this laughing and blushing was keeping Chiho's circulatory system fairly well occupied. Emi breathed a sigh of relief, yesterday's misunderstandings now a thing of the past. Maou and Ashiya, looking on, couldn't help to smile to themselves.

"You know, though…" Maou furrowed his brows, his face betraying his embarrassment.

"I guess it's pointless asking now, but Emi, if you had that much power left, why didn't you attack me before now? Like, until yesterday, you could've reduced me to a pile of ash any time you wanted."

"Oh, that?"

Emi shrugged, as if the idea meant nothing to her.

"Well, a Devil King as cowardly as you are, you might have been pretending to be a weak, helpless human being until the moment you decided to bare your fangs, right? Plus, like I told you, if I fought at full power like that, even if I managed to defeat you, there's no guarantee I'd have enough power left to control the Gate. That's pretty much it."

"Oh. Makes sense."

Maou nodded his agreement. Then his face turned white as he grasped the meaning behind her words.

To put it another way, if Emi had decided to give up on returning home, she could have utterly destroyed him at any moment. She had every chance in the world to pull it off before now.

Emi, perhaps noticing this, sulkily turned her back to Maou.

"I know I don't act like it sometimes, but I'm a Hero. A leader. My people respected me. I can't just prey on the weak and defenseless like that."

"The weak and...? That's kind of mean."

"It's the truth, isn't it?"

"Yeah, well, what about *now*, huh? I got all my power back, and you used all of yours up! I could crush you like a bug! How about *them* apples?"

Maou struck a semiserious battle pose.

"Oh, suuuuuuure."

But Emi was totally unfazed. Grabbing Chiho at her side, she held her close, while Maou's potential love interest hid behind her shadow.

"Hey, Chiho, that guy's using his 'I have my power back' crutch to try and pick on me."

The tactic was as barefaced as it was effective.

"...Really, Maou?"

And what's more, Chiho looked honestly crestfallen as she looked toward Maou. He cringed, shielding his face against her sheer innocence.

"D-don't look at me like that! I... There's no *way* I'd actually do it! I am the proud, noble king of the demons! When it's time to fight,

I fight fair and square! So stop looking all sad like that, Chi, okay? Also, that was *low*, Emi!"

Ashiya sighed, looking even sadder than Chiho as he watched Maou frantically make excuses from the rear.

Lucifer, for his part, seemed utterly lost, as if viewing a scene from another dimension.

"What has *happened* to all of you?"

The question brought Emi and Maou back to reality. In tandem, they planted a foot upon Lucifer's head for speaking without permission.

"Nnrgh!"

"Yeah, that reminds me, this guy comes before any of that. That and Sasazuka. What're we gonna do?"

Maou looked around his surroundings as Ashiya crossed his arms in intense thought.

"As they say, Your Demonic Highness, if you make a mess, it's your job to clean it up. This world's been very kind to us. Leaving it in chaos before returning home would make even a demon's conscience feel guilty."

Ashiya's response could not have been less demonlike. But it was the reference to "returning home" that made Emi's face stiffen.

"…So you *are* going back?"

"Of course we are. With my liege's powers restored, we no longer have anything chaining us to Earth. Ente Isla is always our first and foremost target."

The words from Ashiya's mouth were cold and frank.

"Going back? Back to your family, or…?"

Chiho's question, a justifiable one for a girl with an incomplete knowledge of Maou's world, went ignored.

"Well, hang on. I'm signed up for a bunch of shifts this month, and *grnh!*"

"Your Demonic Highness, is your part-time job at MgRonald more important to you than the conquest of Ente Isla?!"

A swift swat with Ashiya's flattened hand was enough to momentarily rearrange Maou's face.

"Listen to me, my liege. I will grant you that without your hard work for Ms. Kisaki and the Hatagaya rail-station MgRonald, our time in Japan would have been far more difficult than it was. But what possible value does a contract with the human race hold, one written without the benefit of demonic force behind it? I know we will both miss the thousand-yen hourly pay you were receiving—"

"Wow, a thousand yen at MgRonald? They must've *loved* you."

"You stay out of this, Emilia! Your Demonic Highness, how saddened would your former compatriots of the darkness be if they knew how apparently elated it makes the almighty Devil King to cook beef and pork and chicken and potatoes all day? I understand you have made a work promise to Ms. Sasaki here, one you are loath to break. But it is the very sadness, the negative emotion, from such a harmless young girl upon seeing this promise broken that we demons *thrive* upon!"

"Hah! You think that bum's work friend will be *that* disappointed? Missing her big chance to learn how to clean the soft-serve machine?"

"Wait...what? You aren't quitting, are you, Maou?"

"The one desire that drives us demons forward is the subjugation of Ente Isla. That is something I have repeated to you endless times since we were banished to Japan. We have a mission, and it simply must be completed! Your Demonic Highness, I beg you to show me your resolve. You must deal Lucifer his just punishment, settle matters with the weakened Hero Emilia, and bid a final farewell to Sasazuka!"

"Man, I don't remember you mouthing off at me that much as a demon..."

Ashiya's rapid whining wearied Maou's ears.

"Okay, so how're we gonna clean this up *and* get back home?"

"We have done nothing wrong here, my liege. Your only responsibility as Devil King is to give Ms. Kisaki formal notice of your departure. It wouldn't do to make her think you bailed out without telling anyone."

"Aww…but we almost hit the top for regional sales for the last special promotion—"

"Enough about Hatagaya! You have another entire *world* to be concerned about!"

"We only just bought that fridge, too. And the washer. *And* my bike."

"And you now have the power to navigate across the Gate, Your Demonic Highness! You no longer have any *need* for home appliances!"

"Um…so, what do you want from me?"

Lucifer, wallowing in self-pity after being knelt down and stomped upon, spoke up, his face still being held against the rubble. Instead of his former demon cohorts, it was Emi who responded first.

"Oh! Now that you mention it! Lucifer, were you the guy who called me up at work?"

"Uh, yeah…?"

What remained of Lucifer's demonic pride made him quick to admit the crime.

"How did you find out where I worked?"

"Oh, yeah. You got, like, harassed at work, didn't you?" As Maou lifted his foot, Lucifer gingerly turned his face upward.

"Yeah I did!" Emi snapped. "What was *that* all about?!"

"That, uh… Well, you dropped this, Emilia, didn't you? During the first attack?" With Emi's foot still firmly upon his head, Lucifer took out a folding wallet illustrated on the outside with brown bears, white bear cubs, and yellow birds.

"Ahhh! My wallet!"

Emi snatched the fancily decorated wallet from Lucifer's hand.

"You had some kind of work ID in there, so I used that to track you down…"

"Oh, eww, Lucifer, you poked around inside a girl's wallet?"

"Simply disgraceful. That could be grounds for a lawsuit in this day and age."

The looks of disgust on Maou's and Ashiya's faces were sincere.

"You can't just look inside people's wallets like that. That's *personal*."

"I always knew you were a bad seed, Lucifer, but who could have known how depraved you truly were?" Chiho turned toward Lucifer, her previous pangs of fear now transformed into utter disdain.

"Hey, Ashiya, what's the name of that character on her wallet?"

"Um, Re…relax-a-Bear, or something like that? I've seen it quite a bit lately."

Maou's face contorted itself, as if showing pity for Emi.

"Chiho carries around a Louis Videon wallet, you know. I don't know if it's fake or what, but *Videon*, man. What's *this* thing?"

"It's *real*, Maou! …Uh, but I like Relax-a-Bear, too! He's cute!"

The harried addendum to Chiho's frantic response failed to make Emi feel any better.

"Just shut *up*, you guys! I like that design! So what?" Emi blushed slightly as she looked through the wallet's contents. "…Ahh!"

"Wh-what?! I didn't take anything from it!"

"Then where's my stamp card from Subwave?! That was a full card, too! I *hate* you!"

Now Emi's face shone a bright red.

"I…I had never eaten a sandwich with 'buffalo chicken' inside of it before! I was merely curious!"

The conversation had descended into unorganized chaos, one that went off on wilder and wilder tangents as it continued. But no one demonstrated any willingness to rein it in.

"Erf, I feel sick… What the hell's all this about? Why's it all stopped?"

"Don't ask me about thaaaat! It must be some kind of magical barrier!"

"Who's that standin' over there?"

"It looks like Emilia to me…"

"And who's buried in that pile?"

"…That would be Olba."

"And who're those other guys?"

"Couldn't saaaaay…"

Upon discovering the Church's plot, Albert Ende, martial artist and friend of Emilia, and Emeralda Etuva, court alchemist for the Western Continent empire of Saint Aile, immediately sprang into action. They had pursued Lucifer and Olba's trail across the Gate, and they chose this exact moment to descend into Sasazuka.

"So, what, you're Satan? *That* Satan?"

The dark-skinned man, somewhere around thirty, easily towered over Ashiya. He boasted well-kept white hair and a white beard, but what stood out the most was his golden-colored eyes. And now Albert, arms still crossed, was looking straight down upon the Devil King. His lightweight leather suit was designed to accentuate the musculature of his body, making him look like a pro wrestler staring down a sixth grader.

"And you are his general, Alciel? Reeeeeeally?"

Emeralda was far smaller in build, her short, rounded blue-green hair rustling in the wind as her similarly light-green eyes stared up at Ashiya. Her clerical robe resembled Olba's, but instead of the archibishop's simple design, she preferred a more striking arrangement of red and orange, the national seal of Saint Aile stitched in gold on the back. Neither of them seemed to be armed.

"Indeed. Cower in fear!"

Maou tried his best to act the part, confident that these interlopers had no intention of fighting.

"Oh, stop being so siiiilly!"

But the way Emeralda instantly brushed it off disheartened him.

"Well, doesn't this just beat everything, Emer? I ain't got much strength left… Wasn't planning on sizing up the Devil King so quickly and all."

"You knoooow, I would advise against saying that in front of the enemy…"

"Yeah? Yeah. Well, whoops on me!"

Albert bared his white teeth and laughed heartily, hand behind his head.

Chiho had remained silent since their arrival, but the loud laughter made her immediately notice something. She launched an accusatory finger at the giant man.

"M-Maou! That's the voice! The voice that talked to me in my brain!"

"Oh? Hey, little lady, did you pick up on my idea link?"

The conversation had already been derailed; now it was in danger of all but falling off the cliff. Emi swooped in.

"Listen! Listen, everyone. I know we're all a little confused here, so let's just calm down and talk things over so we're on the same page. Let's go back to your apartment, Alciel. We can't just talk here amid all this rubble." ·

"Ridiculous! I would never invite the Hero's cohorts to Devil's Castle!"

Maou intervened before Ashiya could chide Emi any further for attempting to take command.

"Nah, she's right. We're in an emergency, Ashiya; we need to be flexible. I'm getting kinda sick of keeping this barrier going. Plus, it wouldn't be a good idea to waste all my new power on fighting these guys."

Ashiya nodded ruefully. To him, Maou was suddenly making sense again.

"...But what about Olba, buried under that rubble?"

"Leave him. He carried out all those robberies with Lucifer, right? The police'll ID him and lock him up soon enough."

It was true. Within the rules of Japanese society, Olba and Lucifer were criminals. Neither Emi, whom Olba had betrayed, nor the demons, his original enemies, had any reason to show him mercy.

"You remember where it is, right, Emi? You go on ahead. Take Chi and these guys with you."

Maou tossed the apartment's door key toward Emi.

"Huh?"

"I'll come over once I clean things up."

"...You aren't gonna jump back to Ente Isla, are you?"

"*No*, Emi! Your pals would chase right after me if I did. Just go, all right?"

Emi's eyes were filled with suspicion, but she nonetheless motioned toward Chiho, Emeralda, and the others as she began to walk off.

"So what's up with that? You folks gettin' along now, or what?"

"Emilia the Hero, making friends with the Devil King! Myyyy, wonders never cease!"

"I firmly deny that, and *only* that, all right? Let's get going."

For a moment, Emi turned back toward Maou before proceeding down a Sasazuka back alley with her heroic band.

Ashiya watched them go before speaking. "And what do you intend, Your Demonic Highness?"

Maou pointed toward the Shuto Expressway. "We can't just leave it like that. Ashiya, Lucifer, help me out."

Ashiya hesitated for a moment, but sighed, a resigned smile on his face. Lucifer, however, was shocked.

"You, you don't mean..."

"Mm-hmm. I know I just got my powers back, but..."

"But...but if you do that...!"

"...So be it. My liege has made his choice. I am bound to follow him."

"...Can you at least tell me what has possessed you? You, and our lord, as well?"

"I cannot say. I find it difficult to understand myself."

"You two mind knocking off the chitchat for me?"

"My apologies, Your Demonic Highness. Here you are."

Taking Ashiya's hand, Maou began to speak, the excitement plain in his voice.

"As the lord of demons, I must take responsibility for the actions of my minions. Whether it be Ente Isla or the MgRonald Corporation, that must always apply. I rule all that I see, and a ruler's burden is a heavy one."

Maou smiled as he watched over the ruined Sasazuka.

✳

The sight of Villa Rosa Sasazuka was enough to make Emeralda and Albert blanch. Even for someone who had just arrived on Earth half an hour ago, this structure was nowhere near what one's imagination conjured upon hearing the words "the Devil's Castle."

"Ermm... Emilia?"

"I know what you're thinking, Emeralda. But that room over there, upstairs... That's the Devil's Castle, the lair of Satan himself. In Japan, anyway."

"'That room'? Just the one?"

"Yep. All the others are empty."

The two newcomers fell silent for a moment. Suddenly, Emeralda clapped her hands in realization.

"Ah! Of coooourse! They've disguised the exterior as a shoddy, cramped hovel, but once you step inside, you're transported to another dimension, one that extends boundlessly across—"

"Nope. One hundred square feet. If I had to guess, it's about half the size of the mountain shack you lived in, Albert. No bath, either."

"Eesh. Well, *that's* a disappointment."

"And he still calls himself Devil Kiiiing?"

Both had to struggle for the words.

"Oh, I don't know. If you ask me, this apartment really jives with the image I had of Maou, so..."

Chiho's observation was, in its own way, even crueler.

"You'll see what we mean once we're inside. Let's go."

Carefully, Emi ascended the stairway she had so blithely tossed her body down that morning.

Turning the cylinder lock, the group was greeted by the familiar smells of life inside a well-worn building. This time, Emeralda and Albert were at a total loss for words.

Chiho, noticing the paper bag with the can of *senbei* rice crackers she dropped earlier, walked over to pick it up. She turned toward Emeralda and Albert, brushing the dust off the bag.

"Um, so in Japan, the custom's to take off your shoes before you enter someone's home. So you can do that here…"

As she spoke, she removed her loafers as she stood in the front foyer, one about the size of a hamster cage. Emi followed, and then Emeralda and Albert copied the motion, removing their boots. Four pairs of footwear were enough to completely occupy the cramped space in front of the door.

"I'd take my old mountain shack over this heap any day. There ain't even enough space to put up any traps!"

"Forget about traps. There isn't even enough space for the bare minimum of furniture. Feel free to sit down wherever, I guess."

The group settled to the tatami floor, none looking very comfortable with themselves.

"…Oh, um, I'll go make some tea or something!"

Chiho suddenly thought to travel over to the kitchen counter. Emi stopped her.

"Don't bother, Chiho. They don't have any teapots or cups or anything. The fridge and the shelves are completely empty, too. I have no idea what they live off of."

"Oh…?" Chiho, standing by the sink, turned toward Emi. The look on her face was less of surprise and more of disbelief.

"How do you know all of that, Yusa?"

"Oh, uh, the other day I st—"

Emi stopped herself midsentence, all too aware of the blunder she had just made. Chiho wasn't stupid. She knew what it meant when a woman knew a man's kitchen inside and out. Her seemingly comprehensive knowledge of the Devil Castle's interior likely struck Emeralda and Albert as suspicious, too.

"The other day you…what, Yusa?"

"Um…well, this was a *total* accident, but…"

The Hero was just about to plow forward with her highly unheroic excuse when she was interrupted.

"Hmm?"

"Oooh!"

Albert and Emeralda both reacted simultaneously. It wasn't

to pick on Emi. Emi herself immediately knew what caught their eye.

"Um...is there something...?"

Albert and Emeralda glanced at each other instead of answering Chiho.

"What was *thaaaat*, just now?"

"One damned powerful wave of magic power, if I know it. Hey, Emilia, you sure we should really be trusting the Devil King and the rest?"

"I...think so."

The strain was obvious in Emi's voice.

The magical force the three of them had picked up on was absolutely enormous in scope. It felt like the blast wave of a gigantic bomb centered on Sasazuka rail station, lapping across the apartment roof as it spread wider and wider. It was a mammoth explosion of magic, one Emi hadn't even felt in the previous battle.

"...Are you guys hiding something from me?"

Chiho, unaware of all this, was more than a bit put off at her question being ignored. But the sheer, impalpable quantity of magic was all but impossible to wrap one's head around.

Maou said he wouldn't do anything. Was believing him the right move? Was that weird affinity he seemed to have for Japan and its people up to this point all just a farce? A wave of anxiety flashed through Emi's mind, before being very suddenly interrupted.

"Yo! Emi, open up! We're back!"

Emi tensed herself up tightly at the sudden bang—or kick, to be exact—on the door. All of them except Chiho looked at each other, then at the door.

"...Shall I open it?"

Emeralda squinted at the door.

"It's kind of his place, innit?"

"Yes, but the *Devvvvil King's* place. To say nothing of that unusual bolt of maaaagic..."

"Pfft. Whadda we got to be scared of? A Devil King that lives in this piddlin' little pigsty? 'Sides, if that magic was his, no way he's got any of that stuff left. I could beat 'im down inna blink of an eye."

"Oh, thanks a *lot*, Albert! Let's see if you keep on saying that once you open the damn door!"

From the other side, Maou railed at them. Only a few thin pieces of plywood separated them, and yet they couldn't detect a single spark of magic.

"'Open the door,' hmm? You and what arrrrmy?"

"……"

Emi could feel the exhaustion pour over her as this exchange continued. Maybe she was overthinking things after all.

"Just open up! I'm gonna call the landlord if you don't!"

"Open the door for him, Albert."

Reluctantly, Albert stood up.

"Why? What's a 'landlord'? That strong of a monster, or…?"

Maou answered the question from the other side as Albert unlocked the door.

"Ohhh yeah. She's *real* strong. You try to cross her, and one look's all it'll take to crush your soul."

Emi knew Maou wasn't entirely joking. Come to think of it, what had Shiba the landlord been doing since they detected Lucifer's rampage and flew out the door?

That lady had acted like she knew everything about their true colors.

As Emi thought this over, Albert opened the door. Maou clumsily lurched inside, supporting the limp, unresponsive Ashiya and Lucifer with both arms.

"Get outta my way. These guys're heavy."

Maou dragged his companions inside, throwing them down on the tatami floor. Chiho gasped lightly as she realized Ashiya was apparently unconscious.

"Ah…uh…what happened to Ashiya?"

"Oh, nothing much. I squeezed all the magic out of him, he almost died, that sort of thing."

With a great sigh, Maou sat down and looked at Albert and Emeralda.

"So. Guess we all know each other now. Why are *you* people here? Judging by the looks of things, you're not here to kill me, at least."

"Nope. Not really. Fact is, we had no inclination to even run into you. We just came to help out Emilia."

Albert shrugged, his eyes turned toward Emi.

"Olba wasn't the only one. The whole Churrrch was in on it." Emeralda was stern as she spoke, face scrunched, both hands balled into fists.

"What?!"

"The Church bishops all but bullied us into joinin' their side. They had us captured, their spies watchin' us day and night. Took a lot of work to escape, lemme tell you."

"They guaranteed our securrrrity as long as we didn't do anything against them. They wanted me to retire out of court life in the Emm-mmpire. That's how scared they were, apparently, of their Hero and savior seizing political power."

The sad story was high entertainment to Maou's ears.

"Yeah, that's what you get from people who don't lift a finger to actually *do* anything. The demon world's got you beat there. Total merit-based system, all the way down. You guys wanna be my new minions?"

Emeralda, her face still pained, stuck out her tongue at this maybe-joking, maybe-real attempt at scouting new talent.

"*Thpbbt!* I'd never be the minion to someone *thiiiis* broke."

Albert, meanwhile, sized up Maou from head to toe.

"You ain't got enough muscle on you, boy. Anyone who wants to boss me around, well, he better be a damn level bigger than I am."

He flexed his biceps to the audience in a pointless bit of bravado, demonstrating the brawn that usually backed up his words. He followed it up with several more poses, to the appreciative admiration of Chiho.

"So that's all you two care about? Muscles and money?"

Emi's plaintive question went unanswered.

"Okay, enough screwin' around. So anyway, Emilia, we wanted to letcha know that danger was about to be on its way. We traced you and the Devil King's path down to Japan pretty quick, too."

"The problem, though, was that if we could find you, Olba and the Church could, too. It was a race to see who could reach you firrrrst."

Emeralda and Albert stared off into space, recalling the trials they went through to reach their Hero.

"We both fired out a whole mess of sonar bolts. Pretty well caused a bunch of havoc in this world, too, I reckon. Did you have a lot of earthquakes and stuff?"

Everything so far was exactly as Maou had guessed.

"In that case, Albert, why did I hear your message?"

Albert replied nonchalantly to Chiho's query. "Well, the idea link works by linkin' up between people's consciousnesses, so the sender can narrow down the range of folks he sends messages to. So when I sent out that message, I narrowed down the people receivin' it to 'human beings who think about nothing but the Devil King all day.'"

Both Emi and Chiho required some time before they fully understood what the apparently straightforward reply meant.

Emi would naturally fall into that group, having traveled to Japan to slay the Devil King. She just happened to be out of range at the time the communication made its way to Japan.

But Chiho?

"Wha...! That... I, uh..."

Her face grew redder with every moment as she stammered. Of *course* she was thinking about him. All day, to boot.

She didn't need to explain why. Everyone understood that much. The problem was that someone revealed that before she could. That, and Maou was in the room.

"Oh, myyyy! Quite the player, aren't you, Devil King?"

Emeralda's choosing to take the innuendo to the next level made the emotion-o-meter attached to Chiho's brain go off the charts, blinking and blowing off steam.

"Ahh..."

With a groan, Chiho fainted in embarrassment, falling to the ground in a neat row alongside Ashiya and Lucifer.

"...Okay! So! What are you guys gonna do now?"

Maou, unable to decide how to react, turned toward the Hero's party, each one reacting in wildly divergent ways. If he let *his* true colors come to the surface as well, that would truly be an embarrassment for all time.

"Don't ask me. We just came 'cause we thought Olba and Lucifer were gonna do somethin' to Emilia. We weren't countin' on the Devil King to be here, too."

"Our general idea was to take Emilia back home and help Ente Isla realize who should *reeeeally* be leading the recovery effort... but..."

Albert and Emeralda exchanged glances.

"...but the Church's probably got us all on their wanted list by now."

"Indeed, indeed."

"So, what, you're screwed anyway?"

"No, not necessarily. Remember, we still got part of the realm of heaven on our side."

"Very much so! And this let us travel through the Gate without expending any hooooly power." Emeralda took a feather pen out of her robe.

Maou's eyes widened a stretch. "Huh. Look at that. That's the pen angels use when drawing rainbow bridges to other worlds, isn't it?"

"H-hey! You can't just show that to the Devil King!"

Sadao shook his head at Emi's frantic warning. "Demon-realmers can't use it. Quit worrying so much. That's a gadget from heaven; only angels and people recognized by the angels can wield it."

"Oh... But, wait, why do you even *know* about that?"

"I heard about it a while ago. So whose feather did you use for that pen? No, wait, let me guess. Laila, right?"

"Ooh, well done."

"Don't expect any priiiizes!"

Albert and Emeralda freely copped to it.

"Hah! That tomboy get away with something like that again?"

Maou smiled to himself as he recalled the distant past.

"She's walkin' on some danged thin ice up in heaven, I'd guess. Not that I know the details."

"But honestly, who wouldn't want to take action if they knew their daughter was in daaaanger?"

Emi was the only one to blink at Emeralda's words.

"Their...daughter?"

"Oh? Wait, you didn't know, Emilia?"

"Yeah, she told us she was your mom."

Emi's mind went blank in an instant.

"I... Wow. For real?"

"*That's* how you react, Emi?"

Emi's eyes were still unfocused, not quite able to take in the reality yet.

"Well, anyway, this's all yours now. Any way you wanna use it, it's up to you."

The feather pen loomed large, its feather a pure shade of white. A dim light seemed to encircle it, a smaller dot of luminescence centered upon its tip. It emitted an odd warmth when held in the hand, the same feeling Emi experienced in Rika's shower.

Her father had said she would learn of her mother someday. That was repeated to her countless times during her Church Guard days. She knew she was half angel, and if her father was human, the conclusion to make was obivous. But she never expected to not only learn the truth like this, but even grasp a physical piece of her so quickly.

"Oh, yeah, I got a message from her, too."

"From my mother...?"

Emi's heart skipped a beat. The blood collected around her face.

"She said 'Your father was a good man.'"

Both Emi and Maou rolled their eyes.

"She...she didn't have to tell me that *now*..."

"*That's* what you tell your daughter?"

"So there you have it. The message, and the feather pen. So..."

Sitting back down, Albert confronted Emi.

"When are you going back?"

"…What?"

"I ain't askin' for today or anythin'. I imagine you got assorted things to settle over here. But if you stick around here too long, the Church's gonna have their say over the whole bit. Sooner you can get home, the better, I'd reckon."

Emi found herself unable to respond.

"I…"

"You knoooow, I'm not sure this is a conversation we should have in the Devil's Castle…"

Realizing that her mind was currently a whirlpool of extraneous thoughts, Emi turned toward Maou, unable to calm herself.

"When…when're *you* going back?"

"Uh?"

Maou blew his nose, tossing the used tissue at the wastebasket. He missed.

"What're you talking about? I'm not going anywhere."

This made the eyes of all three members of the room who remained conscious grow as big as saucers.

"…Huh?"

"Like, even if I did, I can't now."

"???"

Noticing the enormous question marks perched atop the heads of everyone else, Maou chuckled to himself.

"How much magic power did you think it took to bring that disaster area back to how it was before? You knew I built the whole Devil's Castle on Ente Isla by myself, right?"

Emi, Emeralda, and Albert gaped at the wide arc of the Shuto Expressway above them. The Koshu-Kaido road and Sasazuka rail station were completely back to normal, the lack of traffic whizzing to and fro the only thing missing. No battle damage remained on any nearby building.

Dozens upon dozens of emergency vehicles were stopped, but the paramedics and police officers themselves seemed to have no idea why they were deployed to the area.

There were a few civilians here and there, no doubt caught up in the previous fight, but there were no deaths, no injuries—neither in the area beneath the formerly collapsed rail bridge, nor within the buildings blown apart by errant attacks.

In other words, everything was as it was, before the battle. The only difference were the people nearby with no memory of the past several hours, as if someone had anesthetized them without warning.

"Uh… This what I think it is, Emilia?"

"Probably."

"Is this man *reeeeally* the Devil King?"

"He *should* be."

The shopping mall that faced Sasazuka station was already returning to its typical hustle and bustle. All of the nearby pedestrians had quizzical looks on their faces, as if using their tongues to coax an obstinate bit of food out from between their teeth.

"So if we wanted to, we coulda…?"

"Could *you* have done it?"

Albert responded with silence.


"When someone's known for being evil all the time, you know… When he starts doing good things, it's like the slate's totally wiped clean."

"Yes…"

"So I figured there was no way those guys would attack me."

"Yes…"

"Whadaya think? I had it all worked out, huh?"

"So, can we ever get back?"

"Well, off to work! I'll still be on time if I leave now."

"Your Demonic Highness…"

"Oh, yeah. Tie up Lucifer for me, could you? I don't want him doing anything weird."

The fallen angel was still unconscious, lacking the strength to do much of anything for a while. Ashiya was awake, to his credit, but failed to muster enough power to stop Maou.

"...Hey! Chiiiii... Chi, wake up! C'mon, you got a shift today!"

Chiho had steadfastly refused to leave with Emi (or, to be more exact, with Albert). She squirmed, facedown, on the tatami floor.

"Nnngh... Albert, you're such an idiot..."

Maou sighed, his face troubled to the core.

"Ugh... This is what you get when you mess around with Heroes."

✳

Sales for the Hatagaya MgRonald restaurant were beyond awful that day.

And for today, at least, it was pretty clear who was at fault.

The local streets were empty. Maou had wiped every last bit of damage clean and used wide-area hypnosis to convince everyone that nothing had happened, but deep in their hearts, everyone still held the nagging impression that something ominous had just happened nearby.

Chiho was in a bad mood all day, never even trying to approach Maou. Figuring this was due to the battle with Lucifer and the misunderstanding between her and Emi before that, he finally decided to speak up.

"Hey. Chi?"

"...Yes?"

The voice was frigid. She didn't appear to be scared of sharing a fast-food workplace with the Devil King, but if that wasn't the case, Maou couldn't figure out what was riling her so much. *Is it because I got her involved in all of this? At any rate, if this keeps up, it'll start to interfere with work.* Maou pressed onward.

"You know, with my power, I could erase all the bad memories... you...uh, have."

He realized midway this statement would come back to bite him. He could tell because, the moment she heard it, Chiho's eyes welled up to the point where she appeared ready to bawl at any minute. She glared straight up at Maou as he stumbled his way to the end of the sentence.

"No thanks."

"Huh?"

"You're so *stupid*, Maou!"

"Huuuuhh?"

This response was completely unanticipated. Chiho turned her back to him, not saying another word until ten in the evening.

"Thanks. See you next shift."

Then she left, without a trace of hesitation.

Sadly for Sadao Maou, he lacked even a shred of the Devil King Satan's overwhelming sense of presence. The day's work ended with him painfully failing at the task of understanding a teenage girl's heart.

Crestfallen, he mounted his mighty steed Dullahan and set off for home, only to find Emi standing at the restaurant intersection where it all began. They nodded at each other, as if the meeting was arranged beforehand, and exchanged glances as they politely kept their distance.

"...Hey."

"Oh, *that's* how you greet your mortal enemy?... Why're you acting so downtrodden?"

Emi, in street clothes, held her hands behind her back for some reason. Carrying something, no doubt.

"I'm not. It's nothing. Why're you out so late? If they cut the train schedule short tonight, you're not sleeping at my place."

"Then I'll take a taxi home, okay? I've got my wallet back."

"Man, look at Miss Moneybags here. You know the fares go up 30 percent for late-night, right?"

The empty conversation not going much of anywhere, Maou dismounted from Dullahan. There was nothing disquieting or potentially lethal about this meeting, but he always defaulted to keeping his trusty steed between the two of them.

"So, what? You here to thank me, or...?"

He meant it as a joke, but Emi's response was beyond what he expected.

"You didn't do anything bad to Chiho, did you?"

Maou paused, thrown off balance, but then heaved a complex sigh.

"I asked if I could erase her memories from today and yesterday. She called me stupid."

"...Ugh."

Maou wholly overlooked the meaning behind Emi's grunt.

"Was that bad or something, you think? She hasn't said a word to me since." He drooped his shoulders, already disappointed in himself.

Emi figured Maou must have known how Chiho felt, and yet he'd tromped right into the no-man's-land of her heart and said it. It was a crass, crass move, one that exasperated her. But nothing required her to give romantic advice, so she moved on to the main topic at hand.

"Look, do you want to go back at all?"

"...Didn't you already ask me that? Why're you asking again? I'd be *more* than happy to go back."

"I see. Well, for now, at least, *I* can go back anytime I want to."

"Hmm?"

Emi's voice was bright, almost overtly boastful.

"I don't have to go on a wild-goose chase in search of holy power to control the Gate with, either."

"Hey, come on—"

"I can just keep going with my job and pop on back home whenever I feel like it...but..."

Emi's face soured as she came to the *but*.

"...but I'm still worried. As long as the Devil King is alive, I still need to step up, to be the Hero for everyone. And as long as you're staying here, I'm duty-bound to keep pursuing you."

"Yeah, well, you can feel free to drop that anytime you want. I won't complain."

"You might try to plot something with Lucifer and Alciel again. So unless you give up on Ente Isla or I defeat you first, I can't go back."

"...So you're staying here? Even though you're totally free to go?"

She was obfuscating the point, but to sum up, Emi was staying in Japan for as long as Maou was. Emi took her eyes a short distance away from Maou's and continued, this time oddly apologetic. "I don't really care what the archbishops and so on think about me over there, and it'd be kind of mean to just disappear from my friends' lives over here."

"Do your war mates accept that?"

"They understand. How I can't just let the Devil King roam free. So Albert and Emeralda are going to support me from the other side. They'll send me a way to replenish my holy force so I can keep it charged over here."

"'Roam free'? What am I, a lion from the zoo?"

"You *are* a monster."

"Yeah, uh…yeah."

Emi had him there.

"So, what, then? I'm pretty much totally out of magic force. You gonna take me on right now?"

Taking Emi's words at face value, if she took Maou's life right now, she could immediately return to Ente Isla with no regrets whatsoever. The muscles in his body tensed.

It was a golden opportunity. One that Emi laughed off.

"How many times do I have to say it? I am a Hero. Once I get the chance to pulverize you, fair and square, at your full power, I'm taking it."

She smiled like a beam of sunlight, just as she did that rainy afternoon they first encountered each other in Japan. It was enough to take Maou aback. He reacted curtly, not expecting her to ever show that smile to him again.

"So what did you ambush me here for again? How does telling me *that* help you at all?"

Emi chewed over this for a moment, her face suddenly troubled once more.

"Well...um. You know. That was a freebie, all right? A freebie. You just got vital intel on your enemy for free. I don't wanna hear you complaining about it."

The words came out haltingly. Maou couldn't make heads or tails of it.

"Uh, sure, but if that was a freebie, what's the *real* reason you're here for?"

"Mngh..."

Emi tried her hardest to say something. In Maou's mind, she overlapped neatly with Chiho in front of the Shinjuku Alita big-screen display, asking him to hold hands.

But there was no way Emi would ever be so friendly with him. For the first time in the conversation, she brought her hands to the forefront. They gripped a long, sticklike object, and now, quite suddenly, she thrust it toward Maou.

Maou edged back, fearing another kitchen knife and/or holy sword.

But then, realizing what the object was, he tilted his head, puzzled.

It was the handle of an umbrella.

Through her pained expression and bright-red cheeks, Emi had pointed the handle of a brand-new men's umbrella toward him. It was wrapped in protective paper from a high-end department store, one even Maou knew the name of, and the logo of a famous menswear brand was stamped on the handle.

"An...umbrella? Wha?"

"I...you know, I threw out the one I borrowed from you, right? I thought that was...kind of mean of me, so..."

She was right. The plastic umbrella he lent to Emi before realizing she was the Hero Emilia was tossed away once she realized he was Satan, the Devil King. So she was...repaying him?

"Now let me just say one thing!"

Emi glared at Maou, still debating with himself over what to do.

"All I'm doing is repaying your favor! Borrowing an umbrella from you is a deep, deep wound to my personal virtue and honor!

One that will never heal in thousands of years! But letting any favor go undone would be an even greater blemish upon my reputation! That's *it*!"

She jabbed the edge of Maou's nose several times with the handle end of the umbrella as she half-shouted her diatribe.

"So just *take* it! This thing's getting heavy!"

"Uh...sure."

He took the handle, and Emi dropped her end, all but throwing it at him. It was a firm, weighted wooden grip, one like nothing Maou ever touched. The fabric was thick and shiny, and the ribs felt reinforced and durable beneath it. Its simple charcoal-gray color was a decent match for any outfit, and it was large enough to comfortably protect a couple when open.

"Hey, isn't this expensive?"

"You are *such* a thick Devil King. Is *that* all you can think of? Five thousand yen or so isn't something someone your age should be sweating about!"

Maou was shocked into silence. The price was completely beyond comprehension for him, yet Emi just tossed it out like yesterday's trash.

"F-five...?! You...you spent five thousand on some stupid umbrella?! I mean, I just gave you this old thing I found hanging off a mailbox!"

"I don't care! Shut up! I just couldn't stand seeing my eternal nemesis going around with some half-broken piece of crap all day! If you call yourself Devil King, you could at least *try* to act the part a little!"

"Uh...yeah. Good point. But...still, five thousand, huh? Wow. Funny to think this is even in the same category as the junk I was using. Mind if I take off the wrapping?"

"I *gave* it to you. Do whatever you want!"

Emi no longer even looked at Maou. Her back was turned, brows furrowed as she crossed her arms disgustedly.

Carefully removing the tape, Maou neatly folded up the wrapping paper and placed it in his pocket before opening his new umbrella.

"Whoa! It's *huge*! Looks really sturdy, too! Now *this* is what I call an umbrella!"

Maou's excitement was sincere as he looked on in wonderment. Emi, catching this from the corner of her eye for just a moment, raised the edges of her lips, her look one of ever-so-slight satisfaction.

"...Well, that's all I needed to do."

With that, Emi turned away from Maou. He called back to her.

"Oh? Well, thanks! Sorry for the trouble."

For some strange reason, the expression of thanks that escaped the Devil King's lips planted themselves deep into Emi's heart. They made her turn back around, just one more time.

"I almost forgot."

"Hmm? Forgot what?"

No one will likely ever know what lay behind the smile that crossed her lips.

"Try to patch things up with Chiho, all right?"

That was the last thing he was expecting from her. His eyes lit up in surprise, leaving him unable to answer. Apparently satisfied by this display, Emi smiled, then turned around once more.

"See you later."

Then the Hero and Devil King turned their backs to each other, both of them heading for home.

"Oh, good evening, Your Demonic Highness! I've prepared some egg pancakes for dinner."

"You could at least *call* it an omelet. I don't care if you lie to me."

Ashiya, his strength (if nothing else) recovered, was waiting for him at the apartment, eyebrows twitched upward at the sight of the new umbrella in his hand. Maou preempted his question.

"It's a gift, okay? A gift! I didn't use any money!"

"A gift? My liege, you have a benefactor willing to give you such a fancy umbrella?

"If you're being sarcastic, Ashiya, then zip it! It's one of those... you know, 'what goes around comes around' things, right?"

Maou propped the umbrella against the wall on the front foyer.

This wasn't some cheap umbrella he could toss around with abandon. He'd need to buy an umbrella stand soon, he thought unconsciously.

Suddenly Maou looked upward, feeling sullen eyes upon him. It was Lucifer, in the form of a typical short, long-haired Japanese man, kneeling in the corner and gnawing on some fried eggs.

Their eyes met, but he didn't say a word. Maou was nonplussed.

"You got any place to go, or…?"

"…If I did, I wouldn't be eating fried eggs in this dump, would I?"

"Probably not. Come to think of it, you're a wanted man in Japan, aren't you?"

He had yet to hear anything about Olba, but if he were ever arrested for armed robbery, the archbishop would no doubt be ready to spill the beans about his accomplice Lucifer.

It was doubtful that the Tokyo police would accept the story at face value, but either way, Lucifer was in a dangerous spot.

"Hey, let me ask you something. How did you find your way into Emi's workplace? Like, into her phone line?"

"…What?"

Lucifer blinked in puzzlement.

"'Cause depending on how you did it, we might be able to use that for something. You help me get my power back, I'll help you in return. How 'bout it?"

✳

Soon, the not-so-normal routine of Maou's daily life in Sasazuka, part of the Shibuya ward of Tokyo, Japan, returned.

The morning after Maou and Ashiya's battle, they visited the home of Miki Shiba, their landlord. They felt the need to get to the bottom of this woman, one who had to know the truth about both of thema landlord who, in multiple meanings of the term, seemed superhuman.

If she had her pulse on everything that happened to them, there was an extremely good chance she was the mystery texter who sent that earthquake warning alongside Chiho's.

They were fully prepared for a heart-to-heart chat as they gingerly pushed the call button, but no matter how much they tried, the landlord never answered. After a while, Ashiya noticed a slip of paper tacked to the gate.

**From:** Mikitty

**To:** Villa Rosa Sasazuka residents

Due to personal business, I will be based overseas for an extended period of time. Please contact the property management company below with any issues.

That wasn't what made Maou and Ashiya wince. What did was the crimson-red kiss mark she had closed the note with.

If she went overseas, she likely wouldn't be back for a while. For a moment, they wondered if she'd be held up at the security line. Her body and looks, after all, were patently lethal weapons.

Maou was on the afternoon swing shift that day as well. Things were still a touch awkward between him and Chiho when she reported in that evening, but by and large, she was back to her usual self.

And once he wrapped up the cleaning and laundry around the apartment, Ashiya was off on a grand tour of the museum, then the supermarket.

"Mornin', Emi! Hope nothing bad happens today, huh?"

From the moment Emi reported to work, Rika was joking with her. Emi looked straight at her.

"Listen, Rika, I…"

In as apologetic a tone as she could muster, Emi explained that she got in an accident after leaving Rika yesterday, ruining the blouse she borrowed in the process. Rika let out a wry laugh, completely unfazed.

"Ooh, you're right. I can still see a couple bruises on you. I tell you, Emi, it's a miracle you aren't dead yet!"

Emi had deliberately kept herself unhealed after the battle against Lucifer. It would raise too many eyebrows if she had completely healed up just two days after being scarred in the underground corridor.

"Well, that blouse was pretty worn out anyway, so you don't have to worry about it. Although, if you really wanted to make it up to me, you could keep me company while I stand in line for lunch, huh?"

With a laugh, Rika patted Emi on the shoulder. Emi agreed, honestly relieved on the inside, and as they continued to chat about this, that, and the other thing, their work shift began.

An incoming call suddenly arrived at Emi's station, giving her barely enough time to skim the regular morning mail. She picked it up, mentally switching her brain to work mode.

"Thank you for your patience! This is Yusa from the Dokodemo customer—"

"Whoa! Dang! It actually connected!"

"…Uh?"

The voice on the other end was familiar to Emi, no matter how much she wished otherwise.

"Yo! Emi! Can you hear me?"

"Kkhhh—"

The blood flowed into Emi's head as she painfully groaned through her teeth.

"Man, I had no idea you could really aim at people like that. This is gonna be a lot more useful than I thought!"

"Look, what are you doing?! I'm at *work* right now!"

"Aww, calm down. It's just an experiment."

"What *kind* of experiment?!"

"Hackin'."

"Ha… What?"

"I mean, like, Urushihara got himself directly connected to your booth 'cause he went to an Internet café and hacked into your company's main computer. So I figured if we had a PC at home, we could do a lot more than that…so I made the first big purchase of my life! Monthly installments on my credit card, baby!"

Emi could feel her heartbeat thud against both of her temples. She was unable to stop it.

"Well, there's a lot I'd like to ask you, but first, who the hell is Urushihara?!"

"Oh, I mean Lucifer. He's, like, a total whiz with computers."

"Well, great! Fine! So what do you want?!"

"Oh, I just thought it be safer if I tried it with someone I was pretty familiar with, so… Sorry to bother you!"

Maou could not have sounded less apologetic. Emi irritably slammed her hand down on her desk.

"Someone you're *pretty familiar* with?! Don't give me that BS! Why do I have to be your—"

"Oh, chill out! You're the only girl who could ever take me on! I'd call that 'familiar' enough, y'know? Sorry! Anyway, later!"

Having said his fill, Maou hung up.

Emi groaned, there being no place nearby to let her raging emotions explode.

"Uh… What's wrong, Emi?"

Rika's voice was anxious from the other booth.

"Nothing!!"

The screech was enough to unnerve the entire office.

"Man, that was *awesome*! Anyway, I gotta go to work, so try to get used to that PC a little more in the meantime, okay, Urushihara?" Maou beamed as he removed his headset.

"…This piece of crap?" Hanzo Urushihara—aka Lucifer, newly readmitted into Maou's Devil's Castle after agreeing to head up his new IT department—was plainly dissatisfied with the laptop Maou had purchased on the cheap in Akihabara; its OS was a good two versions behind the times. The computer he had at the Internet café was newer in every possible way.

"Hey, I bought that for *you*, okay? You should be glad I got same-day activation on that Internet line, too! How much do you think that cost me?"

"I thought they gave you a discount on net service once you bought the hardware! They didn't give you any of that?"

"Hey, you can stop whining once you're not wanted for robbery, okay? If you want a brand-new PC, then how 'bout finding a way to recharge my magic power first? Then you'll have the time to clear your name *and* work for one."

"This is ridiculous. Why must I be bound to the laws of these mere humans?"

Maou and Ashiya glanced at each other, then laughed as Urushihara's whining continued.

"Remember when *we* said stuff like that?"

"Indeed. Seems like such an oddly long time ago, doesn't it?"

Suddenly, Ashiya's eyes darted toward the five-hundred-yen wall clock he had purchased at the hundred-yen shop.

"Your Demonic Highness! It's time for work!"

He bowed deferentially as he opened the door.

"Hey, I'm getting sick of those black-pepper fries, okay? Bring something different home with you!"

"I will be preparing egg-drop soup for dinner tonight. Be safe on your bicycle!"

Maou set off for work amid Urushihara's selfish whining and Ashiya's househusbandlike farewell. His resignation toward the role had risen to the point where it formed his overall philosophy in life.

It would be another peaceful day for the hundred-square-foot Devil's Castle, a mere five minutes' walk from Sasazuka station.

# THE AUTHOR, THE AFTERWORD, AND YOU!

When you sign a pact with the devil, you usually wind up paying for it with your life, or your soul, or something else that makes the wish you receive in return seem pretty pointless after the fact.

Satoshi Wagahara, the Author, is a demon among demons, a writer who has forged a deal with the Devil King himself.

Thanks to a Hero with the blood of an angel glaring at the hapless demon lord to the side, the Author was lucky enough to avoid having to hand over his soul on the spot. The price demanded, however, was just as dear: The Devil King and the Hero said "Give us your lifetime" in tandem.

Thanks to this pact, the Author was able to write. He toiled in the craft, considering it fair compensation for what he gave up. But then the demands escalated. First it was the place he lived. Then what he ate. Then what he wore. Then the place he worked.

Now well used to his profession, even granted silvery wings to propel him into the world of human expression, the Author meekly handed it all over, one after the other.

As time wore on, it transpired that the Author, in the end, had given up his life as well. He had used up the entirety of his lifetime, all for the sake of them. That's what a deal with the devil gets you. Before you know it, he's got your soul anyway.

But the Devil King is a greedy one, as befits the lord of all demons. As he explained to the Author, his mortal life was not enough for him to survive upon.

Soon, he demanded the Editor, Mr. Araki, who acted as mediator for every demonic pact. He demanded the Artist, 029 (Oniku), who drew every bit of home, clothing, workspace, and physical corpus of the Author's that was handed over to them. And he demanded the mortal soul of everyone involved with Binding and Printing the Author's work.

Everyone graciously accepted his demands, signing off a portion of their lives to the Devil King and the Hero.

Then, the Author spoke. "Surely," he said, "this must be enough for both of you to survive on."

But now, it was the Hero who thrust another demand in his face.

"Yet we lack the most important thing of all. Without it, one cannot say that we are alive at all."

The Author protested, asking what such a thing could be. The Devil King and the Hero responded as one.

"We demand the souls of the Readers."

Without the very lives of the Readers, their world could never establish itself. Without them, none of the other things the Author had signed away would hold any value.

And now I, the Author, have helped myself to a small sliver of time from all of my Readers.

I can only hope that I have provided a world, a set of lives, and a story that stays in your heart long enough to befit the time spent.

An impertinent, outrageous thing to say, no doubt, for an Author so new to the game.

Also, on behalf of the Hero, I sincerely apologize for everyone named "Sadao" in the nation of Japan.

The Author's tale, one based upon his pact with the Devil King, is filled with people living frenetic, exciting, fun lives.

And maybe, just maybe, that certain someone in *your* town is a visitor from another world.

# THE DEVIL IS A PART-TIMER!
## SPECIAL END-OF-BOOK BONUS

## RÉSUMÉ COLLECTION

# RÉSUMÉ

**NAME**
SADAO MAOU

| DATE OF BIRTH | AGE | GENDER |
|---|---|---|
| NEVER THOUGHT ABOUT IT | 300 (OR SO) | M |

**ADDRESS**
DEVIL'S CASTLE
VILLA ROSA SASAZUKA #201
SASAZUKA X-X-X, SHIBUYA-KU, TOKYO

**TELEPHONE NUMBER**
060-0000-0666

| PAST EXPERIENCE | |
|---|---|
| 1741—AROUND 1799 | WAGED WAR ACROSS THE DEMON REALMS |
| 1870 | ACHIEVED POST OF DEVIL KING |
| 200X | LEFT POSITION OF DEVIL KING |
| 201X | PART-TIME CLERK, MGRONALD HATAGAYA STATION BRANCH |
| 201X | CURRENTLY HERE |
| | |
| | |

**QUALIFICATIONS/CERTIFICATIONS**
LEVEL 1 ARCHITECT (DEMON REALM), DULLAHAN CHARIOT DRIVER'S LICENSE (STANDARD), HANDLER OF
DANGEROUS MAGICAL POTIONS, WYVERN LICENSE, DEMONIC-MEDICINE LICENSE, CERTIFIED DEMONIC
ACCOUNTANT LICENSE, CONSULTANT (SMALL- TO MIDLEVEL IMP HORDES), WARLOCK ANALYST

**SKILLS/HOBBIES**
WORLD DOMINATION, CUSTOMER SERVICE, LANGUAGE STUDIES

**REASON FOR APPLICATION**
I AM SEEKING TO USE THE EXPERIENCES I'VE HAD WORKING AT MGRONALD IN MY QUEST
FOR WORLD SUBJUGATION.

**PERSONAL GOALS**
I WANT TO EAT BETTER.

| COMMUTE TIME | FAMILY/DEPENDENTS | NAME OF GUARDIAN |
|---|---|---|
| WITH MY TRUSTY DULLA-HAN BENT TO MY WILL, IT TAKES BUT 10 MINUTES. | COLLECTED FORCES OF MY DEMONIC ARMY | Shiro Ashiya |

DON'T JUST WRITE THAT IN! —MAOU

# RÉSUMÉ

**NAME**
Emi Yusa

*17, BUT LET'S CALL IT 20.*

| ~~DATE OF BIRTH~~ | AGE | GENDER |
|---|---|---|
| Autumn | | F |

*THINK OF SOMETHING, MAN. —MAOU*
↑
*Don't write on my résumé! —Emi*

**ADDRESS**
Urban Heights Eifukusho #501
Eifukucho D-D-D, Suginami-ku, Tokyo

**TELEPHONE NUMBER**
090-XXXX-0211

## PAST EXPERIENCE

| | |
|---|---|
| 19XX | born on Western Continent, Ente Isla |
| 20XX | assisted with family chores |
| 20XX | assumed role of Captain, Church Knights |
| 20XX | assumed role of Hero |
| 201X — Present | contract employee, Dokodemo Group Customer Service Center |

## QUALIFICATIONS/CERTIFICATIONS

event planning assistant; crop selection, wheat staples; 700 points, Test of English for International Communication (TOEIC)

## SKILLS/HOBBIES

blade sharpening, spirit dispelling, watching samurai dramas, language studies, Devil King destroying

*THAT'S YOUR HOBBY?! —MAOU*
*No, it's my skill. —Emi*

## REASON FOR APPLICATION

As Hero, this is only the most natural of positions for me to take.

*OH, COME ON! —MAOU*

## PERSONAL GOALS

I will submit myself to any hazard, no matter how perilous, in order to defeat the Devil King. I wouldn't mind a bit larger bathtub, though.

| COMMUTE TIME | FAMILY/DEPENDENTS | NAME OF GUARDIAN |
|---|---|---|
| Nearest station: Eifukucho, Keio Inokashira Line; approx. twenty-five-minute commute | None | Rika Suzuki |

*DUDE... —MAOU* *Got a problem with that? —Emi*

**NAME**
# Shiro Ashiya

| DATE OF BIRTH | AGE | GENDER |
|---|---|---|
| | 1500 (ish) | M |

*Don't remember when I arrived in Japan.*

**ADDRESS**
Inside Devil's Castle
Villa Rosa Sasazuka #201
Sasazuka X-X-X, Shibuya-ku, Tokyo

**TELEPHONE NUMBER**
Unnecessary   ← GET A PHONE ALREADY. —MAOU

| PAST EXPERIENCE | |
|---|---|
| | fought in numerous wars in demon realm as a foot soldier before modern time measurement began |
| Circa 1750s | joined demon officer corps as staff member of Devil King Satan |
| Circa 1850s | Four Great Empires formed |
| 1870–1910 | promoted to Great Demon General and chief commander of invading forces, Eastern Continent, Ente Isla |
| 201X | relieved of post as chief commander of invading forces, Eastern Continent, Ente Isla |
| 201X | unemployed/househusband |
| | |

**QUALIFICATIONS/CERTIFICATIONS**
magical incantation license; large wyvern wrangler license; magical toolsmith; handler of dangerous magical potions; demonic welfare agent; dark live-in assistant; magic instructor license; level 1, Demon Realm Literature Proficiency Examination; level 1, Devil's Castle Secretary Examination; demonic interior decorator

**SKILLS/HOBBIES**
Assisting in world domination. Cleaning, laundry, cooking, telekinesis.

**REASON FOR APPLICATION**
I don't remember asking for any of this...

**PERSONAL GOALS**
I wish to return ourselves to the former glories of world conquest and make our domain worthy of the "Devil's Castle" title. An induction-heated electric range is also in the works, as well as a fish grill.

| COMMUTE TIME | FAMILY/DEPENDENTS | NAME OF GUARDIAN |
|---|---|---|
| A househusband begins work from the moment he awakens. | My existence helps reduce the Devil King's tax burden. | I'm the guardian here! ↑ WHOSE?! —MAOU |

**NAME**
*Chiho Sasaki*

| DATE OF BIRTH | AGE | GENDER |
|---|---|---|
| September 10, 19XX | 16 | F |

**ADDRESS**
Hatagaya□-□-□
Shibuya-ku, Tokyo

**TELEPHONE NUMBER**
090-△△△△-1000

| PAST EXPERIENCE | |
|---|---|
| March 20XX | graduated from Sasahata Middle School, Shibuya ward |
| April 20XX | enrolled in Sasahata High School, Tokyo |
| 20XX | currently in second year of studies |
| | |
| | |
| | |
| | |

**QUALIFICATIONS/CERTIFICATIONS**
Level 3, English Proficiency Test
Level 2A, Kanji Character Examination

**SKILLS/HOBBIES**
archery (1st dan), cleaning, cooking, listening to music

**REASON FOR APPLICATION**
I wish to build experience in society through part-time work, in order to contribute to my studies. From a young age, I've always admired the older girls working at MgR.

**PERSONAL GOALS**
I'm going to do my very best! And, um, if you could put me on the same shifts as Maou, that...uh...never mind!

| COMMUTE TIME | FAMILY/DEPENDENTS | NAME OF GUARDIAN |
|---|---|---|
| ten minutes walking | None | Sen'ichi Sasaki (father) Riho Sasaki (mother) |

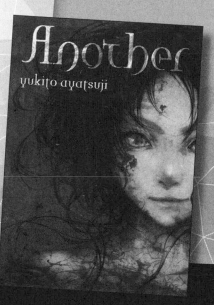